STRUCK

RACHEL LANGLEY

STRUCK

Palmetto Publishing Group
Charleston, SC

Struck
Copyright © 2018 by Rachel Langley
All rights reserved

First Edition

Printed in the United States

Hardcover ISBN: 978-1-64111-079-2
Paperback ISBN: 978-0-578-44664-6

To the ones who championed me on

CHAPTER 1

(LANEY)

The biggest days of your life always start out as ordinary. The days that you plan for, the days that hold anticipation, the days that are supposed to be the biggest, rarely meet your expectations. It's the unexpected, seemingly normal days that change your life.

It was a completely normal day when we went camping in the cave, something we had done countless times. We had found the cave with our father when we were children, hiking through the woods and fields near our home. In the spring and summer months, it was something we did almost every weekend.

That day, my younger brother, Corey, led the way; his light-auburn head was my guide. My boyfriend Hollister reached out to hold my hand while he carried my little sister, Annabelle, on his shoulders. Leela, my twin sister, trailed behind us.

There were a few spare clouds, and even though the forecast called for clear skies, there were more clouds rolling in. They provided the perfect amount of shade at just the right moments.

Annabelle chatted on about everything, as four-year-olds tend to do, asking a million questions, which Hollister answered with patience. I smiled at his kindness; it was like he never ceased to have more to give. I didn't deserve him.

These were the trivial thoughts that occupied my mind on that ordinary day. That's what I was thinking about when it happened—when the lightning first struck.

"Was that lightning?" Leela shouted to us. She ran to catch up.

There was another crack in the distance, far behind us. We couldn't see anything; there were no flashes of light. We only heard the thunder that followed. Leela was by my side now.

"I can't see any lightning," Hollister said, "but let's hustle to the cave just in case the storm is headed our way." We all sprinted through the field, Annabelle laughing at the unexpected joy ride, her arms open wide as if she were flying.

We reached the creek. Corey and Leela crossed on a fallen tree, showing off their skills. Hollister and I found our usual path of stepping stones. The sound of another loud crack, closer now, almost caused me to slip off the second to last one. I caught my balance and hurried to Hollister's outstretched arm. Corey and Leela watched in amusement; I rolled my eyes at them.

"Come on!" Corey beckoned. He was so excited. Everything about cave camping thrilled him. It was his favorite thing in the world. He began collecting wood as we walked along so we would have something dry to start a fire with if it began to rain.

Hollister set Annabelle on her feet, and she ran to Leela. Then he turned his back on me, bending over slightly. "Here, hop on." A piggyback ride. I could not refuse, wrapping my arms tightly around his neck. I rested my face against his ear.

"So, are we going to dinner tomorrow night?" he asked.

"I don't know. Are we?" I responded coyly, pretending I didn't know what he was talking about. He acted as if he was going to drop me. "I'm just kidding! Of course we are." It was our sixth anniversary; we had been dating since we were sixteen years old.

"That's what I thought." Satisfied with himself, a smug smile crossed his lips.

We had known each other our entire lives, but I never got tired of seeing him smile. He was my rock. He had always been there, strong and steadfast.

We reached the entrance to the cave. Hollister let me down.

The cave was deep, but we usually set up camp only fifteen feet inside.

The deeper recesses we reserved for exploration—not that there was a crevice we hadn't thoroughly examined through the years. There were many other rooms and tunnels, but we always stayed close to the entrance.

We all set to work, performing our usual tasks of raising the tents and building a fire. Annabelle twirled around in circles, singing and dancing while we worked.

As the sun was setting, we sat around the fire, roasting hot dogs on skewers. We could see the lightning now, and rain had begun to fall.

"Let me text Mom to let her know we're okay," Leela said, walking toward the entrance to get better reception. My twin sister had a keener awareness of others' feelings, always taking the necessary actions to alleviate any stress or worry from our mother when nobody else thought to do so. She planned to attend medical school in the fall, and she would make a great doctor; her patients would be blessed by her.

After stuffing his face with five hot dogs, Corey asked, "Did you bring the MoonPies, Laney?"

"Do I ever forget the MoonPies?" I quipped, tossing the box to him. He caught it and held it like it was precious gold, the fire lighting up his face, making his smile look wicked. Hollister and I laughed at him.

"What is lightning?" Annabelle asked as Leela scooped our little sister up in her arms.

"It's time for you to go to sleep," Leela said as she tickled her and nuzzled her neck, causing her to giggle uncontrollably.

In between laughter and breaths, Annabelle screamed, "But. What. Is. Lightning!" It echoed through the cave.

"I'm sure Corey can explain it to us," Leela said as she sat with Annabelle in her lap.

"Yeah," I encouraged, "didn't you learn about it in school this year?" Corey always had his nose in a book, especially if it had anything to do with nature.

He began to explain, "Well, first of all, there are three kinds of lightning. There's lightning that happens within the same cloud, lightning that happens between two clouds, and lightning that happens between a cloud and the ground."

He paused to make sure everyone was following, mostly looking for Hollister's approval. Hollister gave him a nod to continue.

"Lightning between a cloud and the ground is the rarest, even though it's the kind we're most familiar with . . . "

I zoned out after that, daydreaming about our anniversary dinner for the next evening, excited to spend some time alone with Hollister. It was hard to get alone time with him—everybody loved him so much, they always wanted to be around him. He was the kind of person who could strike up a conversation with anyone, and with genuine interest and attentiveness, he would make them feel like they were the only person in the world.

Most of the time, I admired, and was even jealous, of this ability, but sometimes it was frustrating, waiting around for the conversations to end so he could talk to me. But he would always find a way to let me know with a look or a smile, even in a crowded room, that he was aware of and grateful for my presence.

Just then, Hollister nudged my arm, and laughing, knowing I hadn't been listening, he whispered to me as a test, "What is lightning?"

I elbowed him in the ribs and rolled my eyes, smiling.

Annabelle was asleep, and Corey's science class had ended. Leela rose with Annabelle in her arms and disappeared into our tent. Corey stretched, yawned, and then retreated into the tent that he and Hollister shared.

Before Hollister or I could utter a word, Corey and Leela began mocking us.

"I love you, Laney," Corey said in a deep voice, trying to sound like Hollister.

"I love you more, Hollister," Leela replied, not needing to mimic my voice.

"No, I love you most, Laney," Corey laughed.

"All right, enough, you two." Hollister shook the tent Corey was in, and Corey screamed, pretending to be scared. Then it was silent. He looked at me for a long moment as though he had something to say. But instead, he gave me a quick kiss on the cheek, and then with a direct gaze, he said firmly, "I do love you the most."

I felt so deeply the sincerity of his statement that tears filled my eyes. I was caught off guard, and he disappeared into the tent before I could respond.

Crawling into the other tent, I lay down beside my sisters. Annabelle was breathing heavily, but I could tell Leela was still awake.

"You okay?" she asked.

"Yes," I whispered, wiping my eyes. "Good night."

Then there was the sound of Annabelle screaming. I could feel that her tiny body was no longer beside me. Where was she? What was happening? I struggled to wake up, to make sense of things.

The light was faint, as if the sun had not yet risen over the horizon. Through groggy eyes, I saw Leela shoot out of the tent. I followed close behind her toward the cave opening.

Corey was just unzipping his tent when we passed by.

She wouldn't stop screaming. It was so shrill. I had never heard her scream like that.

I could see her now, standing in the clearing beyond the woods, her mouth wide open, her face red, tears rolling down her cheeks. Leela reached her first, kneeling beside her, embracing her tightly. My twin looked at me with wide, worried eyes that asked, "What do I do?"

But instantly, Annabelle was quiet, as if all she needed was another human's touch. Because of all the screaming, she was having difficulty breathing, taking short, shallow breaths between hiccups. Leela rocked her, trying to soothe her with whispers.

"Annabelle, what's wrong?" Corey asked softly.

She simply pointed to the field, in the direction of home.

We looked but saw nothing. The sky was still overcast, the clouds not allowing much light to seep through.

"You shouldn't be out here without one of us," Leela gently chided.

I demanded, "What happened, Annabelle? Why were you out of the tent? Use your words and explain." That was something our mother often told her—to use her words.

She wouldn't speak. She just looked at me with big, scared, midnight-blue eyes.

"Are you hurt?" Leela asked, examining her body.

Annabelle shook her head.

"Where's Hollister?" Corey asked.

Annabelle whimpered.

How could he have slept through Annabelle's screams?

We began our return to the cave, Leela carrying our little sister.

I expected to find Hollister sound asleep in his tent, so I snuck up to the opening that Corey had only unzipped five minutes ago and stuck my head in, yelling, "BOO!"

But it was empty.

"Where is he?" I demanded, looking at my siblings with concern. Annabelle buried her face in Leela's long, blond waves. They didn't say anything. "Corey? Didn't you see or feel Hollister leave at some point?"

He shook his head.

"How could you *not* feel him leave?"

"Just because your boyfriend is six foot five and stocky doesn't mean he isn't graceful in his movements," he joked. "Like a little ballerina." He flittered around in a circle, mimicking a ballerina.

Leela laughed and teased him, "You've got some graceful moves there yourself, Corey. Although, Annabelle could do better."

"Because she *takes ballet classes*," he replied, rolling his eyes.

"Y'all—this is serious!" I quieted them. "Where is he?"

"Relax," Leela said, handing Annabelle to Corey. She then pushed past me into Corey and Hollister's tent. Rustling around for a minute, she reappeared with a piece of paper in her hand. "Here," she gave it to me, "Holli left a note, but it got covered up with Corey's sleeping bag in all the commotion."

The note read: *I had to leave early to prepare for the day. Go home and put on your best dress. Then meet me in town at noon (with your siblings). Love, Hollister*

"Oh, look," Corey pointed at me, "there's her big, goofy grin again."

"Well, what are we waiting for? Let's get packing!" I exclaimed.

"Hurry! Hurry!"

Corey looked at Leela and said sarcastically, "You see what Hollister left us to deal with?"

She just smiled and rolled her eyes.

Despite my impatience, my siblings didn't move any faster than usual. In fact, it was as though they purposefully moved much slower. When everything was finally packed and they still seemed to be standing around twiddling their thumbs, I had to say something. "Y'all, come on. By the time we get home, I'll only have a couple hours to get ready!"

"Don't even," Leela silenced Corey before he could make a snide remark. "Grab your packs and let's go. I'm worried about Annabelle and want to get her home. She hasn't said a word all morning."

"You're right," I said as we started on our way. "I wonder what scared her."

When we reached the field, the one Annabelle had pointed toward earlier, there were strange markings in the grass that hadn't been there the previous day. They were a lighter green and looked like veins branching off from a center point.

"Oh, cool!" Corey exclaimed, kneeling beside them. "This is what happens when lightning strikes grass! Our teacher showed us a picture of it in class."

Annabelle whimpered again, like before.

Leela pointed at the spot of grass, "Did this scare you? Is this why you were screaming?"

She turned away, hiding her face in Leela's hair.

Leela looked at me, concerned and shaking her head, unsure what to do.

"Let's keep going," I suggested.

As we walked, I attempted to get them to tell me something about Hollister's plans for the day, but they were unusually tight-lipped, and eventually, we all fell silent and kept in step with one another, our feet instinctively knowing the way home.

Our home sat at the top of a small, rolling hill. It was a late-nineteenth-century farmhouse my father had bought and renovated for my mother in the early years of their marriage. We could see it in the distance, and I resisted the urge to take off running. If I was dressed and ready too early, I would be too eager to wait until noon to meet Hollister.

And I didn't want to ruin his plans.

The house was dark and quiet when we bounded up the steps and dropped our camping gear on the back porch. I guessed that my mother and father must have been part of Hollister's plan because they weren't home. I expected that our mother would have left us a delicious, home-made breakfast, like she did most Saturday mornings, but there was no food on the table and nothing in the kitchen out of order.

"I'll make some eggs and sausage," Leela offered. "Then give Anna-belle a bath, so you go take a shower first, Laney."

I was halfway up the stairs already.

There was a beautiful, 1950s-style, bright-blue sundress hanging on my closet door with a note in Hollister's handwriting that said, *Wear this!* He really had thought of all the details, which made me even more ex-cited for the surprise.

Two hours later, I was ready to go. I could hear my siblings in the living room talking in hushed voices, so I crept down the stairs to listen, hoping for some hints about the day.

"It's so weird," I heard Leela say. "I've texted and called Hollister, Mama, and Daddy, but nobody is answering. They told me to call before we left the house."

"Maybe the storm knocked out the cell tower," Corey suggested. It had happened many times before.

I cleared my throat and came around the corner. "Well, they'll just have to assume we'll arrive on time."

"Eavesdropping is not okay," Corey declared.

"But," Leela interjected, "you look absolutely beautiful, Laney."

I did a quick twirl, making my dress flare out. Annabelle's eyes lit up, but she still didn't say a word. I kept suppressing the tinge of worry that tried to surface every time I looked at her. The sooner we got her to our mother, the better.

"Yeah, yeah, you all look great," Corey muttered. "Can we go now?"

We ignored him.

"Leela, you do look great!" I gushed. She wore a high-waisted, red, midi skirt with a floral blouse tucked in. Because she knew Hollister loved my hair down and curled, I knew she purposely wore hers up in a bun. She intended for all eyes to be on me; she loved to make sure others felt special.

"Thank you," she replied absentmindedly, focused on tying a purple bow in Annabelle's hair. "Okay," she stood up, "let's go."

I took one more glance in the hall mirror before following my siblings out the front door, anticipation welling up inside, more anxious to see Hollister than to find out about the surprise.

Leela drove those three miles to town slower than she ever had before. The rolling green hills down that winding country road were so familiar to us all; we knew where every bend was and the names of the people who inhabited each house. This place was home. It didn't feel like we had spent four years away at college.

We were closer to the town center now. I could see the little green road sign that read *Population 243*. They would have to change that soon now that Mrs. Stover had just given birth to a son two weeks ago.

"Okay, we have to blindfold you at this point," Corey exclaimed.

Leela stopped the car.

"What? No." I shook my head.

"Hollister's orders." He pulled a small scarf from his pocket with a mischievous grin.

Leela nodded, affirming that it was indeed Hollister's order. Corey took pleasure in tying the scarf tightly around my head, ensuring I couldn't see anything. The vehicle began moving again, still too slow for my liking. A minute later, we were stopped again; Leela put the car in park and cut the engine.

But something didn't seem right. With my eyesight gone, my sense of hearing was heightened—but I heard nothing except my siblings breathing. Their mouths were silent, but I could feel their hands and arms moving the air (and Corey bumping my seat from behind) as they tried to communicate something to each other without voices while I waited impatiently.

"What's going on?" I finally demanded.

"Nothing," they said simultaneously.

"Just wait here," Leela ordered. "We need to go check something. Annabelle, stay with Laney." Their doors shut behind them. They walked far enough away that I could only make out muffled words between them, but it sounded like they were upset or arguing.

"Annabelle, what do you see?" I asked her gently. No response. "Please tell me," I pleaded. Still, she didn't say a word.

I decided to wait a minute; I actually counted the sixty seconds that I would remain blindfolded. Hoping that Hollister wouldn't be mad at me if I ruined the surprise, I removed the scarf when my siblings had not returned by the time I reached sixty.

We were parked in front of the town square. The sun illuminated the gazebo.

But it was desolate. Not a soul in sight. There were tables and chairs not completely set up, and half-hung decorations. Some tables were covered with tablecloths while others were bare. Chairs were overturned. It looked like a small tornado had passed through.

Throwing open the car door, I startled Leela and Corey, who were huddled in secret discussion nearby. They turned to me.

"Laney! What are you doing?" Corey chastised. I ignored him and, walking toward the square, continued to survey the unfinished party setup. Flowers were wilting in vases from the noon sun; streamers were strewn across the grass.

But the most alarming thing was that all around us—in the grass, on the sidewalks, in the streets—were the same marks we had seen in the field that morning, like veins spread out in all directions across the ground. If Corey was correct about their origin, then there had to have been a major lightning storm.

"Where is everyone? All of their cars are here," Leela said more to herself than to us, knowing we didn't have an answer.

"Hollister should have been here at least two hours ago," Corey calculated.

"And Mama and Daddy were here last night, getting things set up,"

Leela added. "I mean, the whole town was here helping prepare things. Everybody wanted to be a part of it."

"What was *it* supposed to be?" I demanded. They looked at each other and hesitated to answer me. "Look, it's not a surprise anymore. I'm done with surprises." Pointing at the empty scene before us, I said, "Obviously, something happened here. Just tell me."

Leela paused for a long moment, then exhaled. "It was just an anniversary party," she admitted. "Hollister made sure everyone was a part of it."

"Then *where are they?*" I asked, close to tears—worried tears.

Leela just looked at me, shaking her head.

Corey broke the tension by saying, "Maybe they went to the school gym to wait out the storm."

"Storm's over, sun's shining," I stated. "They should be here by now."

"Laney," Leela said, "you stay here and look around. I'll take Corey and Annabelle to check out the school and Hollister's house."

"Fine. Just meet me at home. I'll walk from here and check out places along the way."

"You sure?" she asked, concerned.

"Yes. Just go!" I said with impatience, waving them away, wanting them to find everyone as soon as possible.

They piled into the car and slowly disappeared around the corner.

I saw my father's truck parked next to one of the moving vans, which I assumed had transported the tables, and went to peer through the window. It was unlocked. My mother's purse was in the floorboard. Her cell phone was still inside.

There were several texts from Hollister; he was checking to make sure everything was going well with the setup and thanking her for all their help. The last one he had sent at seven thirty that morning, telling her he would stop by his house and then meet them here around ten. Corey was right—he should have been here two hours ago.

Suddenly, I heard vehicles approaching from the opposite direction. My heart leapt, hoping it would be Hollister. But as I peered around the moving van, I saw it was an SUV followed by a police car. They pulled into parking spaces not far from where I stood, but I quickly retreated behind the van, choosing to observe from my hiding place.

I recognized Angie Stover's SUV. I knew she had been out of town the last couple of days, visiting her mother with the new baby. She and two officers exited their vehicles. The older officer began carefully walking around the area, obviously not wanting to disturb anything, while the younger one questioned Angie.

"Ma'am, you say you were coming here for a town celebration?"

"Yes," she replied nervously. "I drove straight here this morning. I was supposed to meet my husband here at eleven, but when I arrived, there was no one here."

"So, you went home to see if he was there, correct?" the officer asked.

"Yes, that's correct," she confirmed. "And I called him many times, and all of our neighbors too. Nobody answered." She was near tears.

"Mrs. Stover, when is the last time you spoke with your husband?"

"Last night, after dinner . . . around seven. He was coming here to help set up the tables."

Rick Stover was a good friend to Hollister; they spent many hours building furniture together to sell for extra income. Now he was missing also.

The young officer jotted something down on his notepad. The older officer approached and whispered something in his ear.

"Well, ma'am," the officer began, "it's best you return to your mother's house. We've just received orders to check all the homes in the area and evacuate them."

"Evacuate?" Angie asked. "But this is my home! For how long? What about my husband?" She was crying now.

He touched her shoulder in comfort and began leading her back to her vehicle, to her sleeping newborn. "I know this is hard, ma'am," he said soothingly, "but we are going to do our very best to perform a thorough investigation. We don't know what happened here, and we don't want anything to happen to you or your baby. Until we ensure the area is secure, you cannot be here. Can you stop by the station on your way and fill out a witness statement?"

She nodded through tears, confused. "I was just coming home for an engagement party, but there's nobody here. I don't understand."

I stopped listening and my stomach dropped when I heard the word *engagement*. Leela had said it was just an anniversary party. But Hollister had been planning to propose. And apparently everyone knew it.

Angie drove away.

The older officer turned to the younger one, instructing him to go back to the station to meet her and then to return with more officers to help with the investigation. The older officer was going to check the homes in the area.

Once they were gone, I didn't waste any time leaving. I kept off the road, running through yards, constantly listening for any approaching vehicles, praying that the police officers wouldn't run into Leela. I hoped that they were already home, and that Hollister was with them, and that this was all a huge misunderstanding—something with a really simple explanation.

When I reached the end of our long driveway, out of breath, my sandals in my hand, I could see Leela's red car. They were sitting on the front porch, waiting for me, and it was obvious from the expressions on their faces that they didn't have good news. Hollister wasn't there, and he hadn't been at his house either.

I relayed to them the incident I had witnessed between Angie and the police.

"Well, good," Leela responded, "the police will come here soon, and we can tell them what has happened."

"No," I replied firmly, shaking my head.

"No? What do you mean?" she demanded.

"We need to go back to the cave."

She hesitated, trying to figure out what I was thinking. "Why?"

"Because we are not evacuating."

"Yeah! We shouldn't have to leave our home," Corey piped in.

"Y'all. We need to trust the police to do their jobs. If they think it's safest for us to leave, then we should leave," Leela argued.

"I'm not leaving," I countered. "Hollister is here somewhere, and I'm going to find him." I wouldn't be forced to leave like Angie Stover, forced to fill out a witness report, and then forced to sit and wonder.

"Yeah, I'm with Laney," Corey said. "You don't want to leave, do you, Annabelle?"

She shook her head without saying a word.

"So there, three against one!"

"Y'all, how long do you think we can evade the police?" she tried to reason with us.

"Not very long if we keep sitting here talking," I said. "Let's replenish our supplies and get going. They could be here any moment."

"But what if something bad happened to them?" Leela asked. "What if something bad happens to us?"

I thought about them. All of them. The ones I loved.

"For them, that's a risk I'm willing to take," I replied.

She shook her head.

My eyes pleaded with her. "Leela, please do this."

CHAPTER 2

[LEELA]

The sun was setting over the distant mountains, making everything appear more alive —the birds in the trees, the squirrels playing tag, the dandelions swaying in the breeze. It was hard to comprehend how everything could still be so full of life when our town had become so empty.

Annabelle and Corey were together at the tire swing up the hill from the house; he was pushing her as she spun around and around, seemingly out of control. But he was in control. At thirteen, he knew how to take care of her. The wind carried their laughter to the porch, to my ears. At least their laughter was one thing that hadn't disappeared.

It had become our evening ritual—me reading on the porch, them playing within eyesight, and Laney somewhere by herself.

After the first week or two, she had lost all hope, all motivation to do anything except wallow in sadness. I tried to pinpoint the exact moment she'd lost it. I believed it was when we had found the newspaper left behind by one of the detectives.

The headline had read: *A Deserted Town: Where Are the Missing?*

The missing. That's what our friends and family had become. The whole world knew they were missing but could do nothing to find them. Above the fold was an image of the town square, almost exactly the same as the morning we had arrived there to find no one. I could name the owner of every car parked on the street.

The article had complained about the lack of evidence discovered by investigators. It contained quotes from ignorant people voicing their hypotheses about the disappearances. Two theories were similar to our own: alien abduction and government conspiracy. Perhaps both.

There was also a photograph of Angie Stover and her baby. I felt bad for her—as the only known living town resident, she'd been thrust into the limelight, receiving more fame and attention than any one person could ever desire. I could only imagine what would happen to us if they discovered us—the interest we would generate as the last remaining oc- cupants.

The final section of the article—and this is the part that I thought had transformed Laney from hopeful to hopeless—was a list of names of those who were missing. Our names were on the list, which bothered me but didn't seem to affect her. No—it was when she saw Hollister's name that she had changed.

She had become lethargic and distant, no longer waking up early to develop strategic search plans or spy on the detectives. There was no reason to spy on them anyway; they didn't have any new leads for us to follow. They were just as stumped as we were.

That's why they'd left the town abandoned. There would be an oc- casional patrol car drive through at the same time each day. But that was it. So, for the most part, we could travel about freely without fear of being seen. And although it was clear that Laney had given up searching, she would not agree to leave, content to simply wait for our loved ones to return.

I wasn't sure they would.

I called my younger siblings to me. It was time to put Annabelle to bed. These days, the sun maintained our schedule. She reached me, giving me a sweet smile but no words. She still had not spoken a word. She would laugh and nod and shake her head, but she would not utter a syllable.

Carrying her, we reached the top of the stairs and peeked inside the bedroom I shared with my twin. Laney was alseep, although restless—she had been having bad dreams. I closed the door quietly and retreated to Annabelle's room.

The pink walls of her room were covered in pages and pages of her drawings. Ever since that day, ever since she'd stopped speaking, she had begun drawing obsessively. The only time she would put the crayons down was to eat and to play outside in the evenings. Most of the drawings seemed to be depictions of Mama, Daddy, and Hollister.

She struggled out of my arms to continue a drawing from earlier. I sat on the floor beside the plastic kiddie table, looking at her work. It was a figure of a man. He wore blue jeans (which she was currently coloring), a white shirt, and a green jacket. His eyes were black dots, his hair light brown. His mouth was smiling in an odd way, like he was up to no good.

I didn't recognize him as anyone she had drawn before.

"Who's this?" I asked gently, pointing at the figure.

She looked up at me and shrugged.

"Have you seen him before?" I pressed.

She shook her head without looking up from the paper. She was now drawing trees around him. I waited patiently for a few minutes until she was finished. She held the page up before her, surveying it as if it were a masterpiece, and then tacked it to the wall with all the others. After tucking her in, I told Corey good night and then went downstairs to read some more, not wanting to disturb Laney in our room.

I woke up on the couch to a soft tapping on my shoulder. It was dawn; faint sunlight filtered through the window. Slowly opening my eyes, I could see Corey crouched on the floor next to me, his eyes wide with alarm, his hunting rifle slung across his back. He put his finger up to his lips, instructing me not to make a sound. Pointing toward the window, he whispered, "There's a man sleeping in the hammock."

I shot up, trying my best not to be loud. "What do you mean? Who is he? Have we seen him before?"

He shook his head.

"Laney and Annabelle?" I asked.

"Upstairs, still asleep."

I crept up to the window and peered out to where the hammock hung on the front porch. It was empty. Looking at my brother in annoyance, I declared at normal speaking volume, "Corey, there's no one there."

He rushed to the window, throwing back the curtain. "He was there!" he insisted, hurt that I would doubt him.

I ruffled his hair with my hand and said, "Let's just go get breakfast ready for the girls."

"You can do that if you want. But I'm going outside to find him. You'll see."

He slipped out the side door before I could object.

There hadn't been anyone in town for weeks. The investigators had left, or at least we thought they had. If there had been a man out there, he knew we were here. He would make us evacuate like the rest of the residents—that was the last thing my siblings wanted to do because they knew that the answers to what happened wouldn't be found anywhere but here.

Hoping it was just another of Corey's adventure stories, that the man was just a figment of his imagination, I pushed it aside and focused on squeezing the orange juice.

Laney and Annabelle appeared a short time later, and we all sat down to eat. When I told Laney about the man in the hammock, she wasn't as quick to brush it off. "You didn't even go outside to look?" she demanded. "And Corey is out there by himself?"

"Relax. He'll be fine. He has the rifle," I tried to calm her down.

She rolled her eyes. "We need to go look for him now," she commanded.

As we stood from the table to do exactly that, the back screen door opened and slammed shut. A man appeared in the entryway, Corey right behind with the rifle pointed at him.

"I told you there was a man," Corey announced proudly.

His hair was light brown; his skin was tan. But his nearly black eyes were the most noticeable feature, surrounded by thick lashes. He wore jeans, a white t-shirt, and a green jacket. Corey had been wrong when he said none of us had seen him before. I had seen him the night before, in Annabelle's drawing.

"I found him by the creek," Corey explained. "He was trying to catch himself some breakfast, but I caught him instead." He smirked, a bit too proud of himself.

"Who are you? What are you—a cop, FBI, private investigator?" Laney demanded.

"Definitely not," he replied with levity, as though that was an absurd assumption.

"You do realize you have a rifle pointed at you?" I asked, implying he needed to take us seriously and answer honestly.

"Oh, yes," he said calmly. "It's poking into my spine in a most unpleasant way."

"It can get more unpleasant," Corey demonstrated as he jabbed it into him harder. "So, answer the question. Who are you?"

"My name's Curwen. I was in Johnson City on business, and I decided to come see what all the fuss was about with your town and all the missing people."

The missing people were a tragedy, not something for his curiosity or amusement.

"How'd you get past the road closures?" I asked.

He looked at me directly with his intense black eyes. "I hiked through the woods. How did you avoid the evacuation?"

"We're the ones asking the questions here," Laney countered.

"Let's just be real for a moment," Curwen said. "I know you're not going to shoot me. I've been watching you for a week. You ran out of ammo two days ago."

We glanced at each other; our eyes confirmed that we didn't have any bullets.

"That's right," he said, "so you can lower the gun, Corey. And, Laney, please pour me some of that orange juice."

He had been watching us. He knew our names.

I clutched Annabelle's hand and held her close to me.

When Laney didn't move to pour the juice, he did it himself.

"That's right," he said, as though he had just remembered something, pointing at Laney. "You're the twin with an attitude." She glared at him.

"And you're not welcome here," she stated firmly.

"Well, that's obvious. But I think I'll stay a while."

"Like hell you will," Corey said, repositioning his gun. I knew how much he wished it were loaded, but I was grateful it wasn't.

"Listen," Curwen began, pushing the barrel of the gun away, toward the floor, "I can see that you're scared. I'm not here to hurt anyone. But I *will* stay here for a few days at least." Before Laney or Corey could protest too much, Curwen raised his hands to silence them. "If you don't let me stay, I'll tell the authorities you're here."

My stomach dropped. How dare he feel entitled to manipulate us; I was livid to the point of tears. Laney shot a glance in my direction. Then her actions were so quick nobody knew what was happening until the knife was at his throat. "Get out of our house," she ordered through clenched teeth, inches from his face.

They stared each other down in silence, each one calculating their next move. She had the knife positioned perfectly to severe his carotid artery; I had a flashback of the night Hollister and I had taught her that move, when I had been studying for my human anatomy final.

Curwen showed no real fear. Laney showed no hesitation.

"I think you'd better go now," I calmly suggested, knowing how badly this could turn out. "We may not have bullets, but knives—we've got plenty."

He began to step back toward the door, his hands up in surrender. "Look," he said, "I didn't mean to upset you. I really have nowhere else to go, and I'll get out of your house. But I'll be nearby. You never know— maybe I *can* help." He grabbed an orange from the counter and then exited through the front door.

I sat, breathing deeply and clutching Annabelle to myself.

Laney moved quickly to shut the door and secure the lock. That was possibly the first time the door had been locked in our entire lives.

"That. Was. Awesome!" Corey exclaimed, a wide smile on his face.

"Everyone okay?" Laney asked with concern.

I nodded. "That man had some nerve coming in here like that. If he hadn't threatened us . . . if he had asked kindly . . . "

"What?" Laney's head jerked in my direction. "You would have considered letting him stay here? If he had just 'asked kindly'?"

"That's what Mama and Daddy would do."

Her eyes narrowed. "Well, they aren't here, *are they*?"

She was ready for a fight, but I didn't want to argue.

"And we are no closer to figuring out where they are," I replied, softly but firmly. "We've got till the end of the summer."

"What do you mean?" Now she was angry. "You're giving up? You're just forgetting about them?" She paused, and then said more quietly, "About *all of them*? We can't stop looking."

"Laney, we've looked everywhere. We have nowhere else to look. All we've been doing is *waiting*. What else can we do? Keep living like this, like time has stood still? Time hasn't stopped—the world is moving on out there! And if nothing has changed by the end of summer, we're not going to stay here."

I knew she would need time to adjust to the words I'd spoken. I also knew Laney would begin sobbing any second, like she had so many times in the previous weeks. Her grief was much louder than mine, and probably deeper. I had never loved anyone the way she loved Hollister.

I didn't know how to comfort her, though I had tried. So I grabbed Annabelle's hand and Corey's shoulder and led them both into the living room. Laney ran upstairs. How she could switch from one emotion to another in milliseconds had always been a point of tension between us. I knew she needed space.

Peering through the window, I could see Curwen in the distance, lying in the grass beneath the canopy of oak trees up the hill. Who was he really? This mysterious man who wasn't much older than me. Why didn't he have anywhere else to go?

And how had Annabelle drawn him if she had never seen him before? Perhaps she had seen him, since he had been watching us for a week. Had he talked to her without any of us knowing it?

"Don't worry," Corey assured me. "I'll keep an eye on him." He was watching him through the scope on his rifle. "He's just peeling and eating that orange without a care in the world! Let's walk to town and find some bullets."

I rolled my eyes and shook my head at him. He was only half serious, but I wanted to make sure he understood. "Unless our lives are truly in danger, we're not shooting anybody, Corey. Period. You're not going to become a murderer."

"Who said anything about killing him?" he quipped with a laugh. "Just scare him a little."

I gave him my most stern face, to which he rolled his eyes. "Okay, I got it. I won't shoot him." Returning to the scope, he said, "But I am going to watch his every move."

And that's what we did all day.

Curwen, as he had introduced himself, knew Corey didn't have any bullets when he'd held him at gunpoint. But he had gone along with it and had allowed Corey to bring him into our house. What kind of game was he playing? Watching us for an entire week? Coming into our home and demanding a place to stay?

He remained in the shade of the trees most of the morning. Corey would give periodic updates about his movements—he's reading a book, he's fiddling with some kind of electronic device, he's writing something down. I felt better when I could see him because then I had more confidence that he wasn't telling the authorities about us.

"He's on the move again, headed in our direction," Corey proclaimed around noon. I looked up from the book I had been reading. Annabelle glanced up from her paper but then continued drawing, unfazed by Curwen's approach.

Corey and I went out on the porch to meet him.

"I'm just going to the creek to catch some fish for later," Curwen said as he passed by. "Is that all right?"

"Oooh, so we're allowed to say no?" Corey asked sarcastically.

Curwen ignored him, staring at me, waiting for my reply.

I nodded. "Need a fishing rod?" I offered before I could stop myself.

Corey's eyes were burning into me. I'm not sure why I'd said it. Maybe I felt bad for earlier, or maybe after all these weeks, I was somewhat relieved to see another human being, to talk to someone other than my siblings.

Curwen cracked a smile, revealing his dimples. "No thanks, I've got what I need." He disappeared behind the house.

Throwing his hands up, Corey mouthed the words, "What is wrong with you?"

I shook my head and shrugged. "I don't know, but I'm gonna go talk to him," I said confidently.

"Not without me," Corey insisted. He followed me on the wraparound porch to the back, but I stopped him with a hand to his chest.

"You can watch from here. Keep an eye on Annabelle." He wasn't happy about it, but he agreed, seeing that Annabelle had come up behind him. I ran to catch up with Curwen.

Falling in step beside him, I began, "I'm sorry for earlier—"

"No," he cut me off, "I'm sorry. I shouldn't have threatened you. It was the wrong way to go about things."

We were both silent for a long moment; then I spoke. "You said you were in Johnson City for business—what kind of business?"

"Just working to procure something for my boss."

"What are you trying to find?"

"Just something he thinks is valuable."

"But what kind of business?" I pressed. Was it illegal? Was he a criminal? Our eyes met, and I searched his with suspicion.

"I don't feel like I can be dishonest with you, but I can only reveal the basics," he confessed. "I work for a government organization." Seeing my eyes grow wide in fear, he quickly said, "But you have nothing to worry about. I only want to help figure out what happened here."

I believed him. I didn't detect any bad intentions from him.

"How long do you plan to stay?" I asked.

"No longer than a week, I hope. I'll just camp out under the oak trees, if that's okay with you."

"Why are you asking my permission?"

"Well, from my observations this week, it seems like you're the one in charge," he explained. "Your twin doesn't help much. Well, except this morning—that's the first real action I've seen from her."

It bothered me that he had criticized her, but perhaps because it exposed what my own mind had been thinking for weeks. "You don't have a right to judge her," I responded. "You don't know what she's going through."

"I didn't mean to offend you," he spoke softly. "I only meant to acknowledge that I've seen how hard you've been working to hold things together."

I nearly burst into tears. I hadn't cried since it had happened, since everyone had disappeared. I'd been holding it together, as he said, so Laney could fall apart and so Corey and Annabelle wouldn't. As much as this strange man was a threat who could expose or betray us at any second, in that moment, he was a comfort to me with his kind words. I was grateful to have someone else to talk to, someone else who could help us.

We had reached the creek by this point. He had a campsite set up.

"If you had this place," I started, "why were you sleeping on our porch?"

He was taking down his tent and hammock as he spoke, "I heard on my police scanner that some kids were in town, breaking into the empty homes. I wanted to be able to warn you if anything came close to your house. I fell asleep." He stopped and looked at me with his dark eyes. "So, you see, I'm not here to harm you."

When I remained silent, not sure what to say, he continued, "I'll finish up here and catch some fish for dinner."

"I can help," I offered.

"No, no, no. You should go back. I'm sure Corey and Annabelle are worried about you, Leela." It was the first time he had said my name, the first time anyone new had said my name in weeks.

I agreed with him, but before leaving, I asked, "Do you really think you can help us?"

"I hope so," he replied.

And I realized that's what he was—hope. We needed hope.

CHAPTER 3

[LANEY]

There was a storm brewing. Billowing clouds rolled into the valley, covering every inch of blue sky. The wind whipped through the trees and the tall grass.

My hair was everywhere; I squinted to see past it. I stood on the rear side of our wraparound porch, looking out across the empty field, searching for something, someone.

I felt an overwhelming pressure of loneliness and worry filling my lungs, running through my veins. The rain began to fall, slowly at first and then increasing both in speed and size.

Some raindrops were as large as my head. When they hit the ground, the splatter became a million tiny tree frogs hopping in all directions and making the most horrendous and deafening screeching sounds.

There was thunder in the distance, and I knew it wouldn't be long before the lightning struck. Barefooted, I lunged from the porch, running toward whatever I was searching for.

Within two seconds, my clothes were soaked through, but I ran anyway. The frogs hopped at my ankles, their cold, slimy bodies sending shivers up my legs. But I ran anyway.

I slipped on some mud and landed in a mud puddle. My palm came down hard on a jagged rock; I cried out in pain. The rain immediately washed the tears of defeat from my cheeks. A raindrop the size of a balloon fell on my head.

Suddenly, I was angry. Infuriated. Not willing to surrender.

I rose from the mud puddle and continued running toward an unknown destination.

Then I saw it. The cave was in the distance.

Hollister stood in the entrance of the cave. I began shouting his name between deep *breaths, but he couldn't hear me over the roar of the thunder and the screech of the frogs.*

Somehow, I found the energy to run harder and faster. My muscles burned with the effort. My feet were cut up from rocks and twigs.

But I needed to reach him. I wouldn't let him get stuck in the lightning again.

I made it across the field, only thirty feet from him.

"Hollister!"

"Laney!" he yelled back.

The land between us began to tremble and shake. It broke open, shooting up a wall of fire.

"HOLLISTER!" I cried.

I found his face between the flames. It was twisted and pained.

"Don't come here!" he shouted.

Suddenly, the mouth of the cave closed in on itself, swallowing him.

He was gone.

A loud noise startled me awake, my eyes popping open. I stared at Leela's empty bed and glanced at the clock to realize it was only midday. There it was again—that same loud noise, a noise I knew well.

It was the sound of the screen door slamming shut. But why was it being opened? Who was going out after this morning's events? Or worse, who might be coming in?

I rose gently, grabbing the wooden bat from the corner of our closet, a relic from our softball days. Creeping down the stairs, I didn't hear anyone. There were crayons and paper strewn across the living room floor, where Annabelle had obviously been hard at work.

The front door was wide open. Peeking my head out, I could faintly hear Corey's voice. Following the sound around the house, I found my two younger siblings sitting on the back steps, Corey's rifle still slung over his shoulder.

They turned to look at me with wide eyes. Those same wide eyes had been looking at me for weeks, always trying to guess what mood I was in or how I would react to them. I was tired of those wide eyes.

"Where's Leela?" I demanded. When Corey hesitated to answer, I repeated myself.

He glared at me defiantly and then responded nonchalantly, "She went for a walk." He had become more and more dismissive of my authority as the weeks had passed—because I had checked out and abdicated my responsibility. He'd lost respect for me. But I wouldn't tolerate it.

Glaring back at him, I asked forcefully, "Where? And *why?*"

Knowing my twin, I knew I wouldn't want to hear the answer.

He knew it too, which was why he just shrugged his shoulders in response.

I turned to my last resort. "Annabelle," I began sweetly, "can you point me in the direction that Leela went?"

She side-eyed me for a moment, trying to decide if she should tell me. I gave her a big, encouraging smile. Finally, she raised her little arm, pointing toward the right, toward the creek. With the bat still clutched tightly in my hand, I took off in that direction, Corey and Annabelle trailing me.

It wasn't long before we saw Leela walking toward us. She ran to reach us before we could go much farther, as though she didn't want me to discover what she was up to. I was relieved to see she was all right. Relief quickly turned to anger at her decision to come out here by herself with that man in the area.

"Are you okay?" she asked first, out of breath and eyeing the bat.

"Yeah, I'm fine. Where were you?"

"I went to talk to Curwen," she explained as she pushed past me and grabbed Annabelle's hand. Leela was doing it too—acting nonchalant about the situation, as if it were all no big deal.

"You went to talk to Curwen? By yourself? With no weapon?"

We were all walking back to the house.

"I had my pepper spray with me. And Hollister didn't teach us self-defense for no reason." She abruptly paused and looked at me. "I'm sorry."

I was confused. "For what?"

She looked at Corey and then back at me. "For saying his name."

A look of understanding must have crossed my face. I had forgotten. Days ago, in a fit of anger, I had forbidden them from saying his name because it was too painful to hear. Had they really not mentioned his name since that day? I hadn't even noticed.

"I don't care if you say his name," I brushed it off. "I care if you aren't safe, though."

"It was perfectly okay," she assured me. "Curwen is harmless. He can help us. He's catching some fish for us now."

"How can he help us?" I challenged her confidence.

"I don't know. I guess we'll discuss that over dinner."

"He's staying for dinner?"

"If he's providing the food, the least we can do is invite him to join us," she explained, as though it were an obvious answer, as though I had forgotten my manners. She added, "He's also going to set up camp closer to the house."

It was infuriating, but I didn't respond. Instead, I thought about how much safer I would feel if Hollister were there. If Curwen could help make that possible, if he could help us find our loved ones, could I trust him? Or at the very least, could I listen to what he had to say?

Either way, I wouldn't do anything without some bullets in Corey's gun.

When we reached the house, I suggested that Corey and I would go to Mr. Hammond's greenhouse to see what we could find to add to our dinner. Leela agreed to stay, feed Annabelle, and put her down for a nap. I handed her the bat and asked her to keep the doors locked, knowing she probably wouldn't.

After walking for about a mile and not veering in the direction of the greenhouse, Corey became suspicious. "Where we going?" he asked.

"We'll stop at the greenhouse on the way back," I assured him. "First, we're gonna get some ammo." I watched as a huge grin spread across his face. I smirked and shook my head at his excitement. "But you're not shooting anybody," I warned.

He rolled his eyes.

The hardware store was in the town center. We moved with caution along the road, staying close to bushes and houses so we could quickly hide if necessary. It was almost time for the patrol cars to roll through town, so we walked in silence to listen for vehicles.

Corey was almost taller than me now. It made me sad to imagine him growing up without our father or Hollister to help mold him into a man. He would turn out okay, but there would still be something missing.

And Annabelle—I didn't know what to do about her muteness. There was nothing wrong with her vocal abilities. She still laughed, but she wouldn't form words. I assumed, and hoped, that the problem would resolve itself just as soon as we were reunited with our parents. But perhaps Leela was right. Maybe she did need therapy.

I thought about what Leela had declared that morning—that we would only stay until the end of the summer. Where did she want us to go? Would she still go to medical school? Would we go to the police and tell them everything? What would the consequences be for hiding?

Could Curwen really help us find the answers we needed before any of that would happen? Despite my doubts, I found myself hoping for the first time in weeks. But I also mentally developed plenty of punishments to be inflicted upon him if he disappointed us.

As we reached the town square, which looked exactly as it had that day except for some yellow crime scene tape, we heard laughter and breaking glass. I pulled Corey behind the post office building, where we had a good visual of the area but were hidden behind overgrown shrubs.

Two teenagers were vandalizing the vehicles. One had a crowbar, smashing in windows, while the other was tagging them with spray paint. They laughed maniacally at the destruction they were causing in broad daylight, seemingly filled with glee that they didn't need to perform their acts under the cover of darkness. I assumed they felt secure that nobody was watching.

They made their way down the row of cars, getting closer and closer to our parents' car, and I could feel the tension rising in Corey's body as he crouched beside me.

"I wish we already had the bullets," he whispered through gritted teeth. There was no way we could get to the hardware store without the teenage boys seeing us.

"It's better we don't. I can't have you shooting them."

"I wouldn't *shoot* them, just *scare* them," he explained with annoyance. "You and Leela don't seem to understand that concept."

"You might be a good shot, but you would blow our cover," I said, trying to calm him.

They smashed another window in. Corey stood up, gun raised, ready to reveal himself. But just then, we heard sirens. My brother crouched down again. We both glanced at his watch—the patrol car was right on time to catch the vandals.

The teenagers fell all over themselves as they scrambled to their bicycles, attempting to make an escape as the cops approached. They took off at full speed, thankfully headed away from our home. The police car maintained a steady pace right behind them until they all disappeared around the corner.

"This is our one shot before they come back and the whole square will be teeming with cops again," I said. "Let's go. Quick!"

We ran to the hardware store, which Corey quickly unlocked, entering the security system code. He had just started working there before everyone went missing, and the owner trusted him completely. Something else to be thankful for.

I acted as a lookout. Corey knew where everything was and grabbed what we needed in under a minute, stuffing it into his backpack. I could faintly hear the sirens, not sure if they were from the same car or from a second one arriving for backup.

After resetting the alarm and locking the door, Corey and I listened until we could no longer hear any sirens or vehicles.

"Let's take the back road to Mr. Hammond's so we can stay in the woods," I suggested.

"Okay," he said. "I'll race you." He took off, with laughter (and me) trailing behind him.

After we reached the dirt road, tired and out of breath, the remainder of our trek was uneventful. It was the most exercise I had gotten in weeks, now realizing how lethargic I had been. My siblings had walked to Mr. Hammond's three or four times a week to tend to the greenhouse and bring fresh fruits and vegetables back, things that didn't grow in our mother's small garden at home, outside of the greenhouse's controlled environment. I had only gone with them once.

Mr. Hammond was like a grandfather to all the kids in town, inviting classes from the local schools to come to his place to learn about sustainable farming. We were sure he would be grateful we were caring for it, and not mind if we paid ourselves with some of the produce. We stayed just long enough to get what we needed and for Corey to set the irrigation timer; we would have to return another day for maintenance care.

I knew Leela would be wondering where we were, not knowing that we took a detour to the hardware store. We cut through fields and woods on the way home, avoiding any chance of running into the police.

We could smell smoke from the grill before we could see the house. I don't think either of us realized how famished we were. The thought of food made me excited for the first time in a while, but as soon as I could see that Curwen was the one preparing it, my appetite disappeared. I had held a knife to his throat less than twelve hours earlier, yet there he was, standing on my back porch, whistling a merry little tune. I didn't even acknowledge his presence when I walked past him into the house.

"You know, Laney, I'm so glad we stopped for those bullets," Corey said loudly, following me inside.

I suppressed a laugh.

Leela heard his voice and came from the kitchen, worry draining from her face. "Where have y'all been?" she asked, concern in her eyes. "Curwen heard on the police scanner about a couple of teenagers in town. I was so worried."

"We're fine," I replied flatly. "How long has *he* been here?"

"About an hour. But where were you?" she repeated, more firmly. "What did you just say about bullets?"

"We just went to the hardware store before heading to the green-house," Corey replied nonchalantly. And then, becoming animated, "You should have seen those two stupid boys trying to outrun the cops on bicycles!" He laughed at the memory.

"Really, Laney?" she turned to me. "You just had to have bullets?"

"Not gonna take any chances," I said. "Here's some veggies for dinner." I thrust my bag into her arms.

"I'll get right on that." She glared at me as she took the bag into the kitchen.

I went upstairs to change clothes. Returning a few minutes later, I found Annabelle sprawled across the living room floor, as usual, engrossed in her drawing. I sat beside her.

My mouth fell open, dumbfounded, as my mind tried to make sense of what I saw on the paper.

"Corey," I called.

He popped his head in, his mouth and hands both full of potato chips. "What?" he asked through chews.

"Did you tell Annabelle about those teenagers in the square?"

"No." He shook his head. "I haven't even seen her since we've been back."

Annabelle fussed as I took the paper from her, mid-crayon-stroke, and held it for him to see. He squinted at it for a moment, and then his face mirrored mine, mouth agape.

"How?" was all he could utter.

I shook my head, my eyes wide. I tried questioning Annabelle, but she only gave me silence. Snatching the paper back from me, she continued to color the boys' clothing exactly as we had witnessed it that afternoon. She even had the spray-paint colors accurate.

"Maybe Curwen described it from the police scanner report or something," Corey fumbled for an explanation. It seemed logical.

"Dinner's ready!" Leela hollered.

We sat at the table as Curwen entered with a large platter of grilled fish fillets. As much as I despised his presence, I had to admit—to myself—that I was grateful for the provision. Corey hadn't been able to catch anything good for days.

"Curwen," Corey began, "did Annabelle hear a description of the guys who were in town today, from the police scanner or from you?"

"Not that I'm aware of," he replied coolly, sitting down.

"Yeah," Leela piped in, "she was still napping when he gave me the news about that."

"But you said he has only been here for about an hour," I countered.

"Yeah, he came by earlier to drop off most of his gear. Then went back to fish," she explained, annoyed by my implication that she had lied.

How much time had they really spent together, and what had they talked about? How much had she revealed about our situation? I narrowed my eyes at her with suspicion.

"Why do you ask about Annabelle hearing about the guys?" Curwen asked.

"Because she drew a picture of it," Corey answered with his mouth full.

Leela looked surprised. "Really?"

Corey and I nodded.

"You don't believe us?" I became defensive.

"Yes, I believe you. She also drew a picture of Curwen last night," she explained. "Curwen, has she seen you before? Anytime during this past week that you've been watching us?"

Been watching us. She said it like that was completely normal behavior, like it was okay that he had been watching us. More like spying and violating our privacy.

"Not that I'm aware of," he replied again.

He couldn't tell us anything. How could he help us?

"What *are* you aware of?" I demanded sarcastically.

He looked at me for a long moment with those dark, almost black eyes, seeming to weigh his words wisely. I glared back at him, daring him to respond.

Finally, he simply smirked at me and then quietly, to himself, said, "Huh," as though he had just had some great realization or connection of thoughts in his brain. As much as I wanted to know what he was thinking, I wouldn't give him the satisfaction of asking. There were many things I wanted to ask him, like an interrogation, but not with Annabelle around.

We ate in silence for several minutes.

He spoke first, when all our plates were empty. "Have y'all considered that they'll probably cut the power soon?" he asked. We were silent. What a random, stupid question. "Since I'm assuming you're not going to pay the bill and risk being discovered?" he prompted.

"You're right," Leela finally admitted. "It will probably happen sometime in the next week or so."

"We were busy considering other things," I added sharply.

"Well, about these other things you've been considering . . . can you all tell me what happened here?" he asked softly.

"If we knew, we wouldn't need your help," Corey said.

Curwen pressed, "Well, you can tell me about your personal experience of what happened."

I dreaded having to explain anything to him, to a stranger who couldn't comprehend our grief, our loss. He could look at the photographs on our walls and put names with faces, but he didn't know them. He didn't love them.

Leela could sense my feelings, my mood. "It's late, and everyone's tired," she said, rising from the table. "Why don't we call it a night and start first thing in the morning?"

They all nodded in agreement. As I headed upstairs with Annabelle, I noticed Leela and Curwen speaking in hushed voices as she walked with him out the front door. I rolled my eyes, annoyed that she had taken so quickly to this strange man, and whispered for Corey to wait for her to come in and then lock the door.

CHAPTER 4

[LEELA]

Annabelle was curled up in bed with Laney when I woke up in the morning. They were the first things my sleepy eyes focused on. Annabelle had made it a habit to sneak into Laney's bed early in the morning—I think it was her way of showing comfort without words.

Sleeping soundly, less than five feet away, Laney was a mirror image of myself. Her white-blond waves spread across the pillow, the morning sun illuminating her fair skin and freckles. I remembered what she used to be like before, with constant smiles and laughter.

But now, even in sleep, her lips appeared to frown, and her brow was furrowed. She clung tightly to our little sister, and Annabelle didn't mind the smothering. I dressed without a sound and then crept out of the room, leaving them to snooze a bit longer (and desiring an opportunity to speak with Curwen alone).

He was sitting in one of the rocking chairs on the front porch, reading a book. I brought a cup of coffee out to him and then sat down in the hammock.

"What are you reading?" I asked.

He held the book up so I could see. *The Lion, the Witch, and the Wardrobe*.

I smiled softly. "Our father read that to us when we were little. It's Annabelle's favorite now."

"It was recommended to me at a bookstore in Johnson City," he said, still not taking his eyes from the pages. I felt like I was interrupting, but just as I was getting ready to leave him alone, he closed the book and smiled at me. "Just had to finish that chapter."

"What do you think of it?"

"It's good. I like that they can visit Narnia by going through a wardrobe. So simple."

"Yeah," I said with a smile, remembering, "I always wished it were real."

He gave me a look I couldn't interpret, took a sip of his coffee, and then asked, "So, what's the plan for today?"

"Well, you said you wanted to hear about our personal experience of what happened."

He nodded.

"To explain what we know, I think it's probably best that we take you where it all began," I said. "But I'll need to ask my siblings if that's okay."

"I've been to the town square . . . a lot," he confessed. "I don't think there are any more clues to gather there."

"It's a good thing I'm not talking about the town square then, huh?" I asked.

"Well, now I'm intrigued." He smiled back at me.

"I'll have to convince Laney, though. Give me some time," I said, standing.

"Good luck with that!" he said, seeming grateful the task wasn't his.

When I entered the front door, I could hear Corey cooking and whistling in the kitchen. Laney was standing in the living room, holding a cup of coffee and gazing out the window at Curwen; she had obviously been watching us.

"You're too friendly with him," she said with a strange calmness. There was no accusation in her voice, but she stated it like it was a fact, the way you would say the grass is green or the sky is blue.

"Well . . . I trust him," I admitted. "And I'm grateful for any help he may be able to offer."

"What has he done to make you trust him so well?"

"He slept on our porch to warn us about the break-ins, he's provided us with food and intel, he's not turned us in to the authorities, he's—"

"Okay, enough," she cut me off. "All of that could be for his own personal gain. But you can't see it."

"She's too blinded by his good looks," Corey teased as he entered the room, laughing. "I mean, have you *seen* him?"

"Corey, hush," I commanded, shaking my head at him.

Laney added, "He's not *that* good-looking."

Corey rolled his eyes, plopping down on the couch.

"You know what," I began, returning to the topic at hand, "he may very well be doing all of this for his own personal gain, but aren't we doing the same thing? Hoping that he'll be able to personally benefit us? And we all want the *same* thing—to figure out what happened to everyone. So what if he's using us? We can use him." It wasn't necessarily how I felt, but I knew it was an argument that would persuade my twin.

Both siblings were quiet for a long moment.

Laney spoke first. "Then what do you suggest? What were y'all talking about just now?"

I knew she wasn't going to like my suggestion. Internally, I cringed as I slowly said the words out loud, "I think we need to take him to the cave."

They both gaped at me.

"Have you told him about the cave?" She narrowed her eyes, her voice now filled with accusation.

"No," I replied firmly. "I would never do that without all of us agreeing to it."

"That's our safe place. The place where we can hide. And you want us to reveal it to *him*?" She clutched her coffee mug so tightly, I could almost feel the tension in her body.

"We could just blindfold him," Corey suggested. "That way he wouldn't know how to get there or back."

Laney was quiet. She was seriously considering Corey's idea. I didn't want to say anything that would dissuade her, so I waited patiently without a word. It was funny how all my attempts at lofty arguments meant nothing in comparison with Corey's simple solution.

"Okay," she finally said. "As long as *Corey* blindfolds him and *Corey* leads him."

I understood what she was implying. She didn't think I would do it properly, that I would be *too friendly*, that I wouldn't do what was best for the protection of our family. It was hurtful and infuriating, but again I said nothing, not wanting to change her mind.

"You can tell him to be ready in an hour," she said as she headed upstairs.

Corey smiled with glee. "This is gonna be awesome!"

I left him to revel in his excitement, returning to the porch to inform Curwen.

"Good news, she agreed," I began. "Bad news, you have to be blind-folded all the way there."

He was annoyed but not unwilling. "But how do I know you're not going to take me to some remote location and shoot me?"

"I guess you don't," I replied sarcastically.

"If you do, will you at least make sure there's a nice memorial to mark my grave? And bring fresh flowers daily?"

"Ha! Maybe weekly. Be ready in an hour."

It was less than an hour later when he appeared in the kitchen door-way with an announcement for all of us. "I just heard on the scanner that the police are going to make their rounds to all the houses today to check for any burglaries, vandalism, or other activity. So, I suggest we make this place look as un-lived-in as possible and then leave sooner rather than later. I've already packed up my camp."

"Thanks for letting us know," I said as I wiped Annabelle's face clean. Addressing my siblings, I said, "Y'all know the drill."

"How can I help?" Curwen offered.

"Why do you want to help?" Laney countered, still not dropping her attitude.

He replied calmly, "Because I don't believe anyone should have to leave their home unless they choose to."

She didn't respond, but I could tell she was semi-impressed with that answer. Instead, she grabbed Annabelle and bounded up the stairs to take care of her responsibilities as part of the drill we had developed.

She was in charge of our room and Annabelle's. Corey had to take care of his room, the living room, and outside. I straightened up the kitchen and the bathrooms—a trickier task than it seemed. No wet dishes or toothbrushes, no damp towels, no fresh fruit on the counter. Attention to detail was necessary. There had to be no sign of life.

Curwen didn't wait to be told what to do; he just went to work, instinctively knowing what needed to be done. Or perhaps his job had trained him to know these things. Either way, I was relieved there was another set of eyes, eyes that also paid attention to detail, checking over everything.

In ten minutes, we had grabbed our emergency bags from the hall closet and were gathered in the rear of the house.

Corey pulled out the blindfold for Curwen.

"You know," I started, "we'll move faster if he can see."

"Nuh-uh." Laney shook her head. "That wasn't part of the deal."

Before I could protest further, Curwen said, "It's fine, Leela." He crouched down some so Corey could reach to tie the bandana. Corey then spun him around several times in the yard to disrupt his sense of direction before we finally took off.

We walked most of the way in silence. It was sad to see us now, such a quiet bunch, when we used to talk and laugh so much that our parents got sick of the chatter; they had made us play the quiet game more times than I could remember.

Curwen kept his hand on Corey's shoulder, and Corey would have to warn Curwen about a rock or tree stump to keep him from stumbling. They worked well together as a team, even though my brother didn't let go of his rifle. But I could see Corey warming up to him, grateful to have another man around. Occasionally, Corey would see a familiar landmark and delve into a story about one of our adventures, talking mostly to Curwen.

But then Corey saw a landmark that made him stop midsentence. The lone lightning spot in the distance which indicated we weren't far from the cave. We usually tried to avoid it because it upset Annabelle (and Laney too), but today we had neglected to pay attention to our footsteps, more concerned with getting to safety. With each step, we got closer. Laney and Annabelle, holding hands, approached more slowly.

When Corey stopped without an explanation, Curwen was confused.

"What's happening?" he asked.

"Nothing," Corey whispered. "Just stay here." He left him under the shade of a tree.

The rest of us approached the spot and stared at it with sadness. The spot itself didn't mean much to us, but it was a reminder of that day, the day when Annabelle's voice disappeared and Hollister went missing.

Annabelle started to cry softly, so I picked her up and shielded her eyes from the spot. I noticed that Curwen had pulled the bandanna up so he could see what was going on. He leaned against the tree to observe us, recognizing that this was not a moment to interrupt.

Laney fell to her knees beside the spot and began ripping the grass from the ground in an angry frenzy. Corey and I looked at each other, wondering if we should stop her.

But the answer came much too easily.

We joined her.

Setting Annabelle back down, I grabbed clumps of the dead, fried grass in my hands, yanking it from the dry dirt and tossing it away. Corey did the same. Grass was flying all around us. And it felt good.

No, it felt great. We had to get rid of that spot that taunted us, that reminded us of the day we'd lost everyone. We didn't need a physical reminder. We were reminded every morning when we woke to find our parents were still gone.

I was reminded every time I looked at Laney's sad face. I was reminded every time I asked Annabelle a question and didn't hear her little voice respond.

We didn't need that spot.

In a small, very quiet part of my mind, I wondered what Curwen thought, the three of us acting like crazed mental patients. But I didn't care; I was doing it for Laney. She needed this more than any of us, and it was the one thing I could do to help her, the one thing I could do to show that I grieved with her. It was the only reminder we could get rid of.

When we were finished, we all looked at one another, gasping for breath. Suddenly, Laney was smiling, and then she was laughing and throwing grass in the air like it was a celebration. Corey and I laughed too, lying on the ground and holding our stomachs. Annabelle jumped on top of me, and I tickled her until she couldn't breathe either.

It was all over in a matter of minutes, but it felt so freeing, a good form of grief therapy. We lay there, our lungs quickly expanding and deflating. I hadn't felt so alive in weeks or so unified with my siblings. We soaked it in for a couple minutes longer.

Then I rose, offering both my hands to Corey and Laney; they almost pulled me back down. But once we were on our feet, I wrapped my arms around them in a group hug, and Annabelle squeezed her way into the center of our circle.

Finally, we realized how hot we were, the sun beating down on our heads, the sweat mixing from our touching skin. We let go of one another and picked up the things we had dropped—our backpacks, the cooler, and the fishing pole.

Curwen had already replaced the blindfold over his eyes—nobody knew he had seen us except me. He didn't ask any questions as he returned his hand to my brother's shoulder. We were eager to reach the coolness of the cave.

It had been a couple weeks since we'd visited the cave, but seeing it again felt like going home. It had always been a home away from home as long as I could remember. Other than Hollister, we had never brought a non-family-member there. I understood why Laney had so much hesitation about it.

But it was done now. All five of us stood before it, Corey untying the blindfold around Curwen's head. It took a few seconds for his eyes to adjust to the new surroundings. Then he smiled and nodded, impressed with what he saw.

"You asked how we avoided the evacuation. Well," I gestured toward the cave, "we stayed here. Welcome to the Cavern Hotel."

We spent a couple of hours showing him the cave, exploring its depths and beauty. Not since Hollister had been introduced to it years ago, had we witnessed someone new discovering it for the first time, and his fresh eyes brought us a new perspective. Laney didn't join us but sat alone near the unlit fire pit, listening to the police scanner.

When we all gathered around for lunch, Corey asked her, "What's the update?"

"There are a couple of teams out. One's not far from the house—should probably be there shortly—and the other was at Mr. Hammond's."

Corey's eyes grew wide. "What if they can tell we've been taking care of it?"

She shrugged, doing nothing to alleviate his concern.

With a hand on Corey's shoulder for comfort, Curwen added, "They won't look that closely. Don't worry about it."

Relief washed over my brother's face.

As he finished his last bite, Curwen dared to broach the subject. "So, will you tell me now what happened here that day?"

"Not so fast, Curwen. First, you need to answer some of our questions," Laney demanded. She meant some of *her* questions. "How old are you?" the interrogation began.

"Twenty-five," he responded.

"Where are you from?"

"All over. I travel so much for work that I don't really have a home." Curwen remained cool, giving his answers very matter-of-factly.

"Where do your parents live then?" she countered.

"My mother died in childbirth, and I never met my father," he replied without emotion. He probably had to explain it so often that it had become a robotic response, a concise answer that would hopefully avoid, or at least minimize, the sympathy moment that was sure to follow and put an end to further inquiry.

But my twin was persistent. "Well, who raised you?"

"One of my mother's friends."

At this, I gave Laney a look that told her to stop with this line of questioning.

She rolled her eyes at me but did change the subject. "You told Leela you work for the government—doing what?"

"I'm really just an investigator," he downplayed it and quickly followed with, "I go where they send me and conduct inquiries and make reports."

"So, you want our story to be part of your report?" she asked sharply.

"How will that help us? Or keep us from being evacuated?"

He didn't respond immediately but instead inhaled deeply. It was hard to see the expression on his face because he was sitting deeper in the cave, in the darker recesses. I think he liked it that way.

Surprisingly, Laney waited with patience for him to answer.

"I wouldn't include any of you in my report," he admitted. "I just want to hear your story to see if there are any new details you may have seen or experienced other than what I already know." He continued, seeming to choose his words carefully, "It's important for us to know why so many . . . people were taken—I mean, disappeared."

My ears perked up, and my eyes narrowed in suspicion. *Were taken?* Were they *taken?* What did he know? He was quick to cover his slip-up, and Laney didn't seem to catch his word choice—she was too eager to pounce at his other words.

"*WHY* they disappeared?" she nearly yelled, but then calmed herself. "Why don't we focus on *HOW* they disappeared and find them? The *why* can be figured out later."

"You're right," he said. "Let's find them. Help me do that. Tell me what happened here." He gestured with both arms to the cave walls surrounding us.

He had finally convinced her. He was good, able to turn a conversation around with skill. While I grew more wary of him, she became more willing to share.

And that's what she did. She shared the events of that day as we knew them, not sparing any details. I had forgotten what a good storyteller she was. Corey and Annabelle listened intently, as if they didn't know what was going to happen next. I wished for a different ending.

Curwen was captivated as well, his eyes squinted, hanging on to every word, mentally writing down the details. He didn't interrupt once.

"And then," Laney continued, "when I was in the town square and I overheard Mrs. Stover talking to the police, I heard something Leela never told me." She threw an accusatory glance my way, and I knew what she was going to say. In a dramatic revelation meant to make me look bad, she said, "It was supposed to be an *engagement party*—Hollister was going to ask me to marry him." There were tears in her eyes that she swiftly blinked away.

Now it made sense why her behavior toward me had been so distinctly different these past few weeks. Yes, she was depressed and distant with Corey and Annabelle. But with me, she had also been defensive and difficult, ready to argue with every word I spoke and disapproving of every decision I made. She must have thought Corey wasn't aware of the proposal, or she just didn't hold him responsible for telling her.

But I had a hard time feeling guilty for my secrecy when I believed it was best for her. What good would it be for her to know exactly how much she had lost, that she hadn't just lost her boyfriend, but the man who had intended to make her his wife?

Plus, I had made a promise to Hollister.

Focusing my eyes on Corey, I could see he wanted to speak in my defense, but I gently shook my head at him. "I'm gonna go check on things," I said, grabbing the scanner from her and heading outside. Their voices faded behind me as I exited into the sun.

It was only five minutes later when my three siblings appeared.

"So, what did it say?" Laney asked with annoyance, gesturing to the scanner.

"They called an all-clear," I answered. "We can go home now." I headed back into the cave to grab my stuff.

Curwen was just lifting his bag onto his back. "Hey, for what it's worth," he began, "I wouldn't have told her either. Obviously, knowing didn't help her any."

"Yeah, thanks." I forced a smile as I pulled my hair into a bun, preparing for the long, hot hike back.

As we neared the entrance, walking beside each other, he said, "Hey, wait. You've got some dirt on you." Reaching over, he tried to brush it off my neck. The first time he'd touched me.

"Oh, that," I said, realizing what he was talking about. "That's not dirt. It's a birthmark."

He jerked his hand back as if my skin had burned him and stared at it a moment longer, confusion swirling in his dark eyes. Looking away, he mumbled, "Corey's waiting to blindfold me. I better go." He hitched up his backpack and shuffled away quickly.

What was wrong with my birthmark? It was tiny; people hardly ever noticed it, so why had he reacted that way? What other emotion had flashed across the surface of his eyes? There had been confusion, of that much I was certain. But had there also been a hint of anger, a tinge of sadness? Was there regret, betrayal, mistrust? His reaction only served to increase my growing suspicions.

CHAPTER 5

(LANEY)

I didn't trust that strange man with the black eyes, and I wasn't sure that he should know so many details about our lives, but I had decided to do what Leela suggested—use him to get what I so desperately wanted. If he could in any way help us bring back our loved ones, I was willing to talk forever.

It had taken more energy than I thought it would, recounting that day and the days that followed, remembering the pain and loss. I was ready to be home, to take a nap, to escape reality for a short time. Curwen said he had some ideas we could discuss after dinner. I couldn't imagine what they were.

"Looks like a storm is headed our way," Corey hollered as we neared the house.

The sky was growing dark, covered in thick, gray clouds. We needed the rain, but I hoped there wouldn't be any lightning. Ever since that day, Annabelle would scream and cry, inconsolable, whenever lightning would strike. Right then, she was asleep in Leela's arms.

When we arrived home, my twin put Annabelle in her bed and Corey disappeared into his room to nap as well. Curwen said he was going to scope out the property and nearby streets to ensure that the police were really gone.

As I lay down on the couch to rest my eyes, Leela entered—the last person I wanted to talk to. "Listen—," she began.

I cut her off. "No, no, no," I said, shaking my head.

"But—," she tried again.

"No." I held my hand up. "I don't want to hear any apologies."

"I wasn't going to apologize."

"Well, then I definitely don't want to hear anything from you." I shooed her away with a flick of my wrist.

She sighed loudly, aggravated. But instead of pressing on, as I expected she would, she stomped away, letting the rear screen door slam behind her. It was peaceful then, quiet . . .

The frogs were hopping all around me, their slimy bodies rubbing against my bare feet. I had made it past all the huge puddles, and I stood staring at the opening of the cave, waiting for Hollister to appear . . .

My own shouting woke me. I sat straight up into the arms of Curwen; he held me while I calmed my breathing and wiped my tears on his shirt, on my father's shirt, one he had borrowed. But then I remembered who he was—a complete stranger—and I recoiled, pulling away in embarrassment.

He was examining me with those intense, black eyes. I looked down at my hands to avoid his stare. His hands were still holding onto my arms. "Laney," he said in a quiet, but strong voice, "Hollister is okay. I'm sure of it."

Right. I had been screaming Hollister's name again. It had been the same nightmare as before, except this time Hollister wasn't in the cave.

"You can't be sure of anything!" I threw back at him, wrestling my arms free from his grasp, making it clear that I wanted no comfort from him.

Leela was standing in the doorway. I could see her in my peripheral vision, but Curwen was not yet aware of her presence. She was silent and still, just observing us, no expression on her face.

Finally, he stood up to leave. When he noticed Leela, he gave her a fierce glare I didn't understand. Then he squeezed through the doorway, avoiding any physical touch with her. Again, the screen door slammed shut behind him.

After peeling her steel-blue eyes away from the door, she turned to me and asked gently, "Are you okay?"

"Of course I am," I said with sarcasm as I brushed past her and rushed upstairs, not in the mood for any psychological evaluation of my recurring nightmares.

I crept into Annabelle's room to check on her. She was still deep asleep, snoring softly, her chest rising and falling. Tears began to roll down my cheeks as I thought about her sweet voice—yet another thing missing from our lives.

Glancing around the room, sunlight streaming through the window, I began to take notice of all her drawings on the walls. I'd been so distant and depressed that I had previously paid very little attention.

One page caught my eye, made me gasp.

The drawing depicted a man on a mountaintop who I assumed was a king because he wore a crown. Below him in the valley was a mass of people in shackles. In the center of the crowd was Hollister.

There was no mistaking his golden-blond hair and light-green eyes. He was the only one staring right at me—the rest of the people, unrecognizable, looked at the ground, defeated.

Where were these images coming from? She had never been exposed to anything that could put those ideas into her imagination, at least not that I was aware of.

Just then the screen door slammed, and I heard Leela's footsteps on the stairs. I took the picture, closing the door to Annabelle's room, and hurried to meet her at the landing. Shoving her in the direction of our bedroom, I whispered forcefully, "We need to talk."

I showed her the drawing as we sat on our beds across from each other, the same way we had for twenty-two years whenever we had private conversations.

She stared at the drawing for a long time, perplexed. "What do you think this means?" she eventually asked. "She drew a picture of Curwen before he showed up. She drew a picture of those kids in the town square. . . . Do you think this could be . . . I mean," she stuttered, "it can't be true, can it?"

I snatched the paper from her. "It's not true!" I cried frantically. "Hollister is not in chains somewhere."

"Laney, think about it," she prompted. "If he is, at least he's alive!"

"Are we really going to believe that Annabelle is clairvoyant or something?"

We sounded like a couple of crazy people.

She shrugged, not considering it a farfetched idea.

"What did you think of Curwen's story today?" she asked, changing the subject.

"There's nothing to think. He didn't tell us much."

"Exactly," she stated. "But he said enough to rouse my suspicions."

"But I thought you *trusted* him so well," I responded with sarcasm and a smirk.

"I did . . . I do, maybe," she corrected. "But I also just snuck a peek inside his bag. He left it on the porch."

She blushed, embarrassed to the confess this. But I was impressed.

Anxious for her to continue, I coaxed her with as much patience as I could muster, "Well, what did you find?"

She wiggled her hand into her pocket, and pulling out a card, she handed it to me. It was Curwen's picture. I scanned the driver's license.

Andrew Michael Miller. Birth date: January 24. Height: 6'1". Eyes: Brown. *More like black*, I thought. It listed an address for Johnson City.

"It was issued just a few weeks ago," she pointed out. "Do you think his name is really Andrew? Or do you think this is a fake?"

"He does work for the government," I concluded. "I'm sure it's no problem for him to be issued fake IDs and false identities."

"But why would he lie to us?"

She was obviously very bothered by this betrayal, but it didn't surprise me because I'd never trusted him to begin with.

"I don't know. What did you expect from him?" I asked with an attitude. When she had nothing to say, I continued, "He said he wanted to help us find our people, but so far all he has done is bring us fish and offer some info about the cops. We told him everything we know, and he hasn't given us any new leads. *We don't need him.*"

I could almost hear her heart sink when I said those words. Her eyes dropped.

Why—why did she want him here? What had passed between them

all those times when they were alone? What did they talk about? Why had he looked at her with anger earlier, in the living room, and refused to touch her?

She could sense my scrutiny as I examined her. She was uncomfortable.

Standing, she grabbed the license from me. "Let's go make dinner," she suggested.

"Okay," I acquiesced, "but don't think I've forgotten about what you did—not telling me about the engagement."

"Oh," she threw back at me, "I know *that* will never be forgotten."

As we reached the first floor, Curwen was coming inside with a bucket of fish.

"Sorry, it's just a few," he said. "They weren't biting today. I didn't start early enough."

"We'll work with what we got," I said when Leela remained silent.

Glancing down, I saw the ID card in her hand. What was she planning to do with it?

"Put it away," I mouthed to her, slipping my hand into my pocket, demonstrating what she should do. But she gently shook her head at me, narrowing her eyes.

"Um, Andrew?" she said, her voice like steel.

He set the bucket on the kitchen table and turned around slowly, with hesitation.

"You might want this back." She held the card out to him.

He just stared at her, a range of emotions crossing his face. First, there was some kind of remorse, for his lie, I assumed. But it passed, almost instantly. Anger replaced it, perhaps anger that his privacy had been invaded, anger that we hadn't trusted him. And maybe something else, something I couldn't explain.

He shot a quick glance at me, but I shook my head and put my hands up, indicating I had nothing to do with Leela's spy job. I wished I could have taken credit.

The same fierce look he had given her earlier was back. He didn't like being exposed. Who did? I almost felt sorry for him. Almost.

He snatched the card from her and disappeared out the front door, into the sunset.

Would he be back? I honestly didn't care.

Dinner was a quiet affair that evening. Curwen, or Andrew, didn't show up to the table. Corey asked several questions to find out why, but Leela gave him vague responses, and eventually, he ceased talking. I asked my own questions to Annabelle about her drawing, to which she, of course, said nothing.

Story time was after dinner. It was a tradition in our family, one we had failed to maintain since *that* day. Our father would usually read us a couple chapters from a novel or tell us stories about our family that had been passed down from his grandparents.

Our mother would crochet, not looking up much from her work, but always with a soft smile on her face, listening to her husband's voice. Annabelle would be lulled into a deep slumber.

It was a sweet time, every time. But, it was something we had grown unaccustomed to doing while we were away at college. And we had failed to keep it consistent for Corey and Annabelle since that day. Or maybe Leela had been consistent and I just wasn't present.

Tonight, Leela handed the book to me. And I read, for the first time in weeks, trying to embody my father's spirit, feebly attempting to do the job with as much passion as him. At one point during the reading, I heard steps on the porch, aware that Curwen had returned. Leela heard it too, but urged me with hand motions to finish the chapter. So, I did.

"All right, Corey, upstairs," Leela ordered as she picked Annabelle up carefully. "Go to bed. We love you."

He rolled his eyes at us but mumbled that he loved us too.

She followed behind him slowly, not wanting to wake the sleeping child in her arms.

I heard some shuffling on the porch and knew Curwen was still there. What did he want that couldn't wait till morning? I grabbed his plate from dinner out of the fridge. Leela had made it. Even in her anger, she was considerate.

As I stepped out the door, Curwen turned around quickly. "Leela . . . oh, Laney," he greeted me, his heart sinking, trying to cover up his disappointment that I wasn't her. I handed the plate to him; he mumbled his thanks.

"Curwen, we need to talk."

"Okay," he replied.

He had turned his back to me, his hands gripping the porch railing, his plate set between them. I moved to see his face. Light filtering through the living room window was the only thing making it possible to read his expressions.

"Well, first, is your name Curwen or Andrew?"

"Curwen." He hesitated to explain further, but finally did. "That license is just something I need for my job."

"Which is . . . ?"

"Like I told Leela, I work for a government organization. That's all I can say." I wasn't satisfied with that answer, and he knew it. "Look, I haven't lied about anything I've said."

"But there's a whole lot you haven't said," I countered.

"I know." He sighed.

After an excruciatingly long silence, I pressed him, "What's going on? Can you not help us, like you said?" At this thought, it was *my* heart sinking. I hadn't realized how much I'd wanted his help until that moment.

"I don't know." He shook his head softly. He wouldn't look at me. He didn't need to—he could hear the sorrow in my voice.

"Then I think you should leave," I finally said.

He paused for a long moment, silent. Then, turning to look at me, his eyes were sad, and in a defeated voice, he admitted, "You're right. I probably should."

He walked off into the darkness. Any hope I had walked off with him.

CHAPTER 6

(LEELA)

In the morning, the sky was still dark with clouds; no sun shone through our window. Although it was summer, there was a chill in the air, signaling that the rain would begin soon.

Curwen never got to share his ideas with us about how to find our family and friends, as was planned for after dinner. I had ruined it. Why had I done that?

Instead, Laney had told him he should leave, and he had agreed. When she told me about their conversation, I was torn. What if he had the answers we needed? He did say they *were taken*. He knew something he wasn't sharing, and he could be gone. And we would never know the truth.

Everyone was still asleep when I crept downstairs to see if he had left. He hadn't.

The front door was open, and I heard him cough. He was on the porch.

Then I heard his voice. I moved to stand just inside the screen door, to listen and observe. Standing by the railing, he was talking to someone on a phone I had not seen before.

"No, Durham, I haven't found—"

He was interrupted by the voice on the other end. I could tell from Curwen's breathing that he was frustrated with . . . Durham, someone he had never mentioned.

"Durham, please. I'm not stupid. I understand the importance—"

Again, he was interrupted. Curwen flipped the phone shut, dropping his face into his hands.

I moved silently away into the kitchen. Pulling out a bucket of oranges, I began slicing them in half to make juice for breakfast.

Who was Durham? His boss, I assumed. He said he was trying to find something for his boss, something his boss thought was valuable.

Curwen entered the house, startled to see me in the kitchen. "When did you get up?" he asked suspiciously, eyeing the oranges, trying to gauge how long I had been working on them.

"Just a few minutes," I said nonchalantly. "I can't believe everyone is still sleeping."

"Maybe I drugged them," he suggested with bitter sarcasm.

"I didn't find any drugs in your bag," I joked, not looking at him, focusing on the oranges.

"About that . . . " He became serious, sitting down at the table and scrutinizing me. "Why'd you do it, Leela? I thought we had established trust." His eyes searched mine.

I stared into his for a long moment, deciding what would be best to say. Firmly, I asked, "Yesterday, why did you say they *were taken*?"

"You're too observant for your own good, Leela." That wasn't an answer.

"Why did you say they were taken?" I repeated.

Just then, Corey and Annabelle came bounding down the stairs, interrupting us. Their timing was always impeccable.

"I'll go gather the eggs from the chicken coop," he said, standing, taking the opportunity to slip out and escape further questioning.

After breakfast, Corey went to check his traps before the rain arrived, claiming he wanted something for dinner besides fish. Curwen offered to go with him, obviously still desiring to avoid me, but Corey swiftly turned him down.

"No thanks, *Andrew*," he replied as he disappeared out the door. I guessed he paid more attention to what was happening around here than I'd realized.

Curwen settled into my father's armchair in the living room, cracking open the same book from the previous day, returning to Narnia. What was he doing? Why were we idle? Why weren't we searching for our family? Wasn't that the point of him being here?

I shook the thoughts away and turned my attention to Annabelle. I would grill him with questions when she went down for her nap this afternoon. Right then, I wanted to focus on my little sister's language skills, to see if I could coax her into talking.

Sitting beside her on the floor, I examined the words she had just written. Apple. Bird. Cat. Dog. Her penmanship was good for her age. She really was intelligent; I just wished she would speak so her intelligence could be fully appreciated.

"These are good, Annabelle," I said. "Now would you like to practice saying each of these words?"

She shook her head like she always did.

"Please?" I implored her repeatedly. But she still refused, tears beginning to well up in her eyes the harder I pressed. "Okay, okay," I relented. "Then what would you like to do?"

Standing, she held up her index finger, which meant, "One minute. I'll be right back." Then she ran upstairs. It was nearly noon, and Laney still had not shown her face. I would have to check on her once I made sure Annabelle was occupied.

Curwen was watching me, but I pretended not to notice as I cleaned up the toys sprawled across the room. Annabelle returned with her drawing pad, markers, and crayons. Soon, she had completed another drawing.

I almost dreaded looking at it, remembering the image of Hollister in chains. She brought it to me, and I sighed in relief. It was a person who looked like me—or Laney—with a jeweled crown upon her head. There wasn't anything else in the drawing; it was oddly simplistic compared to her usual work.

"This is very pretty, Annabelle. Is it me?" I asked. She looked up at me with her midnight-blue eyes, smiling. "Do I get to keep it?"

She shook her head and took the paper from my hands. Then, tiptoeing over to Curwen, she laid the drawing over the pages he was trying to read.

He stared at it for a minute, his jaw tightening with the tick of every second. But finally he forced himself to say, "Thank you, Annabelle." He folded the paper and put it in the pages of his book, and then continued reading as if he had never been interrupted.

She settled down to begin a new drawing.

"Keep an eye on Annabelle," I told Corey as I passed him in the hall, on my way to check on Laney.

My twin was fidgeting in her sleep again, and sweating. I pulled the blanket back and nudged her shoulder. Her eyes fluttered open.

She looked at me, tears welling up in her eyes, just like Annabelle. "Can you tell me this has all been a bad dream?" she asked.

Frowning at her, I shook my head, unable to make her tears dissipate as easily as Annabelle's.

"We're never going to see them again," she stated with complete assurance. "Is Curwen gone?"

"No."

"He's still here?" she demanded, sitting up. I nodded. "Well, what has he said?"

"Nothing. I haven't had a chance to question him yet."

"You don't wait for a chance," she chastised me, getting out of bed, dressing quickly. "You just make one."

She bounded down the stairs; I followed right behind.

"Where is he?" she demanded when we arrived to find only our siblings.

"Where'd he go?" I asked Corey.

He shrugged. "*Andrew* said he had *things* to do."

"His name really is Curwen," I said softly.

He rolled his eyes and looked at me like I was a fool for believing that. "Andrew is not here," he repeated flatly.

And he didn't return for the entire day. His camp was still set up under the oak trees, so we knew he hadn't left for good. Laney waited on the porch, keeping an eye out. Corey did a quick sweep around the area but came back before the rain started.

When we were cleaning up after dinner, he finally showed up, soaking wet, his clothes plastered to his skin, his hair stuck to his forehead. None of us moved immediately, simply staring at him. He didn't say a word.

Finally, like some grand observation, Corey said, "Dude, you're dripping all over the floor."

I threw the dish rag at my brother. "Then take him upstairs and give him some towels," I ordered. Corey rolled his eyes but stomped off in reluctant obedience, with Curwen following, leaving a trail of water behind him. Annabelle grabbed the dish rag and began wiping the floor.

When all was clean, we moved into the living room. Annabelle and I snuggled into our father's chair as we waited for Corey (and maybe Curwen?) to return for story time. Laney sprawled out across the entire length of the couch, leaving no space for them.

They appeared in the doorway. Curwen's hair was still damp, but he had changed into a set of dry clothes—sweatpants and a t-shirt—that were too big for him, and I realized they belonged to my father. Laney recognized them also, and it was clear from her facial expression that she was not pleased. But she didn't say anything.

Corey plopped down on the floor in his usual spot.

"This evening, I'd like to share a story," Curwen stated. Nobody responded. "Would that be okay?" he pressed for an answer.

Laney and I looked at each other before I said, without interest, "Sure."

He gave me a kind smile. It lasted only a second. It seemed like he realized he had done something he wasn't supposed to do. He brought a chair in from the kitchen table and sat down near the bookcase. He cleared his throat and began, "Once upon a time in a faraway place, there lived a king and his beautiful bride, who ruled over the land with kindness and love."

Corey groaned. "Is this going to be one of *those* stories?"

"What stories?" Curwen asked.

"A lovey-dovey fairy tale."

"No, Corey," Curwen replied. "If it were going to be one of *those* stories, the king and his bride would live happily ever after at the *end* of the story—not the beginning."

His answer satisfied my brother and piqued his curiosity. Mine also.

Laney's eyes were closed, but I knew she was listening, intent on picking apart every word he spoke.

"Well, anyway," Curwen continued, "they *were* living happily ever after. They had a son and a daughter, securing their legacy with two heirs, and the queen was expecting a third child. The people revered them, proud that they were ruled by such genuine and benevolent royalty.

"Crowds would gather outside the palace gates every day to speak with the queen. She would visit with them and find out how she could help them. Many of them were sick or poor, but she still spent her time among them.

"While the king cared for his people, his first concern was for his wife. Every day, he would ask her to stay inside and rest since she was carrying their child, but she would brush off his concerns, believing she would be fine, always putting herself last."

He stared directly at me when he said that—what did that mean?

He looked away and continued. He spoke as though he believed this story was real; Annabelle was transfixed, hanging on to every word.

"Well, one day she should have listened because she fell ill with something the king's physicians could not diagnose or treat. Day after day, night after night, the king sat by his wife's bedside, holding her hand and wiping her brow, waiting for her health to return, watching her stomach grow larger as she faded away.

"When the doctors admitted they couldn't save her, the king shut himself away with her and their unborn child, not even allowing his son or daughter to visit. He starved himself and slept by her side for weeks until one morning he woke to find her body cold and pale. With her death, two hearts had ceased to beat."

Annabelle sunk deeper into the chair, clinging tightly to me. Curwen noticed.

"Are you okay, Annabelle?" he asked softly. She nodded. "Do you want me to keep going?" She nodded again.

The thunder was getting louder now, closer. The lamps flickered for a few seconds but remained on. Soon there would be no lights at all when they cut the power.

Corey was enthralled in the story, lying on his stomach, propped up on his elbows, head in his hands. I squeezed Annabelle to my side, nodding for Curwen to go on.

"To fully understand the king's despair, you must understand how deeply he loved his queen. They had grown up together; they were never apart, and they knew and loved everything about each other—even the things they hated."

Curwen was looking at Laney as he spoke those words. A single tear had escaped from her closed eyes, rolling down her cheek.

"When she died, any part of him that was good and pure died with her; he became a monster, somebody nobody recognized. He was no longer whole, but completely empty.

"His sadness soon turned into bitter anger and hatred toward everyone. He charged the physicians with treason and had them assassinated. He refused to see his young children because they reminded him of their mother. Then he began a quest for knowledge and solutions." At this point, Curwen paused, his eyes conflicted.

Laney gave him a sideways glance. "Don't tell me that's the end of your story," she quipped. He shook his head but still seemed hesitant, perplexed. "Then, continue please. We don't have all night. It's almost Annabelle's bedtime."

"All right . . . " He looked at me with unspoken questions, and I had no answers because I couldn't figure out what he was asking. "Well, like I said, he went on a quest for knowledge and solutions. He found new, young, impressionable physicians and scientists who would carry out his plans. The people didn't know how mad the king had gone; they simply attributed his strange behavior to the immense sadness he felt. They didn't know his sadness had turned into vengeance.

"First, he ordered the scientists to investigate an obsolete form of transportation that could take them to another land. The king wanted to rob the other land of its inhabitants, to use them for experiments. Rather than try to find a cure for his wife's sickness by using his own people, he wanted to find another source, another population that could be guinea pigs."

Annabelle and I shuddered in unison. Where was he getting this story? Was he making it up as he went along, or had he thought of it earlier? Was it a story he had been told as a child? If so, by whom? So many questions that I couldn't ask in that moment.

"Well, the scientists figured out how to use the ancient transportation system with the help of some old seers, and the king began importing people from the other land.

"The scientists injected them with Queen's Disease—that's what they'd named it—and tried many cures and vaccines, but none of them worked. Thousands died, but the king wouldn't stop; he was determined to succeed.

"The captives who survived the experiments were enslaved, used for manual labor in the kingdom so his people could be free to spend their time in study. He believed a lack of education was the reason for his wife's death and for the countless failed experiments for a cure. So, he ordered his people to become smarter in exchange for slaves to do their jobs.

"The king spent his entire life in search of a cure to save someone who was already dead, and in the process, he killed every part of him that was ever human, every part that could give and receive love.

"The only legacy he left behind was the practice of slavery and a new, elite system of transportation. His descendants have reigned now for 150 years." Curwen sat back in his chair, indicating that his story was finished. He looked around at all of us as if there were some message we were supposed to understand—but we were missing it. It wasn't that great of a story, really. There was love, but then it turned to hate.

And what kind of ending was that? The good guys don't always triumph, but that was the entire reason for telling stories—to let good triumph over evil, to give hope.

"Well, that was uplifting," Laney said sarcastically.

Curwen was flabbergasted.

Were we missing something?

"What was the system of transportation?" Corey asked with a look of excitement on his face.

Curwen's eyes lit up, satisfied with the question. He leaned forward, elbows on his knees. "The old seers revealed the secrets of the ancient ones who used the power of lightning to travel from one dimension to another," he whispered, as though revealing a secret. Right then, a bolt of lightning struck one of the trees outside, and a branch fell. Curwen stood up as the lights went out.

That's all Annabelle needed. She screamed and began crying hysterically, like on the day everyone had disappeared. I tried to calm her, to soothe her with gentle words, but nothing worked. It was like a repeat of that day.

My mind was racing, unsure of what to do first. I looked at Laney the same way I had that afternoon, but her eyes offered me no solutions. Thunder boomed, shaking the house and making the girl in my arms cry louder.

It was Corey who saved me. Jumping up, he peeled our clinging little sister from my body and headed upstairs in the dark.

"Good job, Curwen," Laney hissed. "We don't need stories about lightning." She pushed past him to follow our siblings.

We were alone in the dark. His outline was barely visible.

"You can sleep on the couch because of the storm," I said briskly and began to leave.

But Curwen grabbed my arm and pinned me against the wall.

Laney stopped in the middle of the staircase to watch.

His face was inches from mine. Another bolt of lightning illuminated the hall, and I could see the emotion raging in his eyes. "Don't you understand what I told you?" he pleaded with me, willing me to discover something in his words, his story. But I didn't. "I know where your family is and how to get to them."

I could only stare at him, searching his face, trying to comprehend.

But Laney had moved closer now; she stood behind him. "How?" she asked.

I could feel the heat flowing from his fingertips as he wrapped them tighter around my wrist, as if he didn't want to let me go. His eyes were sad; they glistened with unspoken apologies—for what, I did not know.

Still not letting me go, he turned his head to answer Laney. "The lightning, of course."

CHAPTER 7

[LANEY]

"What are you talking about?" Leela demanded.

"Everything I just told you, it's true," he replied softly.

She yanked her arm free from his grasp. "That's insane . . . and stupid," she said. "Why are you toying with us?" She glared at him.

"Leela, I'm not!" he protested.

I felt as if I might faint. My hopes and adrenaline had become so high when he had said those words—*I know where your family is and how to get to them*. Why would he say that? Was this a joke to him?

I slumped down on the cool wood floor, leaning my face against the wall. The toile wallpaper was all I could focus on. The pastoral images were too sweet and innocent for the reality I was trying to comprehend, so I closed my eyes and breathed deeply.

"So, you're saying that entire story you just told us is *true*?" she asked, incredulous. "You want us to believe there is another place where our people are taken—by lightning—and enslaved?"

"Yes!" he said with passion. The lights flickered back on. "Everything I've just told you—it's treason for me to tell you," he explained defensively. "I've been wrestling with this decision for two days now."

My stomach ached with emptiness, and tears began to roll down my cheeks. He had fooled us. He had used us, and we thought we could use him—but he was just an evil man, or a crazy one.

Leela touched my shoulder. "Are you okay?"

I looked up at her, unable to speak. Would I become like Annabelle?

She turned back to Curwen with vengeance. "GET OUT!" She pointed at the door. "Get out, and don't ever come back! You *lied* and led us to believe you could help us! But *you* are the one who needs help. Hope you got some good laughs out of it!"

She began pushing him toward the door; she wasn't strong enough to really make him move, but he allowed her to make some progress toward the exit, all while continuing to plead his case.

"Leela, please believe me," he begged. "This is not a joke. I can help you. I can."

As she was about to shut the door in his face, I said quietly, "Prove it."

Leela jerked her head in my direction. "What did you say?"

What she really meant was, *I dare you to say that again.*

Standing, I said through a shaky voice, "Let him prove it."

Curwen looked from me to her and back again, surprised that I would be the one to give him a chance. He didn't realize this chance was his trial. If he failed, which he would, I would sentence him to Corey's firing squad, maybe.

"You can't prove something that's not true," Leela declared, her hand still on the door, ready to slam it shut.

Corey appeared at the top of the stairs, trying to make sense of what was happening.

"I can prove it," Curwen said quickly, wanting desperately to persuade her. "Let me show you." His eyes pleaded with her some more. "Please."

She looked back at me, angry that I'd given him a foothold. "You want proof," she said to me, "then you deal with it." She dropped her arm from the door and turned to go upstairs. "Don't you come back in this house!" she shouted to him before disappearing into our room.

Corey looked from our closed bedroom door down at me and then at Curwen, still confused and not saying a word. Curwen stood at the threshold, not entering the house, waiting for his next instructions.

"When can you prove it?" I asked.

"Anytime," he answered, eager to please.

"We'll meet you outside in twenty minutes," I ordered, slamming the door in his face.

Corey, exasperated, asked, "What's going on?"

"Come to our room. We'll explain it to you. Annabelle asleep?" I asked, passing him.

"She cried herself to exhaustion," he said. "No lightning should wake her now."

Good. He had no idea how good that was.

But once we explained things to him, he was more excited about the prospect of getting to use his gun than anything else, not believing Curwen's story either and sure he would fail to show any proof.

"Well, don't hope for it not to be true," I chided him. They both looked at me with concern. "Look, I *know* it's not true. But . . . what if it could be? What if we could have our family back?"

"That man came here straight from a psych ward," Corey quipped.

They were unconvinced and unwilling to grasp at false hope. They were right, but I couldn't help myself; the longing to see Hollister again was too strong.

"Let's just go," I ordered. "It's been twenty minutes."

"Let me grab the gun." Corey hurried off.

"Shouldn't we tell him that we're not actually shooting him?" Leela suggested.

"He just wants to scare him."

"You know this is a waste of time, right?" she asked.

"Well, if it is, he can shoot him."

Curwen was pacing on the front steps when we came out of the house. The sun had set thirty minutes earlier, so we stood in the glow of the porch light.

"Well, how are you going to prove it?" I asked.

He exhaled loudly. "I'm going to show you."

"Show us what?" Leela interjected.

"I'm going to travel by lightning while you watch," he said slowly so we wouldn't miss it. "Then I'm going to come back."

Corey laughed. "Yeah, right, dude. This is crazy." He chuckled some more. "But I'm willing to watch you get struck by lightning or look stupid trying . . . so, let's do it!" He selected his favorite rocking chair, and then with a smile, he gestured to the others, saying, "Ladies, front-row seats."

I looked at my hesitant twin. "We've got nothing to lose," I said.

She didn't respond but still took a seat next to our brother.

"Okay." Curwen nodded. "The lightning won't make a sound, so no worries about it bothering Annabelle. And notice that I'm taking nothing with me aside from the transporter." He held up a little black device. "And I'll bring something back to prove that I actually went somewhere."

"Just so we're clear—where is it you're traveling to?" Corey asked with mock sincerity.

"Antonia. My home."

"Okay. Safe travels on your journey, sir," Corey mocked again, saluting him.

But Curwen wasn't fazed; he was shockingly confident. "All right, I'll be right back," he assured us as he began walking away.

Corey whispered, "This is going to be hilarious."

Curwen stopped a little ways up the hill and turned around to face us. Squinting to try to see him against the black, overcast sky—the rain had become a drizzle—it appeared that he pressed some buttons on the . . . transporter.

Then, one second later, just as he'd said it would, a bolt of lightning shot down from the sky. It was so blinding, I had to shield my eyes, and by the time I uncovered them, it was gone.

Leela was gone too. Running to the spot where he had just stood, yelling his name.

We followed close behind.

"Where is he?" she asked frantically, on her knees, feeling the grass that had just been struck. It was still smoking from the heat. "Where is he?" she repeated.

"Surely, he's around here somewhere," Corey finally replied, but sounding dubious. "I'll go take a look around." He sauntered off, his gun slung over his shoulder, a flashlight in hand.

"*Where is he?*" she repeated to me one last time. "This can't be happening."

I had not uttered a sound and didn't know what to say. Speechless.

"He said he'd be back. We just have to wait." She was talking to herself.

"Well, let's not wait here." I tugged at her arm, leading her back to the porch. Looking up at the sky, I feared upon his return that we would get struck by lightning too.

We sat back down in the rockers to wait. Wait. I was so tired of waiting.

Corey came plodding back through the drenched grass, his boots covered in mud, tracking dirt up each step to the porch. "Didn't see him anywhere," he announced, plopping down in the hammock.

Twenty minutes passed. Then thirty. Then forty. Where was he?

"*Where is he?*" Leela said at the same time I thought it. "He said he would be *right* back."

Had he left us like everyone else?

Another thirty minutes passed. Corey was fighting sleep. Leela had retreated into complete silence—something she did when she was nervous. The rain had stopped.

Finally, it happened. Another bolt of lightning appeared. He was right about it not making a sound; if we hadn't been watching, we would have missed it. It was gone as quickly as it came, leaving behind another smoking patch of grass. And Curwen.

It seemed like a magic trick. None of us moved, mesmerized. Leela gasped and then let out a huge sigh, clearly relieved to see Curwen moving toward us, a box in his hands.

When he reached the porch, the three of us were still dumbfounded, silent and unmoving.

He smiled at our reaction, laughing softly. "Now do you believe me?" he challenged us.

Leela finally spoke, revealing her concern. "What. Took. So. Long?"

"Yeah, dude," Corey piped up, "we've been waiting *forever*." He stood up, stretching.

"Sorry," Curwen replied. "I was getting you some of Antonia's finest pastries and ran into a friend who insisted I stay for coffee. Couldn't be rude or he would have known something was up."

"Let me see these pastries," Corey ordered as he grabbed the box and headed inside. We followed behind him, but Curwen stopped at the threshold.

"What are you doing?" I demanded, tired and annoyed.

"Leela, am I allowed to come back in?" he asked her directly.

Cutting her eyes at him, she replied flatly, "Sure, whatever."

So, it *was* true. It *was* happening. I lowered myself to sit on the stairs while Corey stuffed his face with jelly-filled donuts. How could he eat at a time like this?

"This has to be a joke," Leela said, more to herself than us.

Curwen let out a loud, bitter laugh that echoed through the foyer. "No, Leela," he whispered. "Oh, how I wish it were a joke." He was staring at Leela intensely, like they were having a private conversation. "You saw with your own two eyes."

Then it hit me—Annabelle's drawing of Hollister in chains. I knew where Hollister was; Curwen knew how to get there. Relief and worry intermingled in my chest. I felt Leela sit down beside me.

"Are you okay?" she asked.

"I'm more than okay. We can finally get our family back now. We can get Hollister." I smiled through tears.

"You're saying Antonia is *real*?" Leela pressed again.

"It is. As I live and breathe," he replied firmly, with sincerity.

Her doubt wavered.

Before she could utter another word, I stood up and demanded, "So what are we waiting for? Let's go!"

"Wait," Curwen held his hand up. "We need a plan first."

"Haven't you had two days to come up with a plan?" I countered.

"No, I had two days to decide if I was going to tell you anything at all."

"Then why did you?" Leela asked.

"Because," he admitted, "I can't pull off this act of treason by myself."

I rolled my eyes at him. "Please don't call it that. Antonia is *wrong*. You should do what is *right*."

"It's still my home, and I'm still sworn to loyalty," he replied, defeated.

I tried to feel some compassion for the obvious internal dilemma he was experiencing. But I just couldn't. All I could think about was Hollister.

"Hollister is enslaved. We don't have time to waste," I argued.

"Laney, he's been there a month, right? He can wait one more day while we come up with a halfway decent plan that hopefully won't get us all killed," Curwen stated.

Before I could respond, Leela jumped in. "So what's first?"

"Well, first," Curwen said, "I think *you* should stay here."

"What!" she cried in disbelief. "Never. I'm going."

"That's what I thought you'd say." He tried to stare her down, make her change her mind, but she stood tall and determined. He couldn't intimidate her; I was proud. "Fine," he surrendered, "but you're only going to make things more difficult."

"Not that I'm super excited to be struck by lightning," she muttered.

Curwen rolled his eyes. "It doesn't hurt. It's not *actual* lightning. Just travel light, as we call it."

Leela turned to me. "Maybe you should stay here with Corey and Annabelle . . . "

In unison, Corey and I exclaimed, "I'm not staying here!"

"Actually," Curwen began, "Corey, you *are* staying here. I won't take you there."

Corey protested, but Curwen was adamant that he wouldn't take our brother. He was too young, and it was too dangerous.

"You need to stay here with Annabelle," Leela attempted to persuade him. But he was too hurt and too angry to be consoled, and eventually, he stomped off to his room, taking the box of pastries with him. We decided to leave him alone until morning.

The three of us gathered around the kitchen table. Leela had a pen and paper, jotting down notes and making lists. I mostly just listened to their discussion. They were so deep in conversation, they would have forgotten I was there if it weren't for my occasional interjections.

"Does our government know about this place—Antonia?" she asked.

He shrugged. "I'm not privileged to that information. I don't know what intelligence your government has about our activities."

"But if they do know," I thought out loud, "then they know what happened in our town and haven't done anything about it."

"What could they do?" he asked. "If they don't know how to get there."

He seemed smug when he said that, like Antonia was far superior to us.

I just glared at him.

"You said you work for the government—doing what?" Leela continued, trying to gather as much information as she could. She wanted to keep him talking. People had always talked to her, had always felt like they could be open with her, spilling their secrets, even ones she didn't want to know. It was an interrogation that she made look like friendship.

He was silent for a long moment, not looking at either of us, hesitant to divulge the answer. Then he exhaled deeply, something he did often before he revealed things. "I'm actually a member of an anti-government organization, but I'm undercover as a government worker," he admitted quietly.

I burst out laughing at him, at his hypocrisy. My laughter shocked them both, Leela concerned that I would wake Annabelle. "And you're worried about committing treason!" I pointed out, laughing harder.

Curwen looked at Leela, annoyed. "Can you do something with her?" He gestured at me.

She smiled. "I haven't heard her laugh in so long, I kind of don't want to."

"Our organization is not treason," he said in his defense. "We are working to make Antonia a better place. Telling you non-Antonians about Antonia—that is treason."

"Well," Leela countered, "who sent you here—the government or your organization?"

"Both. But my true mission is to investigate what happened here," he explained. "The Procurement Committee has never taken so many bodies before."

"BODIES? Bodies?" I slammed my hand down on the table in anger. "They are more than just BODIES. They are human beings with souls and spirits!"

"You're right," he quickly replied. "I'm sorry. That's just the terminology we use, just one more thing that needs to be changed."

Leela steered the conversation in a different direction. "Who is the leader?"

"King Gigandet."

"So, it's still a monarchy?" she enquired, jotting things down. He nodded. "Is King Gigandet well loved?"

Why does that matter? Get to the plan, Leela.

"There is some unrest, but he is working to make things better."

"Wait," I interrupted. "If he's working to make things better, then what is your organization doing?"

"Working to make things better in a different way." We both looked at him, confused, expecting him to give more explanation. "Look," he began, "there is no reason to try to explain our entire political atmosphere and history. There's no time for that. All I know is there has been a sickness spreading among the people, and the king believes if he can get it under control, then the people will revere him again."

"What kind of sickness?" I asked, concerned. "What if our family gets it?"

He shook his head. "The slaves, I mean, your people seem to be immune to it."

"Is it Queen's Disease?" Leela asked.

"I don't know. Maybe. That's not important. First things first. You both can carry a small backpack. You don't want to be weighed down by anything heavy—maybe one change of clothes, sunglasses, sunscreen, and plenty of water. It's really hot there, and it doesn't get cooler at night. But," he added as an afterthought, "you still need to have your skin covered, not only for protection from the sun, but also for modesty. You don't want to stand out."

"Geez, Curwen," I said sarcastically, "would you like to pick out our clothes for us?"

"Actually . . . that's not a bad idea," he said.

"Are you serious?" I asked.

"Yes. If I'm going to risk taking you both there, then I need to make sure you'll be as safe as possible. I don't think you understand the severity of this risk. I should have done this myself. I should never have told you anything."

"Yes, you should have!" I countered.

"It was the right thing to do," Leela encouraged.

He sighed. "Right for both of you." He dropped his head in his hands and rubbed his temples for a moment. "Let's just get on with it. I can't unring a bell."

He stood up to get himself a glass of water. He was so nervous and fidgety that I began to sense the weight of what we were going to do. A tiny voice in my mind questioned whether any of this was real—whether he was telling the truth or whether he was a delusional madman.

But we had seen it with our own eyes.

If it was real, and therefore very serious, what if Leela and I didn't make it back? What if we ended up in slavery? Or dead? What would Corey and Annabelle do?

Shaking the thoughts and fears away, I asked eagerly, "When are we going to go? Should we go tonight while it's raining?" The sooner, the better.

Leela shook her head. "We're not leaving before we can explain everything to Corey."

"But—," I started to protest.

"No, Laney," Curwen cut me off. "Leela's right. We'll wait until to-morrow. We usually do travel during storms because it's less conspicuous, but since there's no one around for miles, it won't be a problem. Also, it's daytime there right now; we need to wait until nightfall."

"So, it's kind of like living in a different time zone?" Leela concluded.

"Sure, you could think of it that way," Curwen agreed.

"But . . . " She hesitated. "It's not like another planet, is it? I mean, you're not an . . . alien, are you?" She was embarrassed to ask such "stupid" questions.

"No." He grinned. "It's more like another dimension. And we are all very much human. There's a theory that we all came from here originally, but it's not a popular idea, and there is no proof of it."

With melodrama, I responded, "Yes, how awful it would be to descend from such wretched people, I mean *bodies*, as us! O, that Antonians could have *our* blood coursing through their veins!" I waved my fist in the air for added effect.

Leela chuckled, but Curwen was not amused. He said, "Perhaps you're going to be the one to make this more difficult."

"I've always been the difficult twin." I smiled proudly. "You can ask my parents when you meet them. Which you will. Because we're going to rescue them!" I squealed with delight.

"I'm still having a hard time believing all this," Leela said. She laid her head down on the table, physically and mentally exhausted.

Curwen touched her hand for a split second before pulling away. "I'm not lying to you, Leela. I know it must sound absurd and impossible right now. But nothing you four have been dealing with for the past month has been normal. Your lives are beyond the grasp of normal now."

"He's right," I agreed in order to wrap up this interruption to our planning. "Let's quit with these doubts and keep going, please."

Leela cut her eyes at me, annoyed, but sat up straight, ready to continue.

"All right," Curwen began again, "when we arrive, we'll go to my house and sleep until morning. Both of you will need as much rest as possible because the heat is going to drain you. You're not accustomed to it.

"In the morning, we can go to the records headquarters and try to locate your parents and Hollister. One good thing is we keep extensive records, so they shouldn't be hard to find. You two are going to have to blend in, which is not going to be easy."

"Why not?" I demanded.

"Blondes are rare, as are twins. Most of the blondes I've seen are slaves." He could tell from our expressions that we were not pleased about that.

"It's nothing personal; it was just the way things happened genetically, I guess," he explained. "If you both wear hats, it won't be quite so obvious."

"Yeah," Leela agreed, "we can put our hair up and hide it with a hat."

"NO," Curwen commanded abruptly. "You are *never* to put your hair up while you're there! No matter how hot or sweaty you may get. Understood?" He spoke directly to Leela, but I assumed the rule was for me too.

We both just nodded, caught off guard by his sudden outburst and not wanting to do anything that would make him change his mind. He was my only hope of getting to Hollister.

His furrowed brow smoothed out, and he relaxed. "Okay. Well, I can't plan anything else until we know where they're located. Then we'll know the best way to bring them home. Maybe I can call in some favors to get them released."

He didn't sound confident about that. But I decided not to press him further.

He sat back in the chair, waiting for some questions or comments. Neither of us spoke. We had enough new information to process for one night.

"Okay," he concluded. "I think we should pack your bags tonight and figure out if there's anything we need to do to make things easier for Corey. Then we sleep so we can rise with the sun."

I gave up trying to have any ideas of my own, instead following Curwen's advice. He picked out our clothes for us—dark pants and long-sleeved shirts. I could only imagine how hot—no, sweltering—we were going to be, and he wasn't making it any easier.

We quickly prepared a few meals to help Corey out, finishing everything around midnight. The rain had slowed to a light pitter-patter on the roof.

Curwen lay down on the couch and was asleep before we even left the room.

Leela and I decided to sleep in the clothes we would wear the next day so we could spend all our time explaining things to Corey and Annabelle. I hoped Corey would wake up with a new attitude.

Once we were in bed, under the covers, I broke the uncomfortable silence between us. "Leela, are you scared?"

"Sure," she whispered. "But there's no time for fear. We have to do this."

"Right. We have to get them back."

"We will." She reached out her arm to me. We held hands across the gap between our beds, sharing hope and strength through our fingertips. It was a familiar gesture between us. As an afterthought, she added, "I trust Curwen."

CHAPTER 8

[LEELA]

"**C**orey, we have to do this. Please don't be upset," I begged.

Our brother stood in the driveway, kicking the dirt at his feet, hands in his pockets. He was blinking back tears. "I know y'all have to do it. I just don't understand why I can't go too."

I looked at Laney for help. "Corey," she began, "the reason you can't go is up there on that tire swing." She pointed up the hill to Annabelle. "She can't come with us. She needs you."

I added, "You did so well with her last night when she was scared—the way you took control and comforted her when we had no idea what to do. You're an amazing brother, and we have faith that you will take great care of her."

"But what if y'all don't come back?" he said softly.

I grabbed him by the shoulders and looked directly into his eyes. "If we don't come back, you take Annabelle, and you go to the police. Don't stay here. Got it?"

He didn't want to agree to that, but I squeezed his shoulders, demanding a response. Eventually, he nodded, looking at the ground.

Curwen interjected, "They'll come back. I'll make sure of it. If it's the last thing I do, they will come back. Agreed?" He stuck his hand out to give Corey's a firm shake.

Curwen's eyes were fierce with determination; in that moment, I realized that if he weren't fighting for us, I would be very scared of fighting against him. He returned to leaning against the porch railing, arms folded

74

across his chest, watching this goodbye scene.

Laney and I hugged Corey for a long time, all three of us praying this would not be our last embrace. Then we lifted our bags onto our backs and donned the baseball caps Curwen had selected; he wasn't 100 percent satisfied with anything we owned.

Curwen came in for another handshake. "Take care of your little sister," he said, "and I'll take care of these two." He gestured his thumb in our direction.

We walked up the hill to say our farewells to Annabelle. We could hear her humming a sweet tune as the tire swing swayed gently in the morning breeze; it was such a perfect picture, you never would have known she was a mute, little orphan who was about to be left even more alone. A sense of peace surrounded her. Earlier, when we'd told her we were leaving, she had simply nodded in understanding.

But suddenly, when she looked up at me, she burst into tears. Picking her up, I sat down in the swing with her. Laney went around to push us. What if this was the last memory she had of her twin sisters? I tried to pull some assurance from Curwen's words, from his confidence, but it hardly helped.

"I love you with my whole heart, Annabelle," I whispered. "Don't ever forget it." Stopping the swing with my legs, I forced Annabelle to look at me. "And make me a promise: when we return, you're going to speak again."

Annabelle nodded slowly.

"Promise?" I insisted, holding out my pinkie finger. We locked our fingers together.

"Now, come here," Laney said. Annabelle allowed her to pick her up, wrapping her arms and legs tightly around Laney's body, burying her face in my twin's hair. Laney squeezed her back until it seemed like they would both suffocate.

Curwen and Corey had come up behind us. Laney reluctantly set Annabelle on the ground, nudging her toward Corey, and he took her hand. I had never seen more miserable-looking faces in my entire life.

After quick hugs with Corey, we set off in the direction of the cave. We were going to hike far enough from the house that, hopefully, the lightning wouldn't disturb Annabelle and make things difficult for our brother.

They watched until we became tiny specks in the distance, until we could barely see their hands waving against the blue sky. That's when I stopped looking back and focused all my thoughts on the mission before us.

Laney was already sweating. "Curwen, I don't know how you expect me to survive in the heat," she complained, removing her hat and wiping her brow.

"You'll just have to deal with it," he said plainly. She cut her eyes at him; he saw her. "You'll adjust, and until then, you'll have to stay in air-conditioned locations and drink plenty of water."

Her eyes lit up. "There's air conditioning!"

He smirked. "Yes, Laney. We *are* a developed society."

We were passing the spot of grass we had ripped from the ground two days earlier. Everything finally clicked. Laney and I both stopped walking.

"This is where Hollister *was taken*," she stated softly.

I added, sadly, "Annabelle must have seen it happen."

"And *you knew!*" She turned to Curwen in accusation. "You knew, while you were watching us tear up the grass. And you said *nothing.*"

He glanced quickly at both of us and continued walking, still saying nothing.

She was right. He had said nothing. There was so much I longed to ask him, but not with her around—he wouldn't be as honest if she was there judging him. What was it that pushed him to the edge, that made him finally reveal the truth of his identity?

I would have to ask him later, because in that moment I was battling my fear of being struck by lightning. "Curwen," I began, "I know you said this isn't going to hurt. But are you sure about that?"

"Is what going to hurt?"

"Travel light, as you call it," I clarified, annoyed that he didn't understand.

"Oh, no." He shook his head. "It doesn't hurt. I've been traveling by light for almost a decade now—it has never been painful. There might be some tingling, or you might feel a little warm, but nothing that hurts.

Might just be uncomfortable."

"It will be fine. Don't worry so much," Laney chipped in. Suddenly she was so confident and strong. Where had this girl been when I needed her a month ago? Was Hollister the only one who could inspire her to acts of bravery?

I wasn't worried about going to Antonia, just about getting there. With every step forward, I wanted to take two giant leaps backward. We were leaving Corey and Annabelle, and nothing about that seemed okay. We had to make it back, if only for the sole prize of hearing Annabelle speak again.

"All right, I think this is far enough." Curwen stopped.

It was really happening. We were about to travel by lightning to another dimension to rescue our parents from slavery. I was tempted to pinch myself to make sure it was real, or I was waiting for Curwen to start laughing hysterically and say this was all a joke. A cruel joke, but a joke nonetheless.

We had stopped in the middle of a grassy field away from any trees. Laney was actually smiling; I didn't think she quite understood the seriousness of the situation. Her head was somewhere else, probably dreaming about the impending reunion with Hollister.

But what if Hollister was different, like a soldier returning from battle? I thought of Annabelle's drawing of him—his face twisted in agony, his hands and feet in shackles. What if the things he had experienced had changed him forever? Had she thought about that? I could tell from the expression on her freckled face that she hadn't.

I said a little prayer and then looked to Curwen for further instructions.

He pulled out his odd-looking cell phone and began pushing buttons. So it was not only a cell phone, but also a teleportation device. Seeing the phone reminded me of his conversation with Durham. Would we meet Durham?

Durham had yelled at him for not finding whatever it was he was supposed to find. What would happen to Curwen if Durham learned he was helping us? I shuddered to think what their punishment was for treason.

"Okay, both of you need to hold on to my arms," he instructed. We wrapped our arms through his. I must have dug my fingers into him because I saw him wince, but my nerves wouldn't allow me to loosen my grip. He didn't complain. "Are you both ready?"

"Ready!" Laney exclaimed. I just nodded reluctantly. Maybe *I* should have stayed with Annabelle. Corey was much braver than me.

"You should probably close your eyes," he said. "The light, as you can imagine, is pretty blinding." His advice was for Laney—my eyes were already shut tight.

"Okay. On the count of three. One . . . two . . . three."

I looked up for a split second to see the bolt of light breaking through the blue sky, and then I sealed my eyes shut and hid my face in Curwen's shoulder.

He was wrong. Dead wrong.

The tingling was not uncomfortable. The tingling was a burning, and it felt as if my entire body was on fire. *This must be what it feels like to be burned alive.* I could barely breathe.

I was screaming, but I couldn't hear any noise coming from my mouth. Was there no sound inside the light? He hadn't mentioned that. I kept my eyes shut, but tiny tears squeezed their way through the lashes, trying to escape the furnace that my body had become.

My skin was so hot it felt cold. I was shivering while my body cooked from the inside out. And then suddenly, it was over. Mere seconds, yet it had been excruciating. There weren't words to describe the pain.

"Leela. Leela. Wake up." I heard them both whispering my name. Laney and then Curwen, taking turns. I felt the hard ground beneath me, but my eyes wouldn't open; my lips couldn't speak.

"We have to get out of here. I'll carry her," Curwen said, lifting me into his arms. Every place our bodies touched hurt unbearably, as though I had a severe sunburn. The air was very hot, like Curwen said it would be, which helped reduce my shivering.

"Is she going to be okay?" Laney whispered, concerned. I heard her feet on the pavement, struggling to keep up with Curwen.

"I don't know," he replied through clenched teeth. "This has never happened before. Did you feel anything other than hot and tingly?"

"No, nothing. It was uncomfortable, but not painful. Like you said." What was she talking about? It hurt so badly. Couldn't they see that my skin was red and enflamed with burns?

"Should never have brought her here," Curwen muttered to himself. Then to Laney, "Let's get her inside. We can't be seen."

I felt each step he took because every movement hurt my scorched skin. Finally, he stopped. "Here, get the card out of my wallet and unlock the door."

She rustled around in his backpack. I imagined her nervous, fumbling fingers trying to remove the card from the tight slot in the wallet.

Hurry, Laney. I'm dying here.

I heard a beep and then felt a gush of cold air. Goosebumps crawled across my flesh.

Curwen was climbing a flight of stairs, my head bouncing against his arm, a million knives stabbing me with each step. *Could he just be still?*

As if he read my thoughts, he stopped and lowered me onto a bed.

"She's crying," Laney said.

"Just stay with her," he ordered in a rough voice. "I'll see what I can find to help . . . even though I don't know what's wrong." He left, shutting the door behind him. Although my eyes were closed, I knew I was engulfed in complete darkness. I surrendered to its embrace.

I blinked my eyes slowly, trying to remember where I was. Bright rays of sunlight shone through the crack in the black curtains. Above me, the industrial ceiling fan whirred rapidly, revealing the source of the cool breeze that had woken me. I shivered, but otherwise did not move.

My body still hurt some, and my head ached, but it was a manageable pain level, unlike what I had experienced hours earlier. My first instinct was to be incredibly angry with Curwen for lying to me, but then I recalled his and Laney's whispers.

He had never known anyone to experience what I had experienced, and she had come through it unscathed. Why was I different? I would have to suffer through the pain again when we went home—the thought made me groan.

Suddenly, Curwen was there, towering over me. "Are you okay? How do you feel?" he asked in a panic.

"I'm alive," I choked out, realizing how dry and raw my throat was. Before I needed to ask, he held a glass of water with a straw to my lips. The cool liquid settled in my empty stomach. "Thanks."

"Are you sure you're okay?" he asked.

I nodded. I wasn't good. I wasn't great. But I was okay; I could deal. *Now* I was just *uncomfortable*. I sucked down the entire glass of water and attempted to sit up. Curwen helped me, propping pillows behind my back.

"Where's Laney?" I asked.

"Asleep downstairs."

"Did you get any sleep?"

"Some. But don't worry about that. Tell me what happened to you last night, Leela."

I explained the pain to him, including every detail, things I would never forget, trying to express the physical agony with inadequate words. The description came up short with every attempt.

But from the look on his face, I figured I should stop explaining. He appeared guilty and remorseful, even though it wasn't his fault.

"Isn't my skin all red, like burned?" I asked him.

He shook his head. "You look completely fine."

"Well, I feel fine," I assured him, trying to make him feel better. "Don't worry."

"But what about when I take you home?"

I couldn't help but laugh. "Why do you think I groaned when I woke up?"

He was still too serious and concerned to crack a smile.

"It's fine." I attempted a lame joke: "Lightning up, kid."

He simply rolled his eyes. "You need to eat. I'll be back," he said, shutting the door quietly behind him.

Being alone gave me a few moments to observe my surroundings. I assumed this was Curwen's room, but there was nothing to confirm that, no photos or paintings or clothing strewn about, no signs that this ten-by-ten box was his. The walls were a pale gray, like concrete, and the floor was a charcoal-gray tile. In the corner, there was a black chair, the chair from which Curwen had watched me all night.

On the wall opposite me, there was another door, a closet door. I wondered if all the things that made up who he was were hidden behind that door. Before I could rise and take a peek, he returned, carrying a tray full of fruit and bread and cheese and eggs and water.

"You can have something better tomorrow. This is all I had on hand for now," he apologized.

"Are you kidding? This is great!" I exclaimed, my mouth full of bread. "I don't know how you even had this when you haven't been here."

"There's a lady who cleans my house. She makes sure to keep a little food stocked since she never knows when I'll be here."

"Will she be coming while we're here?" I asked.

"I've already messaged her that I'm home and won't need her services this week."

I could see why his boss would find him useful as an undercover agent. His mind could keep up with all the details, like mine. He didn't like that about me, that I was, as he had said, "too observant." It made it hard for him to hide things.

After swallowing my food with another glass of water, I asked, "What's the plan for today?"

"Well, for this morning, you are going to stay here to rest and regain your strength. I think Laney should stay with you. And I'll try to find out where your parents are located."

"I hope you know, that little idea about Laney staying here? Yeah, that's not going to happen." I laughed.

"A guy can hope," he said with a smile as he popped a grape into his mouth.

"False hopes," I teased, shaking my head.

And I was right. When Laney showed up in the doorway five minutes later, she would hear nothing about staying with me. "Leela will be fine by herself for a little while. Won't you, Leela?" Her eyes threatened me to give the right answer.

"Of course." I smiled mischievously at Curwen. He would not enjoy his morning with my bossy, rebellious twin, but I was grateful to remain inside. Laney supplied me with a mirror, and I could see that my skin appeared completely normal, but it still felt sunburned to touch. So I had no complaints about remaining inside the cool, dark house.

They left shortly afterward, with strict instructions not to leave the house and not to open the door for anyone. When I heard the door beep shut behind them, I got up, moving slowly from the pain. But I had to get used to it so I could be useful.

I realized I had no idea what it looked like out there, in the land of Antonia, a place one travels to *by lightning*. I was still wrapping my head around it. I inched my way up to the window and peeked out. At first, the sun was so bright that I couldn't see past its glaring rays, but then my pupils adjusted. Curwen's home must have been on the outskirts of the city because, out the rear window, there were no houses in sight, no other buildings blocking my view.

The land was a flat, green field of wildflowers for a few miles. This came to the edge of a green forest. And beyond that, there was a purple mountain range. It looked like an oil painting, the heat melting all the vibrant colors together, and I wished I had a camera to capture the image for Corey and Annabelle.

I left his room to find another window on the side of the house. From it, I looked down into a wide alleyway. The concrete was blaring white, reflecting the sun's light back into the sky. The house next door was the same stark white.

None of the curtains were open in any of the windows I could see. Nobody sat outside, and nobody walked down the street. The only sign of life were two abandoned bicycles leaning against the house next door. Was it only because of the heat? Or were Antonians extremely private and closed off?

Before I could stop myself, I was back in his room with the closet door open. But it held disappointment. It contained only clothing and shoes, all of which were neutral colors. There was nothing else of interest. Was everything going to be *so boring*?

I made my way downstairs, hoping to find better things. But it was much the same. It was like living in a black-and-white photograph. If this was the way he liked his house, he must have been very uncomfortable and overwhelmed in our bold and clutter-filled home. That was the difference—his was a house, but ours was a home.

The only thing that piqued my curiosity was a small cabinet in the living room. It was locked. If it was locked, there was something worth hiding. Good thing Corey had taught me how to pick locks. Using one of the hair pins from my bag, I had it open in no time.

The last thing I expected to find was a collection of books. All of them were from our dimension. All of them were first editions. *The Wonderful Wizard of Oz, The Great Gatsby, To Kill A Mockingbird, Dracula, The Secret Garden, War and Peace, Great Expectations. . . .*

On and on it went, at least a hundred of our best-loved classics kept locked away. Were these his treasured possessions—or were they forbidden? Were they locked away for their protection—or for his?

I pulled one of the less fragile editions from the shelf—*Jane Eyre,* one of my favorites—shut the cabinet, and sat on the black sofa. I had searched his entire home to discover things about him that would prove him to be completely different and foreign, yet I had only found something we shared in common.

Sometime later, in the middle of page fifty-six, I heard the now-familiar beep of the front door being unlocked. They were back already, sooner than I'd expected. There was no time to put the book away, so I tucked it between the cushions and then turned toward the door to welcome them with a huge smile.

But it wasn't Curwen. Or Laney.

Three strangers stood there, staring at me.

CHAPTER 9
[LANEY]

The sun was blinding. I put on my hat and sunglasses, observing my surroundings. Last night, in the dark, concerned for my sister, I hadn't noticed much. Everywhere I looked, I saw only white, a pure clean white. No dirt or grime soiled the walkway, and there were no stains on the houses.

It reminded me of pictures I had seen of Santorini, Greece, except the roofs weren't blue. They instead looked like the solar panel shingles Mr. Hammond had installed on his home last year. It made sense that they would harness solar energy; I had never been anywhere where the sun felt more intense.

Afraid to make anything dirty, I hoped the bottoms of my shoes weren't covered in mud from yesterday's hike. But when I lifted my feet to check, the soles were spotless, appearing brand-new.

Curwen noticed my amazed and confused expression, quickly explaining, "I had to clean them while you were sleeping. I also had to scrub down the sidewalk—there was a trail of footprints leading right to my door."

"Why does it matter?" I asked.

"The living quarters are to remain clean," he replied, sounding like an automaton, like it was a command he had memorized and repeated many times.

"But why?" I pressed.

"Because the living quarters are sacred." Again, it sounded like a catechism, answers he had been taught since childhood.

I decided to test him further. "But why are they sacred?"

"Because the home is the center of family life. No more questions," he ordered. What family life? There was no one in sight, and I hadn't heard the sound of children either.

He took the flowerpot from his windowsill and set it in the alleyway between his home and the one next door. It was the only thing of color I had seen—a single red flower, a flower I didn't recognize. A quick glance up and down the street showed that none of the other houses had flowers. Why was his the only one?

"Okay, let's go," he said. My curiosity was easily replaced by my excitement to see Hollister again. Curwen took the lead, walking at a brisk pace, and I remained one step behind him.

The heat was agonizing; I was sweating in no time. The underlayers of my hair were wet against my neck. I longed to put it up but knew he wouldn't allow it. I took a sip from my water bottle every two seconds.

Curwen turned down one walkway after another, all of them looking the same, whitewashed houses on both sides. We saw a few people who took little notice of us, but it seemed he was trying to stay away from crowded areas. Every time I would hear a group of people talking loudly and laughing, he would guide me down a different path until the voices grew faint.

Finally, we reached a tall, narrow, metal gate (painted white, of course) in the middle of the white wall. Before Curwen opened it, he turned to me. "This is only one of the gates between the living and working quarters. Once we go through this gate, don't speak to anyone, even if they speak to you. Keep your eyes down, and stay right behind me," he instructed.

He pulled out another key card, different from the one used for his house, inserting it into the slot and entering a code number. I became keenly aware of just how vulnerable I was, how dependent I was on this man who I only partially trusted (is it a thing—to partially trust someone?).

I didn't know where I was or how to get back to where I had come from, back to Leela, back to Corey and Annabelle. Neither did I know what was beyond the gate. Except Hollister, or at least the promise that he was there.

When the gate beeped, I allowed that thought, that hope, to keep my feet moving. Curwen pulled it wide enough for me to slide through and then secured it behind us.

If the living quarters were the clean space, the working quarters were the unclean. The walls had obviously once been white, but now they appeared a faded red clay color. The walkways were dirt rather than stone, and they were much wider here, to make room for all the people.

People everywhere, bustling past us. Street vendors trying to sell their goods shouted at those passing by. The people looked completely normal, except that their clothes were plain, all solid and neutral. No patterns, no vibrant splashes of color. I was not impressed, but I was grateful Curwen had picked out our clothes.

He was also kind enough to give me a moment to adjust. It was sensory overload after the solitude of the living quarters. Across from us was a row of buildings—they weren't houses, but businesses. He waited until there was lull in the crowd before grabbing my arm and leading me across the alleyway, to the buildings. They provided shade, a reprieve from the sun's heat.

There was a butcher's shop, a home goods store, a cell phone place. And a bakery. *The* bakery where he had bought the pastries, the ones Corey had eaten without sharing. I recognized the logo from the box. I paused to look inside the window at all the delicacies on display, but Curwen pulled me along mercilessly.

I didn't complain, though. I had decided that morning not to complain so he wouldn't leave me at his house with Leela. Right now, she wasn't missing much. But I was going to find out where Hollister and our parents were.

I hoped we could see them too, in which case she would miss it all, and may as well have stayed home with our siblings. Hadn't Curwen suggested she stay home anyway? What had he said? That she would make things harder. How? She was the easy twin.

Curwen came to a halt outside the last building. I glanced up to see where we were—the sign read *State Records*. A line of people flowed out the wide doorway. My first thought was to grumble. We would waste the entire day if we had to wait there, and I wasn't sure I could handle the heat for much longer.

Curwen grabbed my hand and squeezed past the waiting people, but didn't cut in line. The cool air immediately revived me. He found an empty seat in the corner and pushed me toward it before someone could steal it. Gladly, I sat down, removing my sunglasses and trying to look inconspicuous.

He went to grab a number from the counter so we would know when it was our turn. Number fifty-six. Great. I settled comfortably into the seat for the long wait, and Curwen leaned against the wall beside me, his eyes constantly scanning the crowd.

It wasn't going to be as long as I'd anticipated. These people were, as Curwen had described, very efficient. The line died down, and the place began to clear out more quickly than I could have hoped.

Until then, nobody had spoken a word to me. But then an old woman sat in the chair beside me. She wouldn't stop staring at me, and I smiled politely back at her, hoping she would look away, but she instead interpreted the smile as an invitation to conversation. I should have kept my eyes down, as Curwen had instructed.

Her voice was soft and sweet, like my mother's. "My sister had hair the color of yours," she said. "It's very rare, you know."

I didn't reply, but noticed Curwen's jaw tighten.

She continued, "I wonder if we have any common ancestry. I haven't noticed you before. What's your name?"

Curwen's dug his fingers into my shoulder—I interpreted that to mean I should keep quiet. I saw him flash our number at a man who caught his eye.

The man shouted, "Number fifty-six!"

I heard grumbles from those around us whose numbers should have been called first. But standing, I turned and smiled at the woman, saying, "I'm so sorry. That's us."

Curwen grabbed my arm and led me to the counter. Another woman quickly took my abandoned seat.

"Good morning, Clive!" Curwen called cheerfully as we approached.

Clive had dark, reddish-brown hair, with bushy eyebrows and a beard to match. He was a huge man who looked like he belonged in the butcher shop down the way rather than in an office. His pale-blue eyes smiled with kindness; he not only reminded me of a big teddy bear, but also of my father.

"Curwen! How nice to see you. I thought you were away on business," the burly man replied, giving Curwen a knowing look.

"I came home for a couple days to do some research, and you're just the man I wanted to see."

"How can I help?" He looked at me and then back at Curwen with an insinuating twinkle in his eye. "Perhaps a marriage license?" He chuckled, a good, jolly laugh.

Curwen and I both cringed with disgust at the idea.

"Okay, I guess not," Clive said, trying to erase his blunder. "So, what can I do for you? We have a busy day today . . . " He gestured around the crowded waiting room, and everyone appeared to be staring at us with annoyance. I looked down at the floor, wishing to be invisible.

"It's a private matter," Curwen said in a low voice, giving Clive a direct stare. Their eyes communicated more than their words. Was this man part of Curwen's underground group?

"Oh, okay. Say no more. Landon," he called to a young man in back, "I need you to cover the counter for a few minutes." The young man didn't say anything, but his face expressed annoyance as he took over Clive's position.

The big man motioned for us to follow him down a dark, narrow hallway. We entered a small office; the nameplate on the door identified it as his. He offered two chairs for us, which we took, and he sat in one behind the large desk.

"What can I do for you?" Clive asked. "Durham didn't tell me you were coming in today, or I would have told him to wait for another day. We've been so busy with all the death certificates and estate documents."

What was happening? Why so much death? Curwen looked slightly confused, but he didn't ask Clive any questions about it.

"Durham didn't know which day I was coming. I know you're busy, so I'll get straight to the point," Curwen stated. "I need to know the location of a few bodies."

When he used that terminology again—*bodies*—I struggled to keep my composure.

Clive's eyes got wide with surprise and then narrowed with suspicion. "Why do you need to know that? You know that information is classified."

"It will help me with the mission Durham currently has me working on," Curwen explained. That wasn't good enough for Clive. "Durham needs me to question them. They have some information he needs." His voice was firmer now, almost threatening.

"Durham's needs are really going to get me into trouble one of these days," Clive mumbled, but began typing into the computer anyway. All I wanted to know was, who the heck was Durham?

Curwen handed Clive a small piece of paper. "These are their names, and that's the date they were struck."

"These are the bodies from . . . " Clive's voice trailed off as he looked at Curwen with questions.

"Yes," Curwen replied curtly, not offering anything more.

Clive didn't ask for more, but continued looking for the information on his computer. I wanted to ask a million questions, though. There was so much mystery in their unspoken words and looks. But I kept quiet and pulled my plain black hat down further to shield my eyes.

The noise from the printer right beside me made me jump. Clive thought that was funny, so he chuckled. "It won't bite you," he joked. I gave a small, tight-lipped smile and then looked down again.

He rose from his seat and grabbed the sheet from the printer, folding and handing it to Curwen. "Please be careful that this doesn't fall into the wrong hands, and burn it when you're done with it," he pleaded.

"Of course, Clive," he assured him, shaking his hand. "Thank you for your time."

We stood to leave. Curwen reached for my hand.

"Are you sure you two don't want a marriage license?" Clive teased again. "It's about time Curwen settled down with a wife."

I grimaced again, but Curwen just laughed. He was a good actor—probably a good reason to only partially trust him.

"Old Clive," Curwen clapped him on the shoulder, "I think you have your hands full today. Mind if we leave out the back way?"

"Sure. Sure. Go ahead. And don't hesitate to come back on a slow day for that marriage license!" he shouted behind us.

Curwen simply waved as he pushed open the back door, and we stepped into the sunlight again.

I quickly pulled my hand from his. "That guy didn't know when to quit, did he?"

"What do you mean?" he asked.

"With all the talk of marriage," I said. Hollister was the only one I wanted to talk about marriage with.

"It's not a big deal," he said, brushing it off. "We both know that's *never* going to happen."

Rolling my eyes, I took a look around. We were in a narrow, empty alley. On one side were the back of the businesses, on the other was a tall stone wall. There were no other people as far as I could see in either direction.

"Where are we going now?" I asked, leaning against the stone wall for shade.

Instead of answering, he pulled the paper from his pocket. Scanning it, he sighed, obviously not happy with the information. "They're all in different locations," he explained. "Your mother is actually working in the palace gardens." That would suit her passion for gardening. "Your father is in the carpentry warehouses." He liked working with wood. "And Hollister is in the fields. I was really hoping he would be with your father in the warehouses."

"Why?" I asked, alarmed, a stab of panic in my stomach.

"It's just going to be a lot harder to get him from the fields."

"Why? What's wrong with the fields?"

Pulling a lighter from his pocket, he set the paper on fire, letting it burn to ashes and then grinding it into the dirt. When he didn't answer me immediately, I felt the familiar tinge of anger boiling just below the surface, but before I could yell at him, he spoke.

"I'll show you. Come on. The guard towers will be on break soon. It's our best shot."

I felt a sense of impending doom that Curwen did nothing to soothe. Was he trying to show me that it would be impossible to save Hollister? Would he give up that easily? Did he think I would?

He led me to the end of the alley. In front of us was another tall, narrow, white gate. Instead of using a card this time, he entered a series of codes on the keypad; it felt like a decade before the gate beeped and he opened it.

As I slipped through, I almost fell, but Curwen caught my arm to steady me. I was at the top of a flight of narrow stone stairs that led far down to a dirt path. We had exited the city gates.

Antonia was raised above the earth (or was it still the earth in an alternate dimension?), like the Athenian Acropolis. Outside of those walls, there was nothing but nature, an immense green field that ended where a forest began. It didn't look inviting, but that's where the path led. To Hollister.

Curwen went before me down the steep stairs, always keeping one arm up that I could grab onto if I stumbled.

"What about the guard towers?" I asked.

"They *shouldn't* be alarmed since I entered the proper codes in the gate. But we just need to be extra careful . . . and quick."

Quick. I couldn't move any faster. Heat exhaustion was taking over my body, and my water bottle was nearly empty. *The spirit is willing, but the flesh is weak*, I heard my mother's voice saying. She would preach those words to me many times through the years in different circumstances, but in that moment, they seemed fitting.

"How do you have the proper codes?" I huffed out. These stairs were more difficult than I had imagined. I didn't want to think about coming back up them.

He hesitated to answer. "You have more access to things when you work for the king." It was clear from his tone that he wouldn't divulge more information.

We were on the dirt path now. I struggled to keep up with his long strides, my muscles burning. I focused on the trees ahead of us, longing for the darkness of the forest. As tempted as I was to glance back at the guard towers, Curwen warned me not to—it would draw attention and make me look suspicious.

"Can you please slow down?" I practically whined, out of breath.

"No." He grabbed my arm, dragging me to keep up with his pace. I had never hated him more. When we finally reached the cover of the trees, he pulled me off the path, behind some bushes, and then let me sit down to rest.

He shook my empty water bottle and then tossed his at me. "Drink," he ordered. "You need to stay hydrated. You should have told me you were out."

"You should have told me we would be trekking through a desert. I didn't—"

He held his hand up, silencing me. He was listening intently to something, so I strained my ears to hear what he heard. There were footsteps and voices coming down the trail. He dropped to the ground, jerking me down with him.

Two men walked by who looked very similar in size and stature to Clive, except they were solid muscle. They wore black pants and black shirts with black, leather combat boots. These men were an intimidating sight as I watched, my belly to the ground, as they trampled the ground beneath their feet.

"Three twenty-seven has it coming," one of them said. "If he so much as looks at me wrong one more time, I'm sending him to the scientists."

The other one chuckled, asking, "Is that right?"

"You know it," the first replied before their voices faded.

I knew what their jobs were without the aid of Curwen's explanation. Those were the ones in charge, the ones who kept my people in line. They didn't have guns or any other weapons I could see, so how did they wield their power?

Curwen let out a deep sigh beside me, but he didn't appear relieved. "Since we're so close, we'll just keep walking from here and not use the path," he whispered after waiting for the men to be out of sight. Walking through the underbrush required more energy—energy I didn't possess. But my anger was building, and I used it as fuel.

"So, you number us?" I demanded.

"*They* number you, yes," he said.

"Did that paper tell you the numbers for my parents, for Hollister?"

He paused a moment, then replied, "It did, but I don't remember them."

"You're lying!" I accused.

"Shhhh." He held his hand up again to silence me. He had stopped at an opening in the trees and crouched down. I did the same.

We looked down into a vast, shallow valley on the bank of a wide, very blue river. Forest to the east, mountains to the west, river to the north. The river snaked away into the distance to some place I would never go. To the south, hundreds, if not thousands, of fields stretched into oblivion. I had never seen that magnitude of farm production in my life.

I glanced up admiringly at the purple mountains, towering so high that their peaks were engulfed in clouds. Suddenly, I heard shouting and began searching the fields to see where it originated. I squinted my eyes, straining to see the tiny people below, like an army of ants busy at their labor.

My eyes settled on one of the guards, identified because of his black clothing (in contrast, the slaves were wearing yellow, the brightest color I had seen in Antonia). The guard was yelling at an olive-skinned young man with black hair. I didn't recognize him as one from my town. The guard raised his hand and struck the man across the face, causing him to fall backward.

The man glared up at him. Then he stood up, in defiance, in strength. The guard raised his hand to strike again, but a very tall slave approached from behind and grabbed his arm, wrapping his fingers tightly around the guard's wrist, holding it in midair.

I smiled with pride. Because Hollister was brave.

The guard shouted for backup, and suddenly Hollister was convulsing on the ground. That's when I noticed he had a collar around his neck—a shock collar.

"HOLLISTER!" I shouted, tears beginning to stream down my cheeks.

Curwen had his hand over my mouth so fast that he knocked me to the ground, landing on top of me. I had never seen anyone look as angry as he did in that moment, his black eyes frightening. I thought he would kill me right there, so close to Hollister. So close.

Was this the moment Hollister and I would both regret what we had just done, the moment that would keep us from ever being together again? I longed to look again, to see what they were doing to him.

Curwen's phone started buzzing, but he wouldn't get off of me, too afraid I would start shouting some more. He sat on top of me with one hand over my mouth, reaching for his phone with the other, all while staring down at me, daring me to move or make a sound. I did neither.

He answered his phone. "Hi, Durham. I can't really talk right now."

"You had better." The volume on his phone was loud enough that I could hear.

"I'll call you back soon."

"No. Come home now."

"I'm still working on the mission. I'll return to Antonia soon."

"I don't mean home to Antonia."

Curwen paused. He asked slowly, "What do you mean then?"

"Come home to your house," Durham ordered. "So you can explain why there is a woman here. She won't say a word. I might have to do something to get her talking."

Curwen's eyes narrowed into two slits, reflecting a million emotions.

Who the heck is Durham? Why was he threatening my sister? And why did Curwen obey him?

"Durham. I'll be there soon. Don't . . . do . . . anything." He flipped his phone shut. "We have to go now. Leela needs us," he explained firmly. "Can you do that? Can you not scream if I let you go?"

I nodded, and he slowly removed his hand from my mouth.

"But what about Hollister?" I asked softly, my eyes pleading. He was still sitting on me.

"You mean 327?" he asked with anger. The guard's words from the woods replayed in my head—*327 has it coming.* "Yeah, that's right. Your boyfriend is 327, and if he doesn't stop trying to be a hero, we won't be able to do anything for him."

I squirmed beneath his body weight. Why was he telling me this? It wouldn't convince me to leave, to abandon Hollister. He lifted me from the ground, holding onto my wrist and putting one hand back over my mouth.

"Look," he said, showing me the valley again. Hollister was nowhere to be seen. "Hollister has already been taken back to the barracks. There's nothing we can do right now. But we'll come back for him."

I looked at him with anger and doubt in my eyes. Partial trust had become almost no trust. He was lying.

"I promise we'll come back for him," he tried to assure me. "Leela needs us right now. And I'm going to help her, whether you come or not. Do you understand?" He released me.

"Stop treating me like a child," I spit out.

"Either I treat you like a child, or they're going to treat you like a slave." He pointed to the valley, to the guards, before he turned and began walking away, leaving me to decide.

CHAPTER 10

[LEELA]

They stared at me with interested but suspicious eyes.

Two males, one female.

The older male, the obvious leader, stood in front. He was in his early forties. He had hazel eyes and light-brown hair that was graying around the temples—my mother would have said he was one of those men who became more handsome with age. But to me, he only appeared threatening. However, unlike the young woman behind him, his face reflected curiosity more than anger.

Her skin was a warm brown with flushed pink cheeks. She was beautiful with almond-shaped eyes that were nearly black. And her thick, dark hair hung in waves around her face. Although she was shorter than me, she had a commanding presence and stood tall with authority.

The second man was in his twenties, with olive skin and long, dark-brown hair pulled back in a bun. His eyes were a striking light green that reminded me of Hollister's. His face was attractive, but maybe only because it held the kindest expression, with a hint of a smile and glimmer of amusement. It gave me the slightest hope that they might not hurt me.

I stared back at them, unable and unwilling to budge from my spot on the couch, trying to assess the situation and make a wise move. Would I need to remember those self-defense techniques Hollister had taught us— the ones Laney had demonstrated so well in her knife-wielding against Curwen?

They wouldn't do any good against three individuals. Would the young woman fight me too? Her glare said yes. I was cornered, though; they blocked the only exit. There was nothing nearby to use as a weapon.

They had a key to enter the house, so Curwen must know them. But why were they here?

I waited for them to speak, to give me a clue to their identities. It seemed like a century before the lead man broke the silence.

"Hi. I'm Durham," he said. So this was the man who had yelled at Curwen on the phone? I instantly didn't like him. When I said nothing, he continued. "This is Sheldon." He gestured to the young man, who lifted a hesitant hand in greeting and flashed a broad smile. "And this," he turned toward the woman, "is Mara." Her head shot in his direction, her glare now falling on him, not happy about being introduced to me.

"Yeah, so who are you?" Mara demanded.

I wanted to answer. I didn't want to sit there quietly, but I didn't know if I was supposed to tell them who I was or why I was there. Curwen hadn't covered this part of the plan—mainly because it wasn't part of the plan. We weren't supposed to interact with the Antonians. We were supposed to get our people back while drawing little, if any, attention to our mission or ourselves.

Did Durham work for the government or the underground organization that was working against the government? That had never been made clear. I didn't know whether he could be trusted. I remained silent. I would have to wait for Curwen to arrive; he would know what to say.

When they realized I wasn't going to speak, Durham pulled out his odd-looking cell phone, exactly the same as Curwen's. "You two, stay with her," he ordered, annoyed with me. "I'm going to make a phone call." Then he disappeared out the front door.

Sheldon slowly walked into the room and sat at the other end of the couch. He appeared much more honest than the other two. Mara, irritated that he would come anywhere near me, remained in the entry, watching us closely.

"Were you reading?" he asked gently, quietly so Mara couldn't hear. He glanced down at the book sticking out from the cushions. "It's okay," he assured me. "Curwen's not supposed to have them, but he lets me borrow them sometimes."

I still said nothing.

Perhaps he was tricking me. Perhaps he and Mara had a good-cop/bad-cop thing they did.

"I've been reading *The Count of Monte Cristo*," he admitted, barely above a whisper.

Just then, the door beeped again, Durham reentering. Sheldon quickly pushed the book farther down in the cushions, so it couldn't be seen, while giving me a wink and a smirk.

Durham sat in the chair opposite me; Mara took the one beside it, still scowling at me. The boss man didn't try to ask any questions or attempt conversation. The four of us sat in silence—Mara in anger, Sheldon in patient amusement, Durham in annoyed curiosity, and me in concern and discomfort.

What were they doing, just waiting here? Who had he called? Curwen, I hoped.

I counted the ticks on the wall clock. It would be the middle of the night at home now. I imagined Corey and Annabelle sleeping in the same bed to comfort each other. I imagined that they had enjoyed the dinner we had premade and that Corey had read his little sister her favorite story before bedtime. I missed them. Would I see them again?

Soon, I heard another beep of the door. It was Curwen this time, holding Laney's hand, who stayed just behind him.

At seeing Laney, Mara said, "Are you kidding me?" Twins were too much for her. Now Laney got to experience the wrath of Mara's eyes.

Everyone ignored her, taking in the scene. A wide grin spread across Sheldon's face, making him even more attractive. Curwen's eyes told him to cut it out, and then he looked at me with reassurance.

Then he and Durham stared each other down, silently communicating.

"Please have a seat and explain yourself, Curwen," Durham ordered. He had said it politely, but there was an undercurrent of threat to his voice that I knew Curwen would obey.

Curwen walked past Sheldon, leading Laney to the empty seat between Sheldon and me. I scooted over as far as I could so she wouldn't have to touch him. She was sunburned and exhausted, and I longed to know what they had discovered that morning without me. But first we had to deal with the boss man.

Curwen perched on the arm of the couch, right beside me. He asked Durham, "What do you want to know?"

"Everything, kid," he said, but what he really meant was *don't play dumb with me.*

Curwen sighed heavily, like he always did before launching into a story. "I came home yesterday . . . just needed to rest and figure out my next moves. All my leads were running dry."

"Why didn't you report this?" Durham asked.

Curwen hesitated before answering. "I didn't want you to think I couldn't do the job."

"All movements must be logged and reported," Durham stated bluntly.

Curwen nodded, looking down, accepting his chastisement.

"So," Durham gestured to me and Laney, "where do these two enter the story?"

Maybe when your people kidnapped and enslaved all of mine? I wanted to punch him. What would Curwen tell him? The truth?

"When I went to State Records to do some research, I met Laney and Leela," Curwen explained. So, not the truth. He continued, "Their parents died, and their home was confiscated . . . you know how things are."

Mara's eyes grew wide with fear. "Why aren't they in quarantine?" she demanded.

"They were. They've been cleared," Curwen said.

Were they talking about the sickness that was spreading among the people? Was that our backstory—that our parents had died from it and we had been quarantined? I wished I had asked Curwen more questions about this place, now that I had to pretend to be one of them.

"Well, what are you going to do with them now?" Durham asked, but it sounded like a test. He didn't seem to believe Curwen's story, but he was willing to go along with it for now, to test his young protégé.

"I was thinking they could help me with the mission," Curwen said.

"What!" Mara interjected. "You wouldn't even let me help you!"

Durham raised his hand to silence her. "This may be a good idea. They look like they could gain people's trust and gather intel easily. That is . . . if they can talk." He looked at us with a twinkle in his eye, sizing us up, daring us to make a sound.

Laney and I looked at each other, not sure what was expected of us or what we were getting ourselves into. If we didn't speak, would he leave us alone? If we did, what would we have to do? What kind of intel would we have to trick out of people?

Curwen seemed to be weighing the options as well. Finally, he turned to us and nodded. "Of course they can talk, Durham," he said, almost in a defeated tone. What was he signing us up for? We just wanted to get our family and go home.

"Good." Durham smiled at us. It was fake. I still wanted to punch him. "But you know they can't stay here. It's not appropriate. And we don't need any rumors drawing attention to this house."

"Where do you propose they stay?" Curwen countered.

Durham smiled. "With Mara, of course."

Before she could protest, I spoke up. "That's not a good idea. We'll stay here."

Curwen gave the slightest shake of his head, indicating I shouldn't have said anything. Everyone was silent for an awkward moment, but I could tell they were surprised, either by my boldness or some social blunder I had no clue about.

Finally, Mara stated, "I don't want them staying with me. They carry disease with them."

"Mara, nobody asked you," Durham replied calmly but with force.

She looked away and wouldn't say another word. How had Durham come to have so much power over these three? Each of them appeared strong, capable, and intelligent, yet they nearly bowed before him. Last I'd heard, Gigandet was king—not him.

"As any good Antonian citizen knows, unmarried men and women do not stay in the same living quarters," Durham stated. He said it like he knew we weren't Antonian. What game was he playing? I didn't want to play.

"Fine," Curwen surrendered. "They can stay with Mara."

"Excellent." Durham smiled again. Still fake. Still wanted to punch him. "We'll discuss everything further tonight, at dinner."

"Dinner?" Curwen asked.

"Yes," the boss man confirmed. "Seven o' clock. Phaedra's house. Don't be late."

He rose to leave. Mara was already at the door, eager to be out of our diseased presence.

"Sheldon, you can stay if you like," Durham said.

Please don't stay. Please don't stay.

But Sheldon smiled broadly. "All right, boss. I'll check in later."

At the door, Durham turned back. "Curwen, put the flowerpot back in your window. Maybe if it had been there, we wouldn't have stopped by."

With those last words, the heavy door clicked shut behind them.

A collective sigh was breathed by all of us, including Sheldon. Why was he relieved?

We sat quietly, letting it sink in that we would be staying with Mara that night. The more I thought about it, the angrier I became. Before I knew it, Laney and I were both glaring at Curwen, who had moved to the chair across from me, the one formerly occupied by Durham.

"Thanks a lot, Curwen," Laney hissed. "We do not have time for dinner."

"Or staying with Mara," I added.

"You said we would go back for Hollister," she accused.

Tears filled my eyes. "You saw Hollister?"

She smiled and nodded as tears filled her eyes as well. We embraced. She whispered in my ear, "He's alive . . . for now." We held each other as we sobbed, only vaguely aware of Sheldon's presence. The guys didn't say a word until we had finished.

"Dude," Sheldon started, "I tried to keep them from coming here. But once they saw the flowerpot had been moved, I couldn't deter them."

"It's okay," Curwen replied. "I thought it would be better moved, but that backfired."

"What's with the flowerpot?" I asked.

Laney added, "And who the heck is Durham? And Mara?" And, turning to Sheldon, "And who are *you*?"

Sheldon laughed.

Curwen said, "Things just became way more complicated than they should have been. Durham is the leader of the underground resistance. Mara, Sheldon, and I work for him."

"But it's more than that," Sheldon added. "Durham is like a father to each of us. We're all orphans, and he practically raised us."

"Raised you? Or trained you to be his puppets?" Laney countered. That was too harsh—I pinched her to let her know it.

But Sheldon was going to let her know also. "Whoa, whoa, whoa. You don't know me. You should be more grateful to the ones who are going to help get your family back."

"Well, you wouldn't have to help us if you didn't take them in the first place!" Laney argued.

"Wait . . . ," I said. Did Laney not hear what he'd said? I looked at Curwen questioningly.

Curwen nodded. "Sheldon knows the truth."

My sister and I looked at Sheldon, trying to determine if he could be trusted.

Curwen continued, "Remember that friend who stopped me at the bakery the other night, the one who kept me from coming back sooner?" Sheldon flashed a smile and pointed to himself. "Well, I told him everything because he can help us. And we *need* help." Again, Sheldon pointed to himself.

He was much more lighthearted than Curwen. He didn't take everything so seriously, and he was able to contend well in arguments with Laney. That morning, he had only shown me kindness and tried to make me feel comfortable.

"Why would you help us?" I asked Sheldon. "It goes against everything you've been taught, and you'd be committing treason, as Curwen has made clear several times."

"I've traveled to your dimension enough to learn that people are people, no matter where they come from," he said. "That's why they limit traveling—our people would realize there is little difference between *us* and *them*. The resistance has a few spies in the government, but Curwen is one of the only ones actually authorized to travel. The rest of us break the law." He laughed.

Curwen watched us closely, analyzing our interaction. He wasn't pleased by how much Sheldon was sharing—I could tell by the tightening of his jaw. Now I knew Sheldon was the forthcoming one, the one to go to with questions.

"Where did you see Hollister?" I asked.

Curwen and Laney recounted the events of that morning. Sheldon listened intently, just as interested as I was, yet not emotionally invested.

"So, in conclusion, after seeing Hollister," Curwen stated, "we need to do more reconnaissance to see what conditions your parents are in. How are you feeling, Leela? Do you need to stay here and rest more?"

My skin still hurt to be touched, feeling like a sunburn, one that couldn't be seen. And the thought of traveling back through the lightning created a large knot of dread in the pit of my stomach.

I doubted I would ever enjoy a lightning storm again. I would be like Annabelle, hiding under the covers. Or I would wonder if they were taking more slaves, if they were taking children from their parents or parents from their children.

It made me angry, and I shook my head vigorously. "No. I want to help."

"Okay," he said, nodding. "Then I think the best plan is for Laney to go with Sheldon to the carpentry warehouses and Leela to come with me to the palace gardens. You'll both need to point out your parents to us, since we don't have pictures of them."

"Yeah," Laney quipped, rolling her eyes. "No pictures. Just numbers."

"Do you know their numbers?" Sheldon asked Curwen. "It could help us to know them."

"Well, Hollister is 327," Laney said with anger.

Ignoring her tone, Curwen added, "Their mother is 3126, and their father is 2916."

Tears came to my eyes at the thought of them being reduced to numbers, but I blinked them away. There was no time for crying now. I cherished the hope of seeing my mother again. Would she look different? Had they hurt her? At the same time, I was jealous that I wouldn't see my father also.

"Why can't we all go together?" I asked.

"We don't have a lot of time left before dinner," Curwen explained. "It will be faster this way."

"Plus," Sheldon added, "the two of you together would draw a ton of unwanted attention. There are only a dozen sets of twins in Antonia. It's safer to keep you separated."

"When do we leave?" Laney and I asked simultaneously.

Sheldon looked at Curwen. "Do they do that often?" he asked.

"Not that I've heard," he said nonchalantly. We hadn't done that in a month. This mission, this hope, was finally uniting us again. "We'll leave after we eat something."

Sheldon went to the kitchen to whip something up. Laney went upstairs to change, rebelliously telling Curwen that she would no longer wear black. He chose not to fight that battle.

"So," I started, "if there are only a dozen sets of twins in Antonia, then why didn't Durham say anything?"

"He doesn't believe us," Curwen said with confidence. "He's just playing along until he can figure out what we're up to."

"Isn't that dangerous? What will he do if he knows?"

"I'm not sure. I don't want to find out. I want to get this done before he can do anything."

He was risking a lot for us, probably more than we realized. We should be more grateful, like Sheldon had said.

Pulling the copy of *Jane Eyre* from between the couch cushions, I handed it to Curwen. "You might want to put this up," I said, a look of apology on my face.

Taking it, he shook his head at me with a slight smirk, not surprised that I had rifled through his things or picked the lock. "You two are gonna be the death of me," he joked.

"I hope not," I replied seriously.

We stared at each other for a long moment until he said, "Go get ready. Make sure you apply plenty of sunscreen."

We all ate quickly, not wanting to waste any more time, knowing that time was limited. When we stepped outside into the afternoon sun, the first thing Curwen did was return the flowerpot to the windowsill.

Laney asked again, "What is with the flowerpot?"

"It lets people know where a safe house is," Sheldon replied quietly. "It indicates who is part of the resistance."

"Okay," Curwen said after locking the door. "Meet back here at six at the latest. If you can't make it by then, then meet at Phaedra's at seven."

Laney and Sheldon headed in the opposite direction. Suddenly, I had a feeling that I might never see her again. Anything could happen at any moment. I ran after her and hugged her tightly despite how much the pressure hurt my skin.

She embraced me and whispered, "Everything will be okay. You'll see." She pulled back and smiled at me with so much confidence, saying, "Hollister is brave, and we can be too."

She had seen more of Antonia than I had. Maybe it wasn't as frightening as I imagined, or maybe she was, as she said, just putting on a brave face.

I knew she was worried for Hollister after what she had witnessed that morning. I knew she didn't trust that Curwen would keep his word and go back for him. But I didn't know how my typically emotional sister was keeping it all under control.

I released her and turned to find Curwen's hand held out for me. I looked into his dark eyes, searching for the same confidence Laney had. It was there, but mixed with doubt and concern. *I believe, help my unbelief,* I heard my father say.

Grabbing his hand, I continued to look over my shoulder as Laney became smaller and smaller. He gave my hand a squeeze, harder than he meant, because he saw me wince and loosened his grip.

"She'll be fine," he assured me. "Sheldon will take care of her. You'll see her soon." Handing me a water bottle, he instructed, "Make sure you keep hydrated. It's the hottest part of the day."

Hot? Did I feel hot? I had to think about it because I had hardly noticed the temperature at all. The weather felt just fine. I tried to feel the heat, to notice any sweat, and I couldn't. There was even a slight chill from the occasional breeze.

"I'm not hot," I stated.

Curwen laughed; he thought I was joking, that I was putting on a façade. But I wasn't. I was burning hot in the lightning when I shouldn't have been, yet I was completely comfortable when I should have been burning hot. I couldn't explain it, so I didn't try.

CHAPTER 11

[LANEY]

The living quarters were more alive now. I saw children for the first time; they were returning home from school. Curwen was right—blondes were rare; I didn't see any.

But they saw me. They stared up at me with brown and green and sometimes blue eyes, scrutinizing me. That morning, all the adults had paid little attention, but the children were unusually curious as they passed.

"They are the advanced ones," Sheldon explained. "They only come home for an afternoon meal. Then they will return to school, where they live. Their parents only see them for an hour each day."

"Advanced ones?"

"They've been tested and have been found to be the smartest and wisest among all the children. They must spend all their time on education. It's their sole focus."

Their sole focus. My sole focus, my soul's focus, was to get back to Hollister. After we saw my father, I would convince Sheldon to help me get back to the fields or barracks or wherever they were keeping Hollister. Or I would do it alone.

Somehow. I didn't know how.

I had tried to pay attention on the way back, when I reluctantly followed Curwen home from the forest, but everything looked the same once we entered the living quarters. I couldn't tell one pathway from another, and they didn't have street signs. It was a series of lefts and rights until it felt like we were going in circles.

Now with Sheldon, the only familiar marker I saw, which indicated that we were going the same way Curwen had brought me back to his house earlier, was a little old lady sitting on a wooden chair outside her home. Her hair was a soft white, and her face was a darkened brown with wrinkles from decades of too much sun.

As we approached, Sheldon called out cheerfully, "Good afternoon, Muriel!"

She smiled broadly, which increased the wrinkles around her eyes. I could see now that she was blind. She reached her hand out for him to grab, which he did with a firm affection.

"Who is this with you?" she asked, still holding his hand. "Don't look surprised," she said to me. "I heard two sets of footsteps . . . and your heavy breathing." She chuckled. I *was* out of breath, trying to keep up with Sheldon in this heat.

"This is our friend Laney," he said. "We're on a mission and can't stay. But I'll come visit soon and bring you some of those oranges you like."

She reached her other hand out for mine. I reluctantly acquiesced, shaking her hand. Her skin was soft like silk petals, but her grasp was strong. Looking at me (but not really looking at me), she said with fortitude, "May your mission be a success."

"Thank you," I replied quietly, pulling my hand back, uncomfortable.

If she knew our mission, would she still want it to succeed? If she knew who I really was, would she still be so kind? Something told me *yes*. As we continued on our way, I glanced back at her and her house. There was a pot in her window with a single red flower. That sweet—yet fierce—little, old woman was part of the resistance. And her house was a safe one.

The sun was directly overhead now; there was no shade to walk in. My hair was wet with perspiration, and I drank from my water bottle every minute or two. But I could slowly feel myself adjusting to the climate. Would I be freezing when we returned home?

Sheldon interrupted the silence, stating, "We'll be there soon. The carpentry warehouses aren't far outside the city." We turned a corner at the end of a corridor and found ourselves facing another tall, white gate.

Sheldon began to input a series of access codes on the keypad.

"Are you also an undercover agent?" I asked.

He had to concentrate; he made me wait until he was done entering the codes before answering. "Kind of," he said. "I'm not at a top level like Curwen—I've never met the king. But they use me for security sometimes, which allows me to learn intel without being noticed."

"Curwen has met the king?" I asked. He had never told us that.

Sheldon nodded hesitantly, realizing he had probably said something he shouldn't have—it was the downfall of his transparency. It was clear he would say no more.

He held the gate open for me. There was another long flight of narrow stone steps to descend before we reached a dirt path. I could see the forest in the distance, and a small part of me was tempted to run toward it so I might get another glimpse of Hollister.

Had the guard from the forest returned to the fields and learned about what 327 had done? *Three twenty-seven has it coming*, his voiced echoed in my head. *I'm sending him to the scientists*, he had said. What did that mean? I was afraid to ask Sheldon, knowing he would give me an honest answer, and knowing it was probably worse than anything I could imagine.

I could not forget the sight of him, standing tall in his bright yellow garb, protecting the younger slave. I hadn't been able to make out the details of his face from such a distance, but I knew the lines and movements of his body. Twenty-two years of knowing him had permanently etched his figure into my brain.

The image of him writhing in pain from the shock collar flashed before my eyes. I shook it away immediately, knowing it would paralyze and distract me. I tried to focus on the mission at hand: devising a plan to free my father.

"How much farther?" I asked.

We had reached the dirt path, which trailed along the outside of the city wall.

"It's just around this corner up here. You'll see all the different warehouses," he said. "You might as well hold my hand and pretend like we're 'together.' Otherwise, the guards might become suspicious."

Great. First I was teased about applying for a marriage license with Curwen. Now I had to pretend to date Sheldon.

He took my hand. "Just let me do the talking."

Fine by me. I didn't respect these people enough to talk kindly to them.

The wall ended, and I saw the warehouses. Maybe ten of them stretched on for a mile. They all had solar panels on their roofs. This was where my father had been working for the past several weeks.

There were dozens of guards surrounding each building, all of them holding what appeared to be electric cattle prods. I winced, imagining one of them being used on my father.

"Do you think you could smile?" Sheldon whispered. "Or at least not look angry." I forced a smile. He grimaced. "Never mind—don't do that. Just show no emotion."

"All right, let's go," I said.

"Okay. But one more thing. If you see your father, *do not say or do anything*," he warned. I nodded, narrowing my eyes. Obviously, Curwen had caught him up on my actions from that morning.

The guards stopped talking and stared as we approached. Sheldon simply nodded at them with confidence as we passed, entering through the double doors of the third warehouse. Inside was a dark and cool lobby. Chairs lined the walls, like they had at the records office, forming a waiting area. But, unlike the records office, nobody was waiting here.

There was a receptionist behind a desk, watching us curiously. Her hair was the color of honey and looked like silk. Her bright-green eyes sparkled with interest . . . and maybe something more. We walked up to the desk, hand in hand.

"Good afternoon. How may I help you?" She smiled broadly, but only directed her attention to Sheldon. She was interested, all right—in him. If he was aware of it, of the way she was looking at him—and I was sure he was—it didn't faze him.

"Yes," he replied coolly. "We'd like to talk to one of your carpenters about a bed."

"Oh. Are you two married?" she asked, searching our hands for wedding bands.

"No." He shook his head slightly, not releasing my hand. "Our friends are getting married."

"Oh! I love when we get orders for marriage beds," she exclaimed. "It's such a sweet tradition."

Her cheerful demeanor (and probably the fact that she ignored my presence) annoyed me. I'm sure it showed on my face because when she finally did glance at me, her smiled faded.

"Let me get Phil for you," she said quickly, exiting through the doorway behind her desk.

We sat in the waiting area. "What is the marriage-bed tradition?" I asked.

"Unmarried couples are not permitted to purchase a bed for themselves . . . because unmarried couples should have no need for a shared bed. So, when a couple is engaged to be married, their family and friends will pull their money together to purchase a marriage bed for them," he explained nonchalantly.

The receptionist came back with a short, middle-aged man with a balding head of mousy-brown hair and pale-blue eyes. He held a clipboard and walked in our direction.

"Good afternoon! I hear you would like to design a bed for a happy couple," he greeted us while he shook both of our hands. "I'm Phil, and I would love to help you."

"I'm Sheldon, and this is Laney."

I smiled a real smile—not something forced—because Phil's goofy smile was contagious. The corners of his large mouth stretched all the way to the corners of his Santa Claus eyes; he reminded me of Mr. Hammond from back home.

"Well," Sheldon began, "we weren't sure if we wanted to design something new or if we wanted to see some of your samples."

He hesitated, then said, "All right . . . I can show you some of our samples, if you don't mind coming into the workhouses."

He looked at me. Was I not supposed to want to go to the workhouses?

"That would be great!" Sheldon exclaimed with a cool, confident smile.

I nodded in agreement, internally steeling myself for whatever I might see.

Phil led us out a side door I hadn't noticed before. We walked down a short, dark tunnel connecting the two buildings. Phil knocked on the door, and a guard, dressed all in black, opened it. I hesitated for a moment; Sheldon gave my hand a squeeze for encouragement.

This building looked like a warehouse was supposed to look. It was noisy with the sounds of hammers and saws. Slabs of unused wood lined the walls. Dozens of long tables lined up in two rows served as workstations.

At each table were several men, several slaves, *bodies*, dressed in bright-orange shirts and pants, like convicts. Some glanced at us from the corners of their eyes, but most kept their heads down, focusing on their work. Guards paced back and forth on each row, watching the men closely, not bothering to look in our direction either.

Phil showed us around, giving us a tour of the place. I zoned out, neglecting to hear his words. Instead, I made note of how many guards there were compared to the number of workers, a one-to-five ratio.

There were two side exits and a door on the opposite side that led into another dark corridor, connecting to another building. Was my father in one of those other buildings? How could we get to him? I ached to run through the other guarded door into another warehouse and search for my father.

"Laney. Laney." Sheldon was calling my name.

I snapped back to reality. "Yes?"

"Phil wants us to meet with one of their designers."

"Yes," Phil said. "Let me warn you. He is a slave, of course, but he's very docile. He's really quite talented. I feel that he could give you what you're looking for."

"That's fine," I said without emotion, attempting to hide my disgust at his description of this slave.

He led us to a back corner, to the last and darkest workstation where a slave was bent over a new wooden chair. It was beautiful, and so familiar. It looked like the chairs from our kitchen table. Looking at the back of the slave's head, I caught my breath.

Sheldon looked at me, warning me with his eyes, and he held my hand more firmly. I would keep my mouth shut, but I couldn't guarantee that my father would do the same when he stood and saw me. *Dad, please don't say anything. Don't blow our cover.*

"Two-nine-one-six!" Phil shouted. His booming voice startled my father and angered me. All the kindness I had felt toward him earlier dissipated.

My father stood and turned around slowly. I held my breath and tried to give him a warning with my eyes. But I didn't need to. When he saw me, when his midnight-blue eyes met mine, there was only a small flicker of recognition before he returned his eyes to the floor.

What had happened to him? I wanted to cry.

He had lost at least twenty pounds, which wasn't necessarily a bad thing because he had been a little overweight, but I almost couldn't recognize his gaunt and disgruntled face, the hollowness in his eyes. Except for its hard expression, my face hadn't changed at all, yet he didn't know me, or at least pretended not to. I prayed he was only pretending.

I wanted to run to him and throw my arms around him in a huge embrace that would never end. Instead, I ventured to do something that would probably still be considered inappropriate.

I pulled my hand from Sheldon's tight grip and took a step forward. Then I reached my hand out to shake my father's hand. I greeted him, "It's nice to meet you."

He glanced at Phil to see if he would be punished, but Phil was too stunned to offer any sort of permission. My father took the momentary lapse in authority to grasp my hand in his.

It was just as I remembered it—rough and calloused from thirty years of hard work, with hairy knuckles and short, dirty, fingernails. It almost wasn't enough, that one little handshake. It tempted me to reach out and hug him, but he took his hand away quickly after giving mine a reassuring squeeze.

I knew he knew me.

Phil cleared his throat, interrupting my moment. "Well, then . . . shall we continue?" he asked rudely.

"Of course," Sheldon replied, grabbing my hand again, communicating his displeasure with my actions by digging his nails into my palm. I repaid the favor, knowing my nails were longer than his, until he loosened his grip.

At that moment, the receptionist entered the room, motioning to Phil.

"Oh," Phil said. "Um . . . uh . . . do you think you two will be okay here for a few minutes? Just describe to 2916 what kind of bed you're looking for, and I'm sure he can come up with a sketch . . . "

He directed all of his words to Sheldon now. Apparently shaking my father's hand had caused me to lose the respect of the man with the Santa Claus eyes. I never knew I could go from liking to loathing someone so instantly, but Phil had shown me how possible that was.

"Yes, we'll be just fine," Sheldon said assertively. "Thanks."

"Okay, I'll be back soon." Phil walked away reluctantly.

Good riddance.

Once he was halfway across the room, my father sat on a stool next to the table. He dropped his face into his hands and began to weep quietly.

"Don't cry, Dad. Shhh," I whispered.

I had never seen my father cry, and I didn't know how to handle his tears. I wanted to cup his face in my hands the same way he had held mine when I was a child, but I restrained myself, aware of the guards eyeing us with curiosity, ready to pounce at any second.

"Yes, please don't cry," Sheldon begged, looking around us. "You're going to get us all in trouble."

My father looked up at him. "Who are you?"

"Dad, he's going to help us get you out of here."

"Us?"

"Me and Leela."

"You're both here?" He seemed angry.

"Yes . . . Leela is trying to find Mom right now."

"Lizzy . . . ," he whispered my mother's name with such sadness.

"Yes, we're going to get you all out of here and back to Corey and Annabelle."

At the sound of their names, he snapped out of his sadness and looked at me through the same strong eyes I remembered. "How do you propose we do that?" he asked, putting on his planning and strategy hat.

But we didn't have time to discuss elaborate plans.

The guards were watching us. A couple of them were walking our way. I looked up at Sheldon to see if he had any bright ideas.

He took control of the situation. Grabbing the pencil and drawing paper on the table, he began to sketch something. "And this here," he pointed with the pencil, "is how we want the headboard to look . . . "

My father caught on quickly. "How wide would you want it? What are the measurements of their bedroom?"

The guards passed by simultaneously, seemingly satisfied that we were not up to anything they couldn't handle. But Sheldon wasn't going to risk any more displays of affection between me and a slave; he remained standing between us, sketching.

"Okay, here's the deal," he spoke under his breath while drawing, strands of his long, dark hair falling into his face. "Try to complete the headboard by tomorrow morning. It doesn't matter what it looks like. Can you do that?"

"Yes, I think so."

"Good. We'll come back then." Then loudly, he added, "Thank you for your time. See that you do a good job."

Sheldon grabbed my hand and pulled me away. I gave one last longing look over my shoulder; my father was already selecting the pieces of wood he would use from a pile leaning against the wall.

He had aged so much in just one month. I hated to leave him. But I took some comfort in knowing, at least from what I had observed, that his conditions weren't as bad as Hollister's.

Hollister. Maybe we could see him now.

We ran into Phil in the dark corridor.

"Did everything go all right?" he asked cheerfully, wanting to make a sale.

"Yes, thank you," Sheldon replied. "We'll come back tomorrow. The slave said he would have something for us by then."

"Oh . . . all right." Phil acted like we were stepping on his toes, taking over his job, telling him what we were going to do. "I guess that will be okay."

Yes, it will be more than okay! I wanted to shout in his face, shout so loud and close that tiny spit particles would land on him. But I didn't.

"Thanks," Sheldon said again with a smile as he opened the door for us.

I needed to get out of that claustrophobic hallway, and away from Phil. I would never like the name *Phil* for as long as I lived.

I wanted to rush past the receptionist without uttering a word, but Sheldon wouldn't let me. Instead, he spent a few minutes filling out some paperwork about our order, all while my insides were fidgeting to leave that place, every bit of me yearning to go see Hollister. To be so close, but so far.

Finally, when he finished and let go of my hand, I busted out the front door, out into the Antonian sun. The guards were so startled that some of them drew their weapons, ready to strike. When they saw it was only me, they lowered them. Yes, only me. If they only knew who I really was, they would strap a collar around my neck and assign me a number.

The sight of them angered me, and I glared at them. They didn't like that. They looked away, ignoring me.

Sheldon was beside me now.

Being serious, I asked, "Can we go back to the forest? To see Hollister."

He eyed me for a long moment, deciding what his answer would be. He shook his head, exasperated, smirked, and said, "Come on, you troublemaker."

CHAPTER 12

[LEELA]

"I should have sent you with Sheldon, since it was the shorter distance. But I just don't know if I could have handled your sister for much longer—at least not without really losing my temper with her," he apologized.

"Honestly, Curwen, I wish you would believe me when I say I'm not hot or tired. Please stop being so concerned," I said.

He sighed deeply. "It's hard not to be. You really scared me last night. I thought you were dying."

"I did too," I joked half-heartedly, trying to lighten the mood. But remembering the pain created dread in my stomach. Would I have to experience that again on the way home?

We had been walking for almost an hour. After leaving the living quarters, we had passed through the working quarters, which I found to be fascinating—the businesses, the street vendors, the people. Just now, we had passed through another gate, entering the meeting quarters.

Curwen explained that the meeting quarters was the social area, where groups could gather together for recreation or celebration. Beautifully paved pathways weaved through an enormous park and garden. We walked these pathways, side by side, not touching though.

There were small groups of people here or there, chatting and laughing. Few of them took notice of us as we passed. I couldn't help wondering what they would think or say or do if they knew I didn't belong there. Would they respond in fear or disgust? Probably both.

Curwen had explained earlier that Antonian and slave were to be kept separate, only interacting when absolutely necessary. I was neither Antonian nor slave. At least, not yet. But with any wrong move or any bit of suspicion, I could easily become one.

"Are you sure you're feeling okay?" Curwen asked, breaking the silence.

Again, I answered, "Yes, I'm fine."

"This long walk isn't taking all of your energy, is it?"

"No, really, I'm fine." Changing the subject, I asked, "So, how do you propose we get Hollister?"

He didn't answer immediately, deep in thought. "I'm not sure, Leela . . . the possibilities are pretty bleak." He stared down at his feet as he walked.

"What are you saying? That we aren't going to try?" I demanded.

I stopped dead in my tracks; he turned to look at me, defeated.

He was the one who looked exhausted. When was the last time he'd had a good night of sleep? Had he slept last night? I had been in his bed; Laney had been on his couch.

Two guards rushed by us. I hadn't seen many of them in the meeting quarters.

"Leela, let's keep moving," he said quietly, grabbing my arm gently. "We are going to get Hollister. I'm just not sure how yet. Right now, I'm focusing on getting your parents back to Corey and Annabelle."

We reached a large, open plaza lined with cedar trees. A beautiful, grand fountain was in the center. Everything was the same white stone, reflecting the sun's light back into the sky.

But suddenly it was very loud, no longer peaceful, tranquil. There was a large crowd at the other end of the plaza, raising signs and shouting in protest. The signs were hard to read from that distance, but they were chanting, "The light is free!"

It was now obvious where those guards were headed when they had sped past us. A dozen guards surrounded the crowd, their weapons drawn, weapons originally designed for animals but currently used for slaves. Laney had described earlier how they used electric cattle prods as well as shock collars to maintain control of the slaves.

But these weren't slaves. These were Antonian citizens. Would they use them on their own people?

Curwen looked surprised, but not shocked. He took my hand, leading me down a different path, away from the commotion. The people started screaming. I glanced over my shoulder and saw a man fall to the ground as he was stuck in the back with one of the prods. My first instinct was to run toward him, to help him, but Curwen would not let go of me, instructing me fiercely, "Leave it, Leela."

Stronger than I realized, he dragged me down a dark, stone path that led into a small forest. He kept going until the plaza was no longer visible due to the trees, and the screams became inaudible. I couldn't tell if that was because we were farther away or because they had been silenced.

Finally, when I stopped resisting him, he freed my arm.

"What was that?" I asked. "Why wouldn't you help them?"

"Keep your voice down," he commanded, concerned about being heard by a couple walking by. "Sit down," he pointed at a bench nearby, "and drink some water." He tossed the bottle at me. I obeyed, but glared up at him.

"You're just like your sister," he complained. "Making things harder."

"Laney and I are not the same," I replied defensively between sips.

"Well, you both try to go running into situations that you know nothing about."

"Trying to help people isn't a bad thing."

"Trying to help *everyone* can be," he countered. "You have to pick your battles. I've made your family my battle right now. Those people back there are not my focus. So stop making it harder."

"But—"

He cut me off, "No. Be a help to me and not a hindrance. *I'm trying to get your parents back to Corey and Annabelle.*"

That's right. He was an orphan. I imagined he didn't want that for my siblings—he was fighting for us. Once again, I took note of how defeated and tired he appeared.

I looked at him with remorse, apologizing with my eyes. "But who were those people?"

"They belong to an activist group called The Strikers. They believe everyone should be allowed to utilize the travel light." He scoffed at the idea.

"You don't agree?"

"It would be horrible," he said without further explanation. "We've got to keep moving if we're going to make it to Phaedra's on time. Let's go."

"How much farther?" I asked, standing.

"Not much. Once we exit these woods, the palace is on the other side. The gardens are open to the public, so we might be able to find your mother. We must be careful though. There will be guards, of course."

"Of course," I quipped with annoyance. They were everywhere. I began to notice the twinkling lights that lined the stone path we walked. The forest was dense; the tree coverage kept out the sun. It could have been scary at night, I imagined, but in the heat of the afternoon, it was a welcome respite.

After a few minutes of silence, after thinking about how we could free Hollister, I whispered, "If you work for the government, don't you have some sort of connections to make this easier?"

"What do you mean?" he asked.

"I mean—couldn't you say, 'Bring me these three slaves—number 327, number 3126, number 2916. I need to interrogate them'?"

He laughed cynically, but it echoed with sadness. "I don't have that kind of power. Making that kind of request would arouse unwanted suspicion and be very dangerous for you."

"You mean dangerous for all of us, right?"

"Right," he agreed quickly. "It's not safe for you here."

"Just because I could become a slave?" I pressed for clarification.

He hesitated, but then nodded. "Exactly." There was something he wasn't saying, but I didn't know the questions to ask to get him talking, to pull the right information out of him.

The trees began to thin until we reached an opening, the end of the forest path.

The palace rose up in the distance, surrounded by what had to have been hundreds of acres of beautiful, rolling, green hills. There was a wide, shallow river snaking around behind it, disappearing into the foothills of the mountains.

The palace was made of pure white stone, like the rest of the city, with a flat roof; the only thing that set it apart from the rest of the living quarters I had seen was its enormous size. It was a rather humble palace, if ever there was one; it didn't have any ostentatious displays of wealth like I'd expected.

There were little black dots on the roof—I knew they were guards. Although they were only specks from that distance, they awoke a fear in me I hadn't realized before then. It was as if Curwen sensed that; he took my hand in his.

We had at least another mile to go before reaching the palace walls. Guards lined the path, standing alert every ten feet, keeping close watch of those coming and going. A few of them nodded at Curwen as we passed.

He knew the king's guard—surely, he had more connections than he had revealed. One of them even addressed him by name. He didn't want to raise their suspicions about us, but mine were raised about him.

We reached the front entrance to the palace but turned left, following the outer wall, also lined with guards, until we could turn the corner. We walked a ways farther until Curwen found the gate he was looking for; he scanned his card and the gate beeped, unlocked. I feared the nearby guards would say something to us, but they didn't. They just gave Curwen a nod of recognition.

Taking a few deep breaths, I prepared myself for what I might see. I didn't know what my mother might look like after all this time. Not sure what kind of conditions she had been living in, I wondered if she would be traumatized. How would she react upon seeing me?

Curwen pushed the gate open wide enough for us to squeeze through.

I felt like I was leaving Kansas and entering Oz; everything was so much more vibrant and colorful within the palace gardens. Fruit trees, flower bushes, and vines covered everything in a beautifully landscaped design. It went on forever.

The guards, however, diminished the beauty of the place. They stood around like a bunch of ugly statues dressed all in black. I took note that the slaves were dressed in red, remembering that Laney had described

Hollister as wearing yellow. Their crimson garments contrasted with the greenery surrounding them, making them easy to spot.

Some of the guards looked our way when we entered, but most ignored us. Did they ignore us because Curwen was such a common visitor, a usual sight in the palace gardens? Or is that what they were trained to do—to pretend to be oblivious to the things happening around them?

What did they do when they weren't working? Did they have families? Were they simply working mothers and fathers? Most of them looked too young to have grown children, though I attempted not to stare too closely or too long at any of them. I didn't want to give them any reason to talk to me.

"We've got a lot of ground to cover," Curwen whispered. "Keep your eyes open. I've only seen one picture of your mother, so . . . "

"She has blond hair, blue eyes, and she's short and a little overweight." I tried to think of how else to describe her, but her facial features had become blurry in my mind.

"I doubt she's overweight anymore," he said quietly, without emotion. Was he implying that they had not fed her well? Or that she had lost weight from her hard labor? He saw the questions on my face, so he explained, "They are very scientific in their approach with the slaves— they feed them the exact caloric intake that they need for the job they do. Therefore, she has probably lost weight."

I nodded my understanding, but a sadness overwhelmed me, a sadness that he could speak so nonchalantly about these things, a sadness that this reality was his normal.

We began to work our way through the garden at a fast pace. Since we weren't there to admire the scenery, it was easy to quickly glance at the few slaves in different areas and know by their size or height that they were not my mother.

"What is your mother's specialty?" Curwen asked. "They assign bodies according to their skills and abilities." There he went again, explaining their system to me with no emotion, just facts. And using that term: *bodies*.

"She does a little bit of everything. You saw our garden; what do you think it is?"

"Hmm . . . I would say fruit trees. We should go to the orchards."

"Lead the way, sir," I said, swooping my arm out in a gentle movement, presenting the path to him.

He walked for so long that I began to think he didn't know where he was going. How many times had he been here? Would he ask somebody for directions so we didn't have to spend the entire afternoon wandering aimlessly? As I was about to question him, we came to another small gate that didn't have secure access. He opened it for both of us.

Stepping into it was like a dream. There were rows upon rows of large trees with magnificent canopies of light pink blossoms. Petals covered the ground. The air was infused with a fragrant, sweet scent.

"Cherry blossoms?" I questioned in an awed whisper.

"No," he replied. "These are Royal Empress trees."

I had never seen such a stunning place in my entire life. Petals floated down like feathers, and I was so tempted to twirl around with arms outstretched, but there were guards nearby who immediately brought me back to reality. This breathtaking place existed because of the work of slaves; it made me sick, and it took the joy out of the beauty.

"Come on," Curwen shook me out of my reverie. "We don't have much longer before the gardens close for the day."

In that place, with the full branches acting as umbrellas, it was easier to ignore the black-dressed guards who I knew were watching us. Very few slaves were in this orchard, as far as I could see, so I didn't understand why there were so many guards.

The slaves were walking around, gathering the fallen petals into baskets. Why couldn't they leave them on the ground? It was pretty, like floral snow.

Suddenly I saw a familiar face. "Ms. Patty?" I whispered.

"You know her?" Curwen asked as we both stared at the woman dressed in red, stooping to scoop up a handful of petals.

"She worked in the florist shop in town . . . she was good friends with my mother."

Ms. Patty hadn't seen me yet; she wouldn't take her eyes from the ground. I had never seen her with such submissive behavior; she was usually a little spitfire. Her cropped, black hair looked disheveled, and she looked thinner, but otherwise healthy.

Seeing her dressed in that color reminded me of the bright red lipstick she always wore. She must have felt naked without it. How much of themselves had been stripped from them?

"What do I do?" I asked, unsure, aware that there was a female guard nearby.

Curwen looked around trying to figure out a plan. "I'll distract the guard," he said.

Before I could respond, he was headed in her direction. I saw the way she instantly perked up and smiled at his greeting. He could easily distract her. And he knew it.

I knelt near Ms. Patty and gathered a handful of petals to put in her bucket. This got her attention. She was startled for a moment.

"Leela . . . or Laney?" She never could tell us apart.

"Leela," I replied.

"What are you doing here? Your mother didn't think you got sucked into this place."

"We didn't, but we came to get them back. Is my mother here?"

Curwen acted as a lookout while we talked. I could see that the guard was hanging on to everything he said. For a man of few words, he certainly knew how to throw on the charm in moments of need. I was grateful for that, but it also made me wonder what parts of him were real.

"Your mama's not here today," she replied with that familiar accent; it sounded like home. "Her health hasn't been great. She was allowed to rest today. But she'll be here tomorrow."

"What's wrong with her health?" I asked, my voice panicked and too loud. After taking a look to make sure nobody had overheard me, I saw Ms. Patty's eyes chastise me.

"Keep it down, girl. I ain't gettin' punished for you."

"Sorry," I mouthed silently.

"Your mama's okay. She's just fatigued from this heat. She ain't adjusting well to it."

Somewhat soothed by her words, I asked, "Where does she usually work?"

"Just past here, in the vineyard." She pointed in the direction.

Curwen began to increase his speaking volume so I could hear that he was ending his conversation with the guard. My time with Ms. Patty was up.

"Please tell her that we'll come for her tomorrow morning. And please tell her I love her." I abruptly threw my arms around the familiar woman in a rough embrace; I had never hugged her before, but somehow that didn't matter. We were connected by circumstance in a new way that transcended boundaries of etiquette and awkward shows of affection. She started to sob.

Curwen coughed loudly in warning. He didn't come in my direction, though; he knew the guard would watch him as he walked away, so he drew her eyes away from us.

I pulled away, still holding her shoulders, and looked directly into her eyes. "You are not alone," I whispered before turning away, walking toward the gate where Curwen waited.

When he grabbed my hand, from the corner of my eye, I saw the guard's face drop in disappointment and jealousy. *If only she knew the half of it.*

This orchard no longer held as much beauty and enchantment as it had five minutes earlier. What were we doing? We were being extremely selfish, and it made me sick to my stomach. Why did we think it was okay to save just our parents and Hollister? What about everyone else—not only from our town, but also from every place they had ever taken *bodies*?

They had families too. Why did they deserve freedom any less? Ms. Patty was a single mother with a fourteen-year-old son and a twelve-year-old daughter. Where were her children? What did Antonians do with the children? I shuddered.

I hadn't allowed myself to think about it before, but I had to now. How many of the people who went missing in our dimension were actually *here* in Antonia? Could we leave them? How could we not?

It was all too overwhelming. I had marveled at the enormous size of the gardens, but now I loathed them because it seemed a never-ending journey to escape from them. These slaves, should they ever return to their normal lives, would probably never want to be gardeners and florists again.

That's what Antonia did to them. It took the things they loved to do the most and transformed them into a punishment and torture. Would my mother ever work in her garden again?

At that moment, I was so full of hatred for everything Antonian that I wanted to tackle every guard I passed. I wanted to do it for every person they had ever hurt. I wanted to stick them with their own cattle prods. I wanted to rip my hand free from Curwen's grasp, disgusted with him simply for *being* Antonian. Seething with anger, I walked with purpose and determination.

But suddenly, a trumpet sounded. Curwen shoved me into a private alcove behind some rose bushes. But he couldn't hide himself fast enough; someone, a man, called his name.

"Stay here. Don't say a word," he ordered softly, then walked away. He greeted this other person cheerfully, "Gigandet, Your Highness, how are you?"

Gigandet? Was he talking to *the king?*

I did my best to peer through the bushes, to see what this king looked like, to see what kind of Antonian ruler he was. I couldn't make out the details of his face, but I could tell that he wasn't unattractive. But he was plain. An average Joe. Not the kind of man you imagine as king.

I already hated him, just from the sound of his voice.

"I am well," he said. "I saw that you had accessed the gardens and wanted to see you. I didn't know you were home yet."

"Just for a day, sir," Curwen replied. "I needed to do some research before traveling back to continue the work."

"How is the work going?"

"It is well. I hope to have a full report for you very soon."

"Good. Make sure to check in with Whirl before you leave. He has some important information for you."

"Yes, sir. I will." He bowed to him. *Suck-up, sycophant.*

Gigandet walked away, a hoard of guards following him.

My line of sight was no longer clear.

But one thing had become very clear—Curwen took his orders directly from the king.

CHAPTER 13

(LANEY)

Sheldon didn't reveal where he was taking me. When we didn't head toward the forest, I protested and attempted to pull my hand from his.

"Please take me to see Hollister," I begged, near tears.

"You will see him in a minute." He kept dragging me. "Stop being so difficult. No wonder Curwen pawned you off on me."

"How will I see him?" I ignored his insult.

We had arrived at another home in the living quarters, though I couldn't tell how we'd gotten there or how to get back to Curwen's. For all I knew, Curwen's house could have been on the same street. It could have been Curwen's house, except there wasn't a flowerpot in sight.

"Where are we?" I asked while he used a key card to unlock the door.

"This is my house."

"Why is there no flowerpot? Is it not a safe home?"

"No, not my place. The government can't find out about my place. If they ever discover what the flowers symbolize, at least they won't come looking here."

We walked inside. It was much the same as Curwen's house—perhaps not quite as neat and clean. It didn't appear that he had anything to hide. What could the government find?

"Don't tell any of the others I brought you here," he ordered. "Okay?" When I hesitated, he added, "Look, you wanted to see Hollister. I'm going to show him to you—but not if I can't trust you to keep this between us. Don't even tell Leela."

"What—do you have him locked up in a closet somewhere?" I joked.

He laughed. "Something like that."

My face instantly became serious.

"You good or not?" he asked, waiting for my vow of silence.

I simply nodded.

We went to the kitchen. He opened the pantry door, pulling a string to turn on the light. It looked like an ordinary pantry, the same as Curwen's, except Sheldon's shelves were fully stocked.

He bent down, reaching underneath the bottom shelf, and pulled some sort of invisible lever; the back wall opened, revealing an entry into another tiny room. He pulled me inside and shut the pantry door behind us.

We stood in the glow of light from several computer monitors. There was a single chair that Sheldon plopped down in, and he began clicking away on the keyboard. I stood behind him, pinned between the chair and wall; this secret room wasn't meant for more than one person.

"Do they know you have all this?" I asked.

"Who is they?" he asked. "You mean Curwen, Durham, Mara . . . ? Yeah. I'm the techie for the resistance. And you're in luck—just last week, I was finally able to hack into the security cameras at the barracks."

"You think that's where Hollister still is?" I asked. "He wouldn't be back in the fields by now?"

"No." He shook his head. "Once a body is stunned the way Hollister was this morning, he won't be any good for the rest of the day."

I didn't like how casually he'd said it. Like it was a normal occurrence. Like a *body* is only good when it can work. That's what they thought, and it made me sick.

"What's his number?" he asked, intently focused on his work.

"Three twenty-seven." *But he's a person. With a name.*

"Okay, so barrack twenty-seven," he said to himself as he continued to click away on the keyboard.

I waited, scanning the different monitors, trying to find Hollister on them. Most of them skimmed through different cameras in the working quarters. I didn't see any scenes from the living quarters, which made sense because I hadn't noticed any cameras in those areas.

"You know," he said while he worked, "when you all arrived last night, I had to erase any trace of you from the security log. Curwen made sure I would be available to keep a lookout."

I couldn't figure out what kind of response he was expecting. Gratitude? He had said I should be more grateful for their help.

When I didn't respond, he suggested, "Maybe next time you can travel from a different location, without cameras."

Next time? "There won't be a next time," I responded defensively.

"Okay, here it is." He pointed to the monitor in the top left corner. "Barrack twenty-seven. Let me scan the place."

He moved the camera around. All the beds were empty so far; everyone was still in the fields. Finally, we saw him in one of the bottom bunks. The camera quality was grainy and in black and white, but I knew it was him. There was no sound, only video. Hollister was so still, his eyes closed; I became concerned that he was dead, but just then he fidgeted in his sleep.

I breathed a sigh of relief. "They haven't taken him to the scientists yet."

"Wait," Sheldon said, concern in his voice. "Who said he was going to the scientists?"

"The guard in the forest—he said he would send Hollister to the scientists if he kept causing problems."

Sheldon's body was tense.

Before I could question him, his phone rang, scaring us, making us jump.

"Yes," he answered it. He listened, then replied, "Yeah, we're on our way."

I didn't want to leave that tiny, dark space, though. I wanted to stay and watch Hollister forever, to ensure that he remained there, that no one took him to the scientists, whatever that meant. After Sheldon's response, I was too afraid to ask.

But Sheldon needed me to move so he could get out of the chair. He had to push me out the secret door. "I'm sorry, but we have to go to Phaedra's now. Curwen and Leela are running late, and he wants us to be there to smooth things over with Durham," he explained.

"Oh, great." I rolled my eyes. "We get to do his work."

"This is *our* work. We are in this *together*," he said.

"Oh, you mean, except for this trip to your secret closet?" I replied as he closed the pantry door.

"The closet isn't secret. They all know about the closet. They just don't need to know that I brought you to it. Got it?" he asked seriously. "You promised."

I nodded. "Let's just go, so we can cover for them," I replied with annoyance, not looking forward to seeing Durham or Mara again. I enquired, "How far away is it?"

"Not very far, but we are all spread out at strategic points throughout the living quarters, so there's always a safe place for us to go no matter where we are," he explained. "Mara's home is next door to Phaedra's, though, so you won't have to travel any farther tonight."

"I can't wait," I replied with sarcasm.

"Hey, give Mara a chance," he chided with a smile. "She's not so bad."

I rolled my eyes at him. "And who is Phaedra?" I asked. "Please tell me she's not another Mara."

"No." He shook his head, his eyes lighting up with admiration. "Phaedra is the best person I have ever known. If Durham is like our father, Phaedra is like our mother. You'll love her."

I wondered if I could ever love anyone in Antonia.

We were outside his home. The living quarters were bustling with life now, with people returning home from work, friends chatting, children playing, the smell of dinner cooking. The delicious aromas wafting from the windows triggered my stomach to realize just how hungry I was.

Some people waved and smiled at Sheldon as we passed, glancing at me with curiosity, but he didn't stop to converse with them. They wanted to know who this blond stranger was, but he wouldn't give them an opportunity to ask.

I kept an eye out for flowerpots as we went. There weren't any more on his row of houses, but after turning onto another walkway, I saw two, one at the beginning and one at the end.

If I went to those houses for safety, would they help me? How would they feel about the secret work Curwen and Sheldon were doing? They had lied to Durham about it, so I assumed that meant they wouldn't approve. But would they turn us over to the government they were determined to undermine?

We took another left and immediately arrived at Phaedra's house. Both her house and Mara's next door contained the pretty red flowers in the windowsills. How welcoming would Phaedra be? The best person Sheldon had ever known—I would have to decide where she ranked on my list.

Sheldon didn't knock. The same access card he had used for his house also unlocked her door. Seeing my questioning look, he explained, "I've linked our key cards so all of us can enter whenever necessary. It's a safety measure."

So much for privacy.

We heard voices and the sound of pots and pans coming from the kitchen. This house had a different layout than the two previous Antonian dwellings I had seen—not a very open floor plan, the kitchen in the rear through a swinging door.

Sheldon had no qualms about announcing our arrival and busting through that door, greeting Phaedra with a big hug and kiss on the cheek, one of the most open displays of affection I had witnessed in that place. Like Mara, Phaedra was beautiful. She had mocha-colored skin and big, brown, expressive eyes with thick lashes; her dark hair was wrapped up in a lavender scarf.

She hugged Sheldon for a long time before turning her attention to me. When she gave her attention to someone, she gave her full attention, as though nobody else was in the room. I expected to shake her hand, but she pulled me in for a tight embrace.

Mara didn't like this; I could see her scrutinizing us over Phaedra's shoulder. Sheldon just grinned, his eyes saying, "I told you so." My eyes teared up at the kindness of her affection, but I blinked them away.

"Welcome to my home!" she exclaimed when she let go and looked into my eyes. "Mara has been telling me all about you."

I bet she has.

"Thank you for having me," I said with a smile. "The food smells wonderful." My stomach cried out for it—how long would we have to wait?

"Mara," Sheldon said, "can I talk to you outside for a few minutes?" He nodded his head toward the back door. What did he need to talk to her about? My eyes narrowed in suspicion.

"I'm helping Phaedra, if you can't tell," she replied.

"Oh, no, you go with him." Phaedra nudged her shoulder. "Laney can take your place."

She didn't like that either, that I could take her place, replace her. But she went, glaring at me on the way out. Phaedra put me to work cutting vegetables for a salad. Holding the knife, I nearly laughed out loud, remembering the day I had held one up to Curwen's neck. He wouldn't have trusted me with a knife, not like Phaedra did.

Had that really only happened a few days ago? *It felt like years.*

"So, Laney, tell me your story," Phaedra requested, truly interested.

"Didn't Mara tell you?"

"Only a little. But I'd like to hear from you."

What was the story Curwen had made up about us when Durham asked? What if I told it wrong, got the details mixed up, blew our cover?

I hesitated but stated the facts as I knew them. "Our parents recently died from the disease. We were in quarantine. They took our home while we were there, so we had nowhere to go when we were released. Curwen saw us and helped us." *That was right, right?*

"Laney," she said, her voice soft but firm.

"Yes?" I focused on chopping the carrots.

"Look at me."

Slowly, I obeyed. "Yes?" I repeated, staring into her eyes.

"I know you and your sister aren't from here." She must have noticed a look of fear cross my face, because she quickly added, "And that's okay. I welcome you. But don't lie to me."

What was I supposed to do now—pour out the truth? Was this a trick, concocted by Durham or Mara—to use *the best person Sheldon had ever known* to get me to confess? I couldn't read people like Leela; I didn't know when they were being dishonest.

"It's okay," she said with a smile when I wouldn't speak. "Why don't you tell me about your sister? Leela, right?"

I nodded.

"And you're twins?" she asked. I nodded again. "Identical?"

"Yes, except for her birthmark."

"I have, or had, a twin sister once," she said sadly.

"What happened to her?"

"She traveled through the light and never returned."

"Oh?" I asked quietly, my ears perked up, attentive. I didn't know how much to press, but now I was curious, hoping she would say more.

"She met someone there, someone she loved. She chose to have a life with him. I often try to imagine the life she may be living, the children she may have had."

"Did you ever travel through the light?"

She hesitated. "Only once. It was not a good experience for me, so I never went back." Changing the subject, she asked, "Do you think there is love growing between Curwen and Leela?"

Caught off guard, I scowled in disgust. "No. Who told you that?"

She gave me a knowing look, her eyes darting to the back door.

"Mara?" I demanded. "Why would she say that?"

"Perhaps she fears it's true."

"Because she likes Curwen . . . ?"

She simply nodded with a soft smile on her lips.

"Well, I haven't heard anything about that from either Leela or Curwen."

"Laney, it's not something you hear," she explained. "It's something you observe."

I hadn't observed *anything*. Had I missed something? Or was Mara jealous, worried about nothing, making something out of nothing?

"Have you ever been in love, Laney?" she asked.

Hollister. I couldn't talk about him. Talking would be impossible because of the tears that would start flowing. Instead, I turned it back on her, "*Have you?*"

She was like an open book. "There was something once, between

Durham and me, something that might have been. But we decided it was best for our cause not to let love be a distraction."

"Did y'all decide that?" I pressed. "Or did he?"

She gave a sad smile—I knew the answer: that hard man had broken her heart. *Another reason not to like him.* How could *this* woman have loved *that* man?

Just then, the front door beeped. Someone had arrived. Was it Durham? Or Leela and Curwen? Phaedra wasted no time plowing through the swinging door to greet whoever it was. By the time I followed her, Leela was wrapped in her embrace, giving me an amused look over Phaedra's shoulder.

Curwen looked exhausted, leaning against the wall. He needed sleep. With us staying at Mara's (I dreaded the thought), hopefully he would get some. "Durham here yet?" he asked.

Phaedra gave him a mischievous grin. "I called him and told him dinner wouldn't be ready until seven thirty."

"You bought us some time?" he teased, wrapping his arm around her shoulder and kissing her cheek, just as Sheldon had. They loved her. I thought she may have been the one person to show them what a family should look like.

When Sheldon and Mara came back inside, Phaedra insisted all of us enjoy some appetizers in the living room while she finished the meal preparations. Mara made sure to grab the only seat beside Curwen, almost like marking her territory—now that I knew, it was hard *not* to observe. Did Mara *have* to be there?

I was dying to ask Leela how her day was. Did she see our mother? If so, how was she? My twin sat in an armchair with me, squished together, and I could tell by her fidgeting that she wanted to ask me the same questions about our father. Instead, we munched on some crackers, staving off the hunger, hoping our stomachs wouldn't growl in the awkward silence.

Finally, Curwen broke the silence. "So, we need to discuss a plan for how to get your father. I already have one for your mother." Leela and I automatically darted our eyes from Curwen to Mara and back to Curwen. "It's okay," he said. "She knows. Sheldon filled her in."

"You know," Leela said with an angry edge to her voice, "I wish you would let us know when you're going to tell people and who you're going to tell."

What had happened between them today?

Mara rolled her eyes, but Curwen did look apologetic. "You're right, Leela," he said with sincerity. "I should keep you both more informed about what's going on."

Curwen hadn't instructed Sheldon to tell Mara on the phone call earlier, but Sheldon did receive a message on our walk to Phaedra's. Was that what it was about? I wished Leela and I had working phones to communicate throughout the day. We could be messaging right this minute as we sat beside each other, writing all the things we weren't able to speak.

The door beeped again. I steeled my heart and mind for the appearance of Durham. I had been no good at fooling Phaedra, but she had been generous to me, not pushing me to reveal anything. I knew Durham wouldn't be so kind. Leela grabbed my hand; she had the same fear of him.

"Good evening, everyone," he greeted us, taking a seat on the couch beside Mara. "You never did check in with me, Sheldon." His voice was calm, but it carried authority and criticism.

Sheldon looked uncomfortable being chastised in front of us. "I'm sorry, boss. I got so caught up helping Curwen train these two," he gestured at us, "that I lost track of time."

"Yeah," Curwen added, "we were just going over some things about the other dimension with the twins so they won't be overwhelmed when they come back with me."

"And when do you plan to go back?" Durham asked.

"Probably tomorrow night."

"And you think these two will be ready, with only two days of training?" he scoffed.

"I do, sir," Curwen replied confidently.

"And you think you'll be able to garner some success this time? We can't afford to waste this much time. I should send you back right this second. It seems to me you're losing sight of the mission. You've got to find—"

Curwen interrupted him, "I know, sir. We will complete the mission by the end of the week. I guarantee it."

Durham's jaw tightened, the same way Curwen's did sometimes. "I'm going to pretend you didn't just interrupt me because our lovely hostess has arrived." He glared at Curwen for a half second and then turned his smiling face to Phaedra. Again, I thought: What did she ever love about him?

"Would everyone like to move into the dining room?" Phaedra asked. "The food is ready to be served."

"Do you need any help?" Leela and I both asked simultaneously.

Durham laughed. "So they *do* speak!" he exclaimed facetiously. "And in unison!"

"Leave them alone," Phaedra ordered him, teasing. "No, thank you, girls. Everything is already on the table."

If we were worried about Durham asking us questions at dinner, we didn't need to be. He practically ignored us, as did everyone else so they wouldn't draw attention to us. But I tried to keep my eyes open and observe, as Phaedra had instructed.

Although Durham didn't speak to us, I could tell he was highly aware of our presence. Did he know we weren't from here, like Phaedra did? I was sure he must. So why was he playing along? What was his game?

I didn't have long to figure it out. He rose to leave immediately after dinner despite Phaedra's insistence for him to stay longer. Did she still love him even now? I wanted to scream, *"Let the man go!"*

Before he left, he turned back to his three worker bees and said, "You can all have the day off tomorrow to train these two. I'm sure they need all the help they can get."

"Thanks," Curwen replied, shutting the door behind him.

Leela released a huge sigh, exclaiming, "That man infuriates me!"

"Tell me about it!" I said.

Everyone stared at us for a long moment before bursting into laughter.

"I think it's time these two got some sleep," Sheldon said.

Curwen nodded in agreement. Mara handed us the key card to her house. Phaedra gave us a hug good night.

Even though it seemed like they just wanted to get rid of us, I couldn't pass up the opportunity to be alone with my sister. I wanted to be rid of them as well. We could plan in the morning.

The sun had set; the stars were out. But I didn't recognize any constellations. They must be different here. The air was warm, but not unbearable. The street was silent and empty. We tiptoed next door, grateful to have some space to ourselves for a short while.

We fell asleep beside each other in the middle of recounting the events of the day.

CHAPTER 14

[LEELA]

I woke up before the sun with a pounding headache, dehydrated; Laney was sound asleep beside me. My skin felt less burned than the day before. But my throat felt like a desert, so dry. I needed a drink, so I slid out of bed as softly as possible, tiptoeing down the hallway and stairs to the kitchen.

In the dark, I found a glass and filled it with water from the faucet. Water tasted different here, more pure, more filtered. Annabelle came to my mind—she refused to drink unfiltered water. How were she and Corey this morning, or rather, this night?

Day two without them. Hopefully by tonight, their morning, we would return to them—with our parents. And Hollister—I had promised myself that I would bring him back for Annabelle's sake, just to hear her voice again, to show her that he was okay.

As I headed back upstairs, I caught a glimpse of someone outside through the window. It was Phaedra, watering Mara's flowerpot. She saw me and bid me come, pointing at the door. Even though Laney had told me about their conversation, about Phaedra suspecting who we really were, I felt she would keep our secret, even if she knew the entire truth.

"Come over for breakfast," she invited when I opened the door. "You'll need a good meal so you can have enough energy for today, for your . . . training." She gave a knowing smile. She knew we weren't training, but did she have a clue what we were really planning to do? Had they told her everything last night, after Laney and I left them?

It was still dark outside. There was no one in the street except for us. I followed her next door, curious to have time alone with her, especially after all that Laney had learned from her.

When I saw the familiar box on her kitchen table, I said without thinking, "These are the pastries Curwen brought us!" The ones Corey had eaten without sharing. Now I could taste them.

She smiled, setting an assortment of fruit on the table as well. "The pastries are from my bakery," she explained.

"They're delicious!" I exclaimed between mouthfuls. She just smiled in return. She and Sheldon were similar in that way, always smiling, a stark contrast to Curwen, Mara, or Durham.

Not one to waste time with small talk, she got straight to the point, asking what she wanted to know. "So," she began, "what happened between you and Curwen yesterday?"

Laney had asked the same thing last night. "What do you mean?" I replied.

"You were cold and distant, unhappy with him for some reason?"

She had been observing us, trying to determine, for Mara's sake, if love was growing between Curwen and me. I had laughed when Laney told me that, that Mara would *fear* such a thing.

I answered her with equal directness, "There is no love growing between Curwen and me." The only thing that was growing in my heart toward Curwen was suspicion. I only trusted him out of necessity—there was no other choice.

She scrutinized me for a long moment. "But why were you so cold?"

How much could I tell her? And why did she need to know?

She stared at me until I finally admitted, "I just don't know how honest he has been or how much I can trust what he has told us."

"Trust grows with time. The nature of his job is to play many roles and to keep many secrets . . . including yours," she said. "If he has said he will do something, you can trust that he will do everything in his power to do it."

But what if it wasn't in his power? Or what if it was, but he wasn't utilizing the power he had?

We heard the door beep; Laney and Mara appeared moments later.

"What are you doing?" Mara was annoyed with me. "You need to let people know where you're going, Leela."

"She's fine. I told her to come over," Phaedra said. "Good morning, Laney," she added with a smile.

"Good morning," she replied. Then she grabbed a pastry with delight in her eyes, and without thinking, she said to me, "These are the pastries that Corey hogged."

"Who's Corey?" Mara asked. I guessed Sheldon hadn't told her everything, or maybe Curwen hadn't told *him* everything. Maybe he was keeping our secrets, like Phaedra had said.

"Who's Corey?" Mara repeated when we didn't answer.

Only the best kid brother a person could hope for.

"Nobody," Laney and I said together.

Mara glared at me, but Phaedra chuckled. She really didn't mind not knowing everything, and that was a quality I admired. Mara, on the other hand . . .

Before she could press further, Curwen and Sheldon arrived. They joined us at the table, stacking their plates high with food. I was glad we'd gotten there first.

"Did Mara fill y'all in on the plan for today?" Curwen asked.

"Did y'all already come up with a plan?" I asked.

"Well, we didn't sit around gossiping last night," Mara quipped.

Directing my words to Curwen, I firmly stated, "I thought we were *all* going to plan this morning. I thought we agreed last night that Laney and I would be kept more informed."

"He said you would be kept *informed*, not that you would be part of the *planning*," Mara answered for him. Curwen cut his eyes in her direction, wanting her to be quiet.

Yes, please.

"We wanted to make the best use of our time," he explained. "If we planned last night, we could get an earlier start this morning. It wasn't intended to exclude you."

Phaedra was standing behind Curwen. She gave me a look that said,

"Give him a break. He meant no harm. Forgive the man." She could say so much with one look. Mara saw her look, too, and didn't like it, perhaps feeling that her mother figure was betraying her.

I was surprised how silent Laney was during the exchange, confident that she had some words for Mara, but she loved the pastries more. Between bites, she finally asked, "So, what is this great plan?"

Curwen looked hesitant to share it now. But if he didn't say something soon, Mara most certainly would. And he knew that, so he spoke up. "Sheldon, Laney, and I are going to get your father while Mara and Leela will get your mother," he said, knowing that last part would not sit well with me.

I wanted to protest. Why wasn't Curwen going back to the gardens with me? What did Mara know about the gardens? *Mara* didn't have a personal relationship with the king—*Curwen did*. Or was he trying to avoid any more run-ins with Gigandet?

I could see on Laney's face that she was sorry, not sorry. She hated that I was stuck with Mara, but grateful that it wasn't her. I smiled devilishly at my twin, thinking maybe we could switch places. She read my mind, speaking before I could, "That makes the most sense, since I've already been to the warehouses and Leela is familiar with the gardens."

My smile quickly fading, I tried to kick her under the table. Sheldon received the blow instead; he didn't make a sound, but gave me a grin and a light kick in return. I shook my head at him, laughing with my eyes. Phaedra was doing her usual observing and analyzing. Surely, now she would think Sheldon and I were *growing in love*.

Curwen cleared his throat before continuing. "Sheldon has created fake IDs for all of you, just in case you need them for anything. He also hacked the codes needed to remove the shock collars."

How much did Phaedra know? Had they told her everything last night? Or was she simply trusted not to pry, not to ask questions, to listen without ever fully knowing? She talked about Curwen knowing and keeping secrets, but I suspected she had a vault of her own.

Curwen peered out the window. "The sun is already coming up. We should get going. Mara can explain the plan to you on the way, Leela." He saw the look on my face. "You'll be in capable hands. I'd trust Mara with my life," he attempted to placate me.

I bet Mara loved his words, but they only annoyed me. Because he trusted someone, that meant I should as well? I didn't even know how much I trusted him anymore.

"I think it's time we get going," Curwen repeated, looking at his watch, urging us to get up and get moving. We all stood. It seemed like one of those moments where we all should have put our hands in and yelled, "1 . . . 2 . . . 3 . . . Go team!" but it didn't feel like much of a team. Laney and I were just there to follow their directions.

"Whatever you're doing today, be quick about it," Phaedra encouraged. "Durham didn't give you the day off to be generous. He's up to something, and he knows you are too."

"Yes," Curwen said. "Let's all try to meet at the usual travel location by noon."

"Wait. What about Hollister?" Laney demanded, ready to burst into tears at any moment.

"I have a plan for him," Curwen said. "But first, your parents." When it appeared Laney wouldn't budge without hearing the plan, he said, "I'll explain it on the way." Then, more firmly, he commanded, *Let's go.*"

Once outside, Laney and I embraced. Like yesterday, it felt like I might never see her again. "I love you, Laney," I whispered.

"Love you too, Leela. See you later. With our parents. And Hollister."

The thought of it made her smile wide, her eyes bright with excitement. I gave her the best smile I could muster and turned to follow Mara. Curwen was looking at me, but I avoided eye contact with him, ready to just put my head down and obey orders.

It was so early that the narrow passages were nearly empty, unlike yesterday. I liked it better this way; it almost made Antonia seem peaceful. Although the city and the surrounding landscape were beyond description in their beauty, there was a darkness and mystery beneath the surface of Antonia, a danger that I feared, that I knew could capture me at any moment.

The only thing that kept me going was the mission and the knowledge that as soon as it was over, we could go home and resume our lives. I tried to imagine what kind of help my parents would need to readjust to their freedom, and I tried *not* to imagine what kind of things had been done to them since they had been in captivity.

"Look," Mara began, jarring me from my thoughts, "I know you don't want to be with me, but we're doing all of this for you and your sister. Show some gratitude."

There it was again. Sheldon had told Laney to be grateful, and now Mara demanded I show some gratitude. Her words made me so angry that I couldn't speak, which always happened when I wanted to explode with rage. Where was Laney when I needed her? She would know exactly what to say *and* have the ability to say it.

"There would be no reason for us to be grateful if they hadn't taken our people in the first place," Laney's reasoning echoed in my head. Didn't they get that? This was on them, not us. We had been wronged, not them.

She was right—I didn't want to go anywhere with her. I wanted it all to be over. I wanted my mother, father, and Hollister safe at home with Corey and Annabelle. And I didn't want to see her ever again.

The longer I stayed in Antonia, the more I loathed it.

I didn't pay attention to my surroundings; I just focused on echoing Mara's footsteps, walking in her shadow, not saying a word. How could she think I wasn't grateful for their help? I wanted to leave that place just as much, if not more, than she wanted me to.

"Okay," Mara began again, "before we become surrounded by crowds, let me tell you the plan." She paused, digging around in her bag. She pulled out a card resembling the ones I had seen Curwen use to access the gates. It simply contained a large barcode—no pictures or words. "This is your ID." She handed it to me. "I've got one for your mother as well."

"How do they know whose ID it is if there isn't a picture or name?" I asked.

"All the guards have scanners. That information will appear on their screens when they scan the barcode. It keeps the information protected," she explained, and for the first time, she didn't sound annoyed.

"So, who does the ID say I am?"

"Not sure," she replied. "Probably someone who has died recently. Hopefully, their death hasn't been logged into the system yet. But we'll still just use my card for the access points. Yours is only for absolute necessity."

"What about the codes for the shock collar?"

"They're all up here," she pointed to her temple, indicating she had memorized them. "So, we'll find your mother. I'll remove the collar, and we'll leave it exactly where we find her—it contains a tracking device. Then we'll slip these clothes," she showed me some in the bag, "over her clothes. And we'll leave out of the nearest exit."

"What about all the guards?" I asked, concerned. "Have you been to the palace gardens before? Do you know them well? Do you know how many guards there are?"

"Keep your voice down," she hissed. "Curwen and I practically grew up in the gardens. I *know* them. And I have plenty of intel about the guards and their shifts."

"It would be better if we both have the intel," I whispered with anger. "Not just you."

She refused to respond. She didn't like me. She didn't like *my kind*. Was that all it was, or did she really think Curwen had a romantic interest in me? Should I tell her that I had no interest in him? Would she treat me better then?

"Women are the same no matter where you go, always putting themselves in competition with one another," I heard my mother say. *"Don't do that,"* she had instructed. *"Champion each other on."* She had told Laney and me that throughout our lives, because others were always comparing us to each other, trying to decide which of us was smarter, prettier, kinder, better.

Remembering her words, I tried to see Mara with new eyes, almost like seeing her for the first time again. I wanted to tell her that she was beautiful and strong and capable. But just then, she glared at me, uncomfortable that I was staring at her, and I knew she wouldn't receive anything from me.

"I don't mean to appear ungrateful. I just meant, it might be beneficial for both of us to have the codes and intel," I said quietly, apologetically.

She didn't answer immediately, but finally said, "Listen, this may not have been the plan you would have developed, but we don't do violent things like your kind. We don't carry guns or bombs or threaten people to achieve our missions. Not if we can help it. We do things as peaceably as possible."

How could she be so blind? I wanted to cry at her ignorance; I could hardly breathe.

There was violence all around her. Though I hadn't seen it, I imagined Hollister writhing on the ground from the shock collar. I remembered the crowd in the courtyard—the same place we were passing through now—and the screams from the people as they were *violently* subdued by the guards.

She was resolved. Nothing I said would change her mind. Had she ever been to our dimension? Was she allowed to travel? Or was everything she thought she knew about "my kind" taught to her?

We had reached the path through the small forest now; I braced myself for the anticipated chill of the darkness.

"Shouldn't you be drinking your water?" Mara asked. I looked down at the full bottle in my hand. "Curwen told me not to let you get dehydrated."

"I'm fine." I really was.

"Don't be stubborn just to spite me. I'll force that water down your throat if I have to," she threatened. What had she *just* said about not threatening people?

I looked at her incredulously, then cut my eyes away and walked ahead of her. I shoved the water bottle into my small bag, daring her to make a move, knowing she wouldn't. If there was anything these Antonians hated, it was making a scene and drawing attention.

"You're really pushing my patience," she called to me.

"Shh . . . keep your voice down," I replied, mimicking her, just loud enough for her to hear me. I smiled to myself, taking some satisfaction in antagonizing her, channeling my inner Corey, laughing under my breath.

We reached the opening in the forest; I could see the palace looming ahead. The nerves were starting to hit me. What would we do if every-thing didn't work out as planned? Would Laney and I end up as slaves also? Would we ever go home again?

As we approached the palace, I kept my eyes down, not wanting to make eye contact with any of the guards.

"Which gate did you and Curwen enter yesterday?" Mara asked as we walked around the wall.

"The first one we came to . . . "

"Well, we're going to go to one that's closer to the vineyard; it will be quicker that way."

"This place is so massive that I don't really think there is a quicker way," I said quietly as we passed a guard. "Does the fruit from these gardens feed the people of Antonia, or just the king?"

"These are the king's personal gardens, reserved for the royal family only." She acted like my question was stupid. "The harvest from the fields is for the people. Some for the bodies."

"How many *bodies* are there in Antonia?" I asked.

"Why do you ask?"

"Do they outnumber the Antonians?"

She narrowed her eyes at me. "Why do you ask that?" she repeated firmly.

I shrugged. "Just wondering." Did she think I would attempt to incite some sort of slave uprising? Like I had that kind of power. What was the end goal of the Resistance? Did they not desire to end the slavery here? I had never asked, but only assumed.

"The Antonian population is about five million, so no, the slaves don't outnumber us. King Gigandet would not allow that to happen." She de-fended the king fiercely for someone who was part of the Resistance. Shouldn't she talk about him with contempt, not pride?

But she was probably right. Laney had said they kept extensive records about the slaves and their locations. Suddenly, the image of a missing per-sons bulletin flashed through my mind—the pictures of so many random people. How many of these photos belonged to the slaves in Antonia? How many families were still searching for their loved ones and fearing the worst, having no clue that they were slaves in another dimension?

The anger and sadness inside me almost couldn't be contained, but it also couldn't be expressed. Because I didn't know how to express such deep and powerful emotions. It was an overwhelming feeling, a tightening in my chest, a sickness in my stomach. *Pull yourself together.* I focused on my breathing and the back of Mara's head.

The sun was high in the sky, beating down on my skin, but still I didn't feel warm. I hadn't figured it out yet—why wasn't I hot like Laney? She constantly had sweat dripping down her forehead, but I had chills instead.

"How do you know when we've gone far enough?" I asked. The white stone sidewalk we were on looked as if it stretched into infinity.

"I know the gardens well," was her only response.

We walked a while longer until we came to a gate where the guard was actually asleep. He was slumped down on the ground, his back against the wall, snoring. On one hand, I could tell Mara was embarrassed by the bad impression he was making of the Antonian people, but on the other hand, she would use it for our advantage.

"Let's enter this gate. You won't have to scan your card since he's asleep—then there will be no record that you were here." She said all of this softly, not daring to wake him. She scanned her ID card, and the solid white gate beeped.

My legs were shaking as I followed close behind her. A guard who stood just inside the gate nodded to us, obviously unaware that his co-worker was unconscious outside. Mara and I shared brief, amused smiles.

Lifting my eyes, I realized we were in the same orchard with the pink Empress trees; we hadn't walked to the right gate, but we didn't have far to go.

For the first time, I noticed cameras along the top of the walls. Was that the only place they were? "What about the surveillance cameras?" I whispered, nodding in the direction of one.

"Sheldon sent some sort of virus to their system . . . so the ones here in the gardens shouldn't be working today," she explained. "He said it will take them a while to fix."

"Y'all would be lost without Sheldon, huh?"

"He has a vital role to fill, that's for sure." She cut her eyes to me. "But don't tell him I said that. It'll go to his head."

The red figures were scattered all over the place, but none of them were my mother. I searched for Ms. Patty again to confirm that my mother had come to work today.

She was in the same location as the previous day, but three guards were in close proximity, so I didn't approach. Our eyes met, though, and she gave the slightest nod, which I interpreted to mean that yes, my mother was there. I passed by her quickly, my head down.

I didn't want to waste any time, my steps quick and determined, possibly drawing more attention to us. People visited the gardens for nice, leisurely strolls and conversations, but I was there for a purpose, with a mission to complete. Mara followed at a slower pace, pretending to admire the scenery whenever a guard was near.

I paused at the entrance to the vineyards, waiting for her, my face showing that I was not pleased with her nonchalant performance. I was anxious and excited to see my mother again, praying that she would be the same, but knowing she wouldn't. How could she?

Mara eventually picked up speed, approaching me.

"Quit messing around," I whispered.

"You're being too obvious," she hissed. Shaking her head in annoyance, she opened the next gate. I sighed at the sight of the vineyard. It was nearly three times the size of all the other orchards and gardens I'd seen.

Alternating rows of green and purple grapes stretched out in all directions; the slaves' red clothes contrasted sharply against them, making it a bit easier. The fact that my mother was blond also made it easier; Curwen was right—there weren't very many of them, even among the slaves.

We started on the left and worked our way up and down each row. The guards made me anxious; there seemed to be a greater number of them here.

"Why are there so many?" I asked Mara.

"They have to make sure the slaves don't eat any of the grapes," she replied matter-of-factly, as if it was such an obvious answer. "These grapes are for the king's wine."

"They shouldn't allow the slaves to touch them either. They'll contaminate them!" I replied with bitter sarcasm.

She stared at me blankly for a few seconds, and then continued on.

As we turned the corner to continue down the next row, I spotted my mother straight ahead several rows over; I heard her faintly humming one of her favorite tunes.

She had lost weight; she was as small as Mara now, but it didn't appear to be a healthy kind of thin. It was clear that her health had been failing. Her eyes were sunken into her face and glazed over as if she was somewhere else in her mind.

Mara looked back at me when she realized I had stopped, staring in a different direction. "Do you see her?" she whispered, standing very close to me, the closest she had ever been. She couldn't see my mother because she was too short.

I nodded; I couldn't speak.

How were we supposed to do this? There were way too many guards. As much as I dreaded any slave being punished, a small part of me wished one would try to escape to create a distraction.

Mara looked at her watch. "They'll be changing shifts soon. Let's keep walking. We'll circle back around so we don't look suspicious just standing here."

It was hard for me to make my feet move and to pull my eyes away. With all my heart, I desired to run to her and embrace her.

Mara sensed that; she grabbed my arm, guiding me in another direction. "You've got to remain calm and act natural," she instructed firmly.

We needed more people to help us. How could the two of us possibly do this? Did either of us have confidence in what we were about to attempt?

She continued her instruction, her arm linked through mine as we strolled down the row next to the one my mother was on. "We will have a very narrow window of opportunity. As soon as the guards take their leave, we must hurry. The new guards will arrive to their posts in two minutes or less. Put the new dress on her first; it should cover all of her slave clothing. Then I'll work on the collar." She looked at her watch again.

"Two minutes until shift change. Let's go ahead and make contact with your mother.

We turned up the next row. There were only two slaves—my mother and another woman. As we passed the other woman, she scrutinized us closely. Had Mara taken into account the other slaves, or had she only planned for the guards?

We stopped a few feet away from my mother, pretending to admire the grapevines. Mara nudged my shoulder, telling me to make contact.

"Mom," I whispered. She didn't hear me. "Mom," I repeated a little louder.

She looked at me, blinking, her eyes still glazed over. "Leela? Is that you?" Her voice sounded soft, weak, like a little girl's, like Annabelle's.

"Yes, Mama, it's me."

"Well, what are you doing here, love?" Her face was sweet and angelic.

"I'm here to take you home."

"Home? Home . . . ," she muttered, staring up into the sky, blinking from the sunlight, as if she expected lightning to strike her again. Had my mother completely lost her mind?

A bell rang, announcing the shift change. Mara pulled me back beside her, handing me the navy linen dress from her bag. As soon as the last guard passed by our row, she said, "Go."

We rushed into action. I explained everything to my mother as quickly and simply as possible, like speaking to a child, while I slipped the dress over her head, clearing a path for Mara to get to the collar.

"Mama, Mama, pay attention. Give me your arm," I pleaded. She was reluctant to remove her work gloves. She was in a confused and scared state of mind, and she didn't like Mara hovering around her neck, pressing buttons on the collar. I was afraid she would call out at any moment.

She kept repeating the questions, "What's going on? What are you doing?"

"Leela, make her be quiet," Mara commanded through clenched teeth. She had to remember and input the codes without my mother's voice ringing in her ears.

I finally had the dress down to her feet. A little of her red garment showed at the neckline. I wished her hair were longer so it could cover it. I would have to hold it at the back as I guided her out of there.

"Shh, Mom. You're fine," I soothed her. "We're taking you home, to see Corey and Annabelle."

At the sound of their names, she began to weep softly.

"Got it," Mara exclaimed, removing the collar. She dropped it under the grapes where my mother had been working. "Let's go. This way will be fastest."

My mother walked slowly but submissively. I kept my hand on her back, bunching up the dress in my fist. Mara flanked her other side.

As we passed the other slave on her row, the one who hadn't taken her eyes off of us, the one who had witnessed everything, Mara handed her a bag of Skittles. "Don't say a word," she ordered her. The slave's eyes lit up, and she nodded in agreement, ripping open the bag of candy.

I didn't have time to think about how disgusted it made me—bribing slaves with candy—because I was too focused on my mother, whispering encouraging things into her ear, trying to comfort her.

We were headed for a gate I had never been through before. Then suddenly, we heard someone, the slave with the candy, shout, "They went that way!" She had betrayed us. We had betrayed her, leaving her behind.

"Run!" Mara ordered. But my mother couldn't, or wouldn't, move that fast. Mara and I, our arms under my mother's arms, lifting her feet off the ground, ran as quickly as we could with the extra weight.

But within seconds, we were surrounded by guards, their cattle prods drawn.

CHAPTER 15

[LANEY]

The sun's heat was completely unbearable. I had thought I would be more accustomed to the climate by the second day, but it only felt hotter. My hair was soaked with sweat at the nape of my neck.

"Curwen," I whined, "can I pleeeease put my hair up?"

Sheldon looked at me funny. "Why are you asking his permission? Of course you can put your hair up."

"But Curwen said—"

"It's fine, Laney," Curwen cut me off. "Put your hair up."

I looked at him questioningly but didn't say anything as I tied my hair into a knot at the back of my head; I didn't want to chance him changing his mind.

We were about halfway to the carpentry warehouses. I was beginning to recognize familiar landmarks somehow, but only by paying attention to the minutest details, like a crack in the pavement or a paint-chipped corner. Details weren't my thing, but in Antonia, they had to be everyone's thing.

"So, what's the plan?" I asked.

"Well, you and I are going to pick up the headboard we ordered. Curwen is going to say we need to hire your father for some labor," Sheldon explained.

"Is that allowed? You can hire a slave?"

"Yes," Sheldon said.

"So, you pay the slave for his work?"

"Not exactly," Curwen replied.

"Then what?"

"We pay the slave owner," Sheldon answered.

"That would be the owner of the warehouses?"

Their short, direct answers didn't contain enough details.

"Well," Curwen paused to think, "I guess the ultimate slave owner would be King Gigandet. Most of what we pay to hire your father will go straight into the royal vault, but the warehouse owner will receive a small percentage."

"So, is that what Leela and Mara are doing? Are they hiring my mother for day labor?"

"No . . . " Sheldon glanced at Curwen cautiously. "You can't hire bodies from the palace. Their first duty is to the king's grounds. They don't have time for other, less important tasks."

"Then what are they doing?" I demanded.

They were being too slow and vague for my patience.

"They're just going to change her clothes and sneak her out like an ordinary citizen," Curwen explained matter-of-factly.

I replayed his words in my head, making sure I understood them correctly. "You know, I may not be an 'intelligent' Antonian," I whispered as a stranger passed by, "but is that really the best plan? Leela told me how many guards there were."

"It's the best plan given the situation," Curwen said.

I didn't have a good feeling about it. "You should call them now and discuss a new plan."

"Don't worry." Sheldon brushed off my concern. "Mara has been on dozens of missions and never failed."

"Y'all are putting a lot of faith in someone who doesn't care one ounce about me and Leela," I said.

"Hey," Curwen stopped me, his hand on my shoulder, "Mara cares about us," indicating Sheldon and himself with his free hand. "She'll do everything she can to complete this mission and reunite you with your family."

I tried another angle. "What if our mom isn't even there? What if she still isn't feeling well enough to work?"

"Then we'll try again another day," Sheldon said.

Leela had described the palace gardens to me, and the one detail she emphasized was how closely guarded they were. Regardless of Mara's mission-completing success, she was no match for dozens of guards. I tried to push the anxiety away.

We were almost to the warehouses, making our way down the narrow stone staircase outside the city walls. Curwen walked in front of me, and Sheldon was behind. I felt safer with the two of them than I had with just Sheldon, but I couldn't help wondering how Leela felt—all she had for protection was Mara.

The same guards stood outside the entrance, and they smirked with amusement when they saw me. I glared back at them until they looked away.

"Hurry up, y'all. Let's get inside," I urged them, eager to escape the scorching heat.

The same secretary sat behind the desk. When she recognized me, the smile faded from her face; my eyes dared her to speak to me. I was too tired and hot to be bothered with superficial cordiality—that was Sheldon's job.

Curwen and Sheldon approached the front desk while I took a seat in the empty waiting area.

"May I help you?" the secretary asked, the huge smile returning to her lips.

"Yes, is Phil here?" Sheldon asked.

"One moment." She disappeared down the dark hallway.

Curwen snapped to get my attention. *So rude.* He pointed at the floor next to him, indicating that I was supposed to go to him like an obedient puppy dog. Sucking up my pride, I rose slowly and went to stand beside Sheldon just as Phil and the secretary returned.

"Good morning!" Phil exclaimed. "How are you today?" He shook hands with Sheldon, and then Sheldon introduced Curwen as the groom-to-be for whom we were purchasing the headboard.

"Oh, really? Congratulations, young man!" He shook Curwen's hand vigorously. "What's the bride's name?"

Curwen paused for a brief moment, obviously drawing a blank on his lovely bride's name. He and Sheldon spoke at the same time.

"Leela."

"Mara."

Curwen had said Mara! Is that who he wanted to marry? Was that the first name that came to his mind when he thought about his future wife? I knew Phaedra was mistaken to think there was anything between Leela and Curwen. Hadn't Curwen said he would trust Mara with his life?

But Sheldon appeared surprised by Curwen's response.

"Well, which is it?" Phil asked, confused. "You can't have two brides."

"I don't," Curwen replied defensively. "Her name is Mara. Leela is just the nickname Sheldon likes to call her."

"Okay . . . " Phil was semi-satisfied with the answer. "Anyway, what can I do for you all today?" He appeared uncomfortable and ready to be done with us, although he had not yet spoken to or made eye contact with me.

"We'd like to pick up the headboard," Sheldon explained. "And Curwen would like to hire the same slave to do some work around their future home."

"How long would you like to hire him?" Phil's eyes narrowed in suspicion. "He's a pretty big slave and could be hard to control if he tried to get violent. It might not be safe."

"When I spoke with him yesterday," Sheldon began, "he seemed to be very levelheaded and accepting of his position. Plus, look at us." He gestured to himself and Curwen. "We can take care of him."

I wanted to roll my eyes and scoff at his statement because they were underestimating my father's strength. But I pasted a fake, amused smile on my face instead.

There was too much tension in the conversation; Phil needed to relax. Maybe my kind face would have a positive influence on him.

It had the effect I'd hoped for. He smiled back at me. "Oh, all right. But only for the day. He needs to be returned by six o'clock sharp." He started filling out some paperwork.

"You two," he spoke to Sheldon and me, "can go on back and look at the headboard. . . . Make sure it is to your satisfaction."

The secretary came around and showed us through the door that led to the dark hallway. She didn't speak to me, but it seemed like she was constantly casting flirtatious glances in Sheldon's direction. If I really were his girlfriend, I would have had some choice words for her blatant disregard of our relationship.

Sheldon held the other door open for both of us, and the secretary explained our presence to the guards before leaving us to fend for ourselves. The men were hard at work, as they had been the previous day.

I spotted my father at the same workstation, finishing a few details on the headboard. He was carving a design in the top of it; he loved to carve intricate designs in his woodwork.

We walked in his direction, and even though our eyes had met when we first entered the room, he kept his eyes on his work as we approached, like any good submissive *body*. I couldn't wait until the moment when I could throw my arms around him in a long embrace.

At any second, I felt like I might burst into tears; the anticipation of freeing my father was too much. They should have left me at Mara's house because the temptation to show my true feelings was almost more than I could control.

Being so close, it's hard to resist.

"Hi," Sheldon said softly to my father. I appreciated his gentleness, his humanity. "Were you able to complete the headboard on time?"

"Yes, I just finished the final details." He kept his eyes down.

"Good. You can help us carry it home."

My father's gaze shifted warily in Sheldon's direction for a split second. "Are you sure that's allowed?" he whispered.

"Oh, yes. Our friend Curwen is hiring you for the day to do some work at his home. We're taking the headboard there."

During Sheldon's explanation, my father seemed to get more and more nervous. His hands shook a little, and I knew from his expression that the idea of leaving that place caused panic in the pit of his stomach.

"It'll be okay," I whispered. "Everything will work out just fine. You'll be back where you belong in no time. Don't worry." I almost reached out to cover his hand with mine, but Sheldon grabbed my hand and squeezed it in reassurance.

A couple of guards were passing by, so I rubbed my free hand across the beautiful cedar headboard and remarked enthusiastically, "This will be a wonderful gift! You did excellent work."

Just then Curwen entered the warehouse, scanning the room for us, though I couldn't imagine it was too difficult to see us among the guards dressed in black and the slaves dressed in orange. He walked directly toward us, folding a packet of papers and stuffing them into his pocket along the way.

He also put a remote in his other pocket. When I realized what it was for—to activate my father's shock collar—I felt sick to my stomach.

"Hey," he said quietly. "Are you all ready to go?"

Sheldon and I nodded. My father was hesitant.

"Is this thing heavy?" Curwen asked my father, putting his hand on the headboard.

My dad shook his head.

"All right," Sheldon said, "then the three of us should have no problem carrying it. Laney, your job will be to open all the doors for us."

"All right," I replied with more confidence than I felt. "Come on, Dad," I whispered. "You can do this."

Firmly, he replied, "I know. I must."

The three of them grabbed the headboard, Curwen and Sheldon on the ends, my father in the center. I hurried ahead of them to open the door. The guards didn't bother to offer any assistance, instead either ignoring us or making snide comments about us to each other.

Neither Phil nor the secretary were in the front office or waiting room, and we continued on our way without trying to find them. Even though the sun's rays were blinding as my eyes adjusted, I could tell that the outside guards watched us with curiosity.

"We'll drop this at my house and then head to the meeting location," Curwen said.

They had to carry the headboard all the way home. I was grateful not to be a part of that. Just carrying my own weight required an enormous amount of energy in the Antonian heat. How long had it taken my father to become accustomed to it?

The three of them moved much faster than I expected; I had to walk at an accelerated pace to keep up. I thought Curwen and Sheldon were surprised by my father as well—he was much stronger than they thought he would be, like I had known.

It was midmorning, so we had the entire day to reunite my mother and father and return them to Corey and Annabelle. I smiled at the image of the happiness that would fill my siblings when they saw their parents again.

And Hollister, the small voice in the back of my mind kept reminding me. What was the plan for him?

"Laney, we need you up front!" Curwen hollered. Already, we had reached the top of the narrow staircase, and Curwen needed me to open the gate. "Come on, Laney, you're not doing your job very well," he complained, but he was barely breaking a sweat under the weight of the headboard.

I had to squeeze past them, pressed up against the stone wall to get in front of them. Curwen told me all the codes to enter, which I did with shaky fingers. The gate beeped, and I opened it as carefully as possible, trying not to knock any of us off the stairs. To be so close to freedom and then accidentally plummet to our deaths—I shuddered at the thought.

They moved past me quickly, and I shut the gate behind us. We were silent along the way. I wanted to ask about Hollister. I wanted to ask Sheldon if he had checked last night or this morning on the barracks security footage. Was Hollister still laid up in bed? Was he back in the fields? Or had he been sent to the scientists?

But I couldn't say any of that in a public space. We needed the privacy of Curwen's home, although Sheldon's would have been closer.

The paths were busy now, filled with people bustling from here to there. They talked softly to one another, but because there were so many of them, it sounded much louder, like a constant hum. We wouldn't have been able to hear one another speak even if we wanted to.

The people instantly moved out of our way, perhaps not desiring to be contaminated by a *body*. Once out of our path, though, many of them stopped and stared. I guess a slave in the living quarters wasn't a common sight, and the attention made my father more uncomfortable and nervous.

Rescuing my father seemed so easy. Was it supposed to be that easy? There had to be a catch somewhere. Was Leela having a harder time than us? Was it just my luck that I was the twin who got to go on the easy mission?

Would freeing our parents prove to be easy, but rescuing Hollister be more difficult? There wasn't anything I wouldn't do for Hollister. I wished he had seen me that day at the fields, that he had heard me shout his name so he would know I was here for him, so he would be filled with hope as well.

We approached Curwen's house. Like the first night as he'd carried Leela, he had me reach into his pocket for the key card. The gush of cool air that hit us as we entered was glorious. They set the headboard in the hallway, leaning it against the wall.

That was it, the moment I had been waiting for. I threw my arms around my father, squeezing him with all the strength I had. His embrace was as I'd always remembered it. We remained that way for a long moment until he pulled away, still unsure about the men who were watching us.

"I'm going back out to get some new clothes for you," Curwen said to him. "Then you can take a shower and change. While I'm gone, Laney, you can fix him something to eat." The door beeped behind him.

There was a basket of food on the kitchen table, obviously delivered from Phaedra's bakery. She must have known how empty and bare Curwen's cupboards and fridge were. What would Durham say about her helping us, even if she didn't know exactly what we were doing?

"So, Laney's dad, what's your name?" Sheldon asked.

"Wouldn't you just like to call me 2916?" my father's gruff voice responded.

"No." Sheldon shook his head. "I'd like to call you by your name, sir."

My father's eyes glossed over, taken aback by the respect Sheldon displayed. "Dan Sachtleben," he answered sheepishly.

Sheldon reached out and shook his hand. "It's nice to meet you, Dan Sachtleben."

I tried not to cry as I watched a tiny shred of my father's dignity be restored.

"Okay, Dan," Sheldon said, "Let me get this collar off of you now. Would you have a seat please?" He pulled out a chair from the kitchen table, and my father took it, perhaps the first time he had been able to rest all day. I turned away, focusing on preparing lunch, not wanting to become emotional.

About an hour later, my father appeared at the top of the stairs, clean and shaven, wearing the clothes Curwen had bought him—some khaki linen pants and a white button-up shirt. He looked like a brand-new person. How easily trauma could be externally erased, but what was happening internally?

"You're looking good, Dan!" Sheldon clapped him on the shoulder.

"Let's head out to the meeting place," Curwen said. "It's almost noon. They should be there by now."

We went to the meeting place, the same place where Leela and I had first entered Antonia. It was in a small clearing near the woods, right outside of the living quarters, very close to Curwen's house.

Nobody was there waiting for us.

We waited for two hours while Curwen and Sheldon repeatedly called Mara's phone.

No answer. Ever.

Finally, Curwen suggested, "Dan, I can go ahead and take you home now. We only have you for a few more hours."

My father shook his head emphatically. "I'm not going anywhere without my wife."

He could not, would not, be persuaded.

So, we made our way back to Curwen's, ever hopeful that maybe the instructions just got crossed, that they didn't realize where we were supposed to meet.

When I recognized our location, I became more anxious with every step. Just thirty more feet, turn the corner, walk twenty more feet, scan his card through the lock, and open the door to find my two favorite women waiting for us. I held Curwen's ID card in my hand, ready.

I rushed ahead of them through the throng of crowded people, too impatient to care what they thought of me. I had reached the door. Looking back, I couldn't see the men; they hadn't turned the corner yet, but I went ahead and unlocked it, wishing with the turn of the handle that they would be waiting on the other side. I gave the door a shove.

Standing in the open doorway, I listened intently for the sound of female voices.

There was nothing but the whir of a ceiling fan.

CHAPTER 16
(LEELA)

"**S**top right there!" one of the guards shouted in a deep and powerful voice as he approached. He didn't have to shout like that—we were already frozen in place; we had nowhere to go. At least a dozen guards surrounded us. If any other slaves wanted to make a run for it, now was their chance.

The one closest to me shouted, "Release 3126, now!" Mara instantly obeyed, but I didn't want to let go of my mother's arm. What if this was the last time we ever touched?

"Wait," another guard, the female guard Curwen had flirted with, said, "she was in here yesterday." She pointed her finger at me. "Nobody comes here two days in a row . . . "

"Release 3126!" the first guard repeated, glaring at me with piercing eyes.

I clutched her arm more tightly. My fingers wouldn't obey.

But my mother wrestled her arm free from my grasp, and she pushed me away. "You don't touch a body," she said loudly, like she was repeating a rule that had been drilled into her head. A look of recognition flashed across her eyes, warning me to stay away from her. She was trying to spare me from the brunt of whatever was about to happen.

Three guards rushed at her, pinning her to the ground. "Where's your collar, 3126?" one of them demanded. Her eyes winced in pain from the way they twisted her wrist behind her back.

I couldn't take it.

I acted without thinking. I knew Mara was shaking her head, telling me not to do it.

But I did it anyway. "She has a name!" I yelled as I swiftly grabbed the stun gun from the belt of the guard who was on top of my mother. Sticking the prongs to his neck, shocking him, I said, "It's Elizabeth."

Instantly, the female guard was on me with the cattle prod, and I fell to the ground in shock, unable to move. While she cuffed my hands, another guard approached, bringing the shock collar for my mother.

They also cuffed Mara; she didn't resist. I glared up at her, and she glared down at me, neither of us happy with the other's actions. Or lack of action.

The guard I had tased also glared at me with anger and disgust. He was strong and tall, towering over me. He was obviously the leader of the group, the others jumping whenever he issued an order. After securing the collar on my mother, he commanded another guard to take her away.

I cried out to her and fought against the arms that held me, but it was no use—she didn't look back at me. They had broken her. Her last act of defiance against them, her last display of affection for me, had been to push me away, to protect me and sacrifice herself.

They searched us and found the identification cards, even the one for my mother.

The guard I had tased handed them to another one, saying, "Scan these."

Mara and I looked at each other, unsure what the scanner would reveal, mentally blaming each other for the situation we were in.

The guard pulled out a hand scanner and ran Mara's ID beneath it. The machine beeped approval. Then he scanned the other two cards; they made a different sound than Mara's. They all looked at me with suspicion. Mara rolled her eyes, exasperated, her jaw tightening in anger.

"Where did you get these fake IDs?" he demanded.

"We got them the same place as everyone else," Mara said. "State Records."

"Really?" he asked sarcastically. "I didn't realize they were issuing IDs to bodies now."

"These IDs were issued to women who were both declared deceased this morning," the female guard explained. "You're Mara." She pointed at Mara. "But who are you?" she asked me.

I remained silent. Most of the guards had returned to their posts. Only four remained.

The lead guard kicked me in my side, knocking the air out of my lungs. He shouted, "Answer us!"

"Or do we need to bring your boyfriend in for questioning?" the female asked with an evil smirk.

Curwen. I saw the look of fear cross Mara's eyes.

"No," she replied instantly. "Her name is Leela."

Would she tell them everything if she thought it would protect Curwen?

Some guards were looking on in amusement. This was probably the highlight of their month. How often did they make citizen arrests?

If I were a true Antonian citizen, I might have felt a tinge of humiliation, but at that moment, I just felt defeated. I could have rose to my feet and tried to make a run for it, knowing I wouldn't make it very far. And I feared the punishment they could inflict.

It was the first time I had felt hot since I had been in Antonia, my cheeks burning. My head was spinning, and the grass was itching my face. It felt like a slow-motion, out-of-body experience, like I was watching it happen without being a part of it.

And then I passed out.

My eyes blinked slowly open, focusing on my surroundings. There was faint sunlight streaming down from high above. My pupils dilated to let in more light, and then I was aware that I was not alone. Rubbing my eyes with the back of my hand, I realized my head was pounding. I groaned in pain.

"Are you awake?" It was Mara's voice, speaking softly. Her tone revealed that she felt defeated as well. Curwen had trusted her, and she had failed the mission; I imagined it was a huge blow to her ego.

"Yeah . . . ," I replied, attempting to prop myself up on my elbows, but feeling too weak. "What happened? Where are we?"

"They have brought us to the prison beneath the palace."

"Why does my head hurt?" I asked.

"They weren't exactly gentle with you during transport. Your head got knocked around a bit—payback for you stun-gunning that guard. I think that's why you've been unconscious for so long."

"How long?" I asked.

"We've been here for three hours . . . we should have met up with everyone else an hour ago. They'll be worried."

They should be worried. "They should be worried," I muttered, my head hurting so badly that tears were trickling down my face.

"I don't want them to do anything stupid though, anything that would get them stuck in here," she said. "They're probably already on their way to question Curwen anyway, since that guard saw you two together yesterday." There was an edge to her voice, like it was my fault.

I remembered her last words before I passed out. *Her name is Leela.* What else had she told them? I couldn't see her well; she was seated in a dark corner opposite from where I lay.

"What did you tell them?" I whispered, in too much pain to demand with a strong voice.

"I told them that we met randomly this morning in the meeting quarter and that you offered to pay me if I helped you. And I didn't know what you were planning until it was happening."

"*Nice.* It's all on me."

"Pretty much," she replied bluntly.

I wanted to cry harder, but resisted, knowing it would cause me more pain.

"So, we're locked in here?" I looked around. The walls were stone, the floor was dirt, and there was a narrow, wrought-iron door. High above, the ceiling contained a few cracks which let in some sunlight.

I sat up, like I was moving in slow motion, and pulled myself back so I could lean against the wall. My body felt like it had been beaten, like all my muscles ached after an extremely vigorous workout. And my stomach cried out for nourishment.

"Can we call anyone?" I asked.

"No," she stated with determination in her eyes. "We got ourselves into this situation, and we have to find a way out of it. If we try to contact anyone, we'll just get them into trouble as well."

"What's going to happen to my mother?" Suddenly, I was panicked. What kind of punishment would my mother have to endure because of our poorly devised escape plan? It wasn't her fault that I had talked to her or touched her. Would they take that into consideration?

"I'm not sure . . . " She paused. "Probably nothing. Your mother seemed pretty out of it. I don't think they will hold her accountable, so long as she doesn't reveal that you're her daughter." She whispered the last part, looking around, worried about being overheard.

"Mara," I was serious, "doesn't any of this seem wrong to you?"

"What do you mean?"

"This entire Antonian system of government. The practice of slavery. Everything! I mean, what is their reason for arresting us? Because I talked to a slave?"

"No, I think we could have gotten away with that. It was the fake IDs that did us in. I'm pretty sure they're charging us with espionage."

"But we weren't spying on the government . . . "

"They don't know that." She sighed. "The plan might have worked if . . . *Elizabeth* had moved faster." She had called her by her name.

"No! It wasn't her fault. Your Skittles weren't enough to keep that other slave silent. She sold us out. We wouldn't have gotten far."

"You're right," she conceded. She had lost all her fight, or she was saving it for when it really mattered.

"Curwen works for the government," I said. "I saw him talk to Gigandet yesterday. Couldn't he help us?"

"No," she hissed. "Do you want him to be killed? Because that's what would happen." She almost couldn't bring herself to say those words; they got choked in her throat on the way out.

Just then, we heard voices down the dark tunnel outside our cell. I moved closer to Mara in the corner; whether she wanted me near her or not meant very little in that moment. I was scared, and I hadn't even realized it before I heard those footsteps. Should I pretend to be unconscious still? Would they take me for questioning if I was awake?

We peeked around the edge of the doorway, trembling, to see who was coming our way. There were two silhouettes moving toward us, holding torches they used to light other torches that lined the tunnel. It was the most medieval-looking place in comparison with the modernity I had seen in the rest of Antonia. Where was the electricity in this place?

As they got closer, we moved back into the corner, as far from the door as possible. I was surprised Mara had not pushed me away from her yet. Her body was tense—she was scared too, and we were each other's only consolation. They were unlocking the door and shining a flashlight in, searching for our location in the dark.

A slave entered first, dressed in a bright-green shirt and matching pants. He carried a tray with food and drinks; the sight of it reminded me of my hunger and thirst. He set it down and then disappeared through the doorway.

"Return from where you came," a hidden, cool voice commanded. The slave's footsteps faded away down the tunnel. We were left alone with a mysterious man who stood just outside the cell.

He closed and locked the wrought-iron door and then sat down against the tunnel wall in a dark spot so we still could not make out the features of his face. "Go ahead and eat," he said. "I know you're both hungry. It's some of Antonia's finest; the king's chef prepared it himself."

I looked at Mara, my eyes questioning whether it was safe to eat the food. She hesitated for a moment but then pulled the tray closer and inspected the food the best she could with our limited light source. First she looked at it, and then she sniffed it.

"It's not poison," the man said. "You two are far too interesting to kill so quickly, before the mystery has been solved."

"There is no mystery," Mara stated with attitude. "We're just two young women who were visiting the palace gardens, and this arrest is a flagrant disregard of our rights."

Was she changing the story now?

"What rights?" He laughed deeply and cynically.

"There are laws," she replied.

"And when you break them, you don't have any rights."

"Who are you?" Mara demanded.

"Who are you?" he asked. I could hear the amusement in his voice, like it was his job to torment us.

I picked up the sandwich from the plate and began nibbling at it. He certainly wasn't going to get me to speak. And the sandwich was one of the most delicious things I had ever tasted. How could anything be so enjoyable when everything was so terrible? It messed with my head.

When we didn't respond, he answered his own question. "So, you're Mara?" He pointed at her, and she nodded. "And," he pointed at me, "you're Leela?" I nodded, my mouth full of food. "Well, I'm Whirl, the king's most trusted advisor."

Whirl. Gigandet had said that name to Curwen yesterday. Curwen was supposed to contact Whirl about some information.

Mara narrowed her eyes at him. "Trusted advisor? Don't you mean the king's puppet?" she demanded.

My eyes flew to her in warning. Why was she deliberately provoking him? Did she know about Whirl? Had Curwen told her things about him?

"Well, if you hadn't broken any laws before, now you have," he said with a smile. "Those words are treason."

Mara swallowed her pride and said no more. She picked up the other sandwich and began to eat, now that she saw it hadn't killed me. I downed the drink after the last bite of food; it was some kind of cucumber juice.

"Is there something you want from us?" Mara asked more politely once she finished eating.

"The truth?" he said. "What did that slave mean to you?" He pointed at me. His long finger cast a shadow on the stone wall. "And how come you," he pointed at Mara, "agreed to help her?"

What *did* she mean to me? Why had he used the past tense? Had they done something to my mother? Could she be . . . dead?

My breathing became rapid. My head was spinning again. The cell seemed so small. Claustrophobia was setting in. My skin was tingling with heat now.

I was going to pass out again. I could feel it, so I pressed my cheek against the cold stone wall, hoping it would revive my sanity. I couldn't ask about that slave without revealing that I did have a relationship with her, so I just kept silent.

Mara glanced at me with what appeared to be genuine concern. "Look, Whirl, we've given you all the truth we're going to offer, so unless you're going to let us out of here, I suggest you take this tray and disappear." She shoved the tray toward the door, causing the empty cups to fall over.

"You know," he remained calm, but threatening, "you're really messing up. You don't realize how bad things can get. I'm your only hope here, and you're throwing our possible alliance away."

She rolled her eyes. "I don't consort with the king's men."

"We're all the king's men . . . unless we're traitors . . . "

I wasn't looking at him, but I imagined if we could have seen his face in the darkness, his eyes would have been piercing into Mara's.

We remained silent. I was still trying to slow my breathing and keep from crying.

"All right," he finally said, "if that's the way you want it." He rose to his feet, but I didn't turn to glimpse his face. "I'll come back later and see if you've changed your minds."

He walked slowly away down the tunnel until he disappeared around a corner. We didn't speak for a long time in case he was still waiting to hear our conversation. I almost didn't have anything to say anyway.

My mother was completely lost to me, to Laney, to Corey, to Annabelle. Who would be a mother to my precious siblings now, especially if Laney didn't make it home?

Were they more successful in rescuing my father? Could he be both mother and father to them? Would Hollister ever be free? Could he and Laney adopt Corey and Annabelle, acting as their substitute parents? So many questions ran through my head, thinking about provision for my younger siblings.

"Do you think my mother's dead?" I finally whispered.

She didn't answer right away, but instead moved to sit next to me for support. "I really can't answer that, and I wish I could. I know what it feels like to wonder what happened to your mother and father."

I pulled my face away from the wall and looked at her curiously. "What happened to your mother and father?"

"When I was just a little girl, I came home from a long day at school to find the house empty. I waited and waited. But they never came home. Eventually Durham came—he was friends with my parents—and he took me home with him."

"So, you don't know where they are?" I asked.

"Durham said the king's men must have taken them. My parents worked for the same organization as Durham, and as Whirl said, that's treason. Whether they're still alive, I don't know for sure. But I like to imagine them somewhere in the mountains, living free, because somehow they escaped."

"Is that why you're helping us?"

"Why did you think I was helping you?"

" . . . Because you care for Curwen."

"It's true that I do. But I never would have carried out such an insane mission solely for that reason. Helping you was the right thing to do." That was the kindest thing she had said yet.

"Even though you're locked in here?"

"Even though I'm locked in here. That sandwich alone was worth being locked in here!" she joked. And we laughed. The first laugh we had ever shared, and perhaps the last.

My head hurt to laugh. I held it in both hands and ended up feeling dried blood in my hair. It had run down the side of my face. I pulled my hair up, tying it into a knot, attempting to cool myself off. It felt like I had a fever.

"How bad does this look?" I asked, pointing at my head.

"Come to the light," she said, moving toward it herself. "They knocked your head on the wall as we were exiting the gardens. That one guard laughed about it. I wanted to punch him." She examined the wound closely. "It could use some stitches. You'll definitely have a scar. But you probably won't have to live with it for long." She laughed with dark humor at the suggestion of our impending deaths.

Then she glanced down at my neck, then back at my eyes, then back at my neck. She tried to wipe it with my shirt. "This isn't blood," she stated in disbelief.

"Oh." I realized what she was looking at. "No, that's just a birthmark."

She was silent for a long moment before finally whispering, "You're the one."

"The one what?"

"The one to break the curse."

"I have no idea what you're talking about."

"Curwen never told you why he was in your town—what his mission was?" she asked, incredulous, shocked.

Had he ever told us what his mission was? He had only stated that he had to find something for his boss. Which boss—did he mean Durham or Gigandet?

"No . . . " I shook my head.

"You have the mark in the shape of three angles and an arc."

She said it as if it was a huge revelation, as if I was supposed to know what it meant. What was I missing? What had Curwen not told us?

"You mean my birthmark?" I pointed to it. I couldn't see it without a mirror. I never paid attention to its shape. It was just something I knew I had, the only thing that made me physically different from Laney.

In my morbid mind, I had always been glad to have it in case I was ever murdered and Laney was missing, they would be able to identify my body from hers. Whenever we had tried to trick our parents about our identities, my father would tackle me, tickling me until I couldn't resist, so he could check my neck and confirm that I was who I said I wasn't.

I smiled at the memory until I realized Mara was still staring at me, her mouth agape. "What curse are you talking about?" I demanded.

"How much do you know about Antonia's history?"

I paused, recalling everything Curwen had told us. "Mainly I just know about the king whose wife died, and how he started lightning travel and the importation of slaves to find a cure for her disease."

She nodded slowly, her eyes wide, as if I was supposed to understand. When I still stared at her, eyes full of confusion, she sighed and started to explain. "Well, one of those slaves put a curse on the descendants of the king. The curse stated that one of the future kings—King Gigandet— would have to deal with mass sickness and suffering unless he married the match of the one whose neck has the mark in the shape of three angles and an arc. If he marries anyone other than the one with the mark, his wife will die from the sickness too."

"And the mark on my neck is . . . ?"

She lifted my hair and looked closely. "It's a perfect triangle connect- ed to a crescent shape." She sat back and looked at me in awe. "It has to be you."

"So, Curwen was supposed to find the one with the mark and bring her here?" I asked in disbelief. My mind flashed back to the day in the cave when Curwen had seen my birthmark.

He knew who I was.

"He never mentioned this," I continued. "Was he finding me for Gi- gandet or Durham?"

"Both."

"But which one would he have given me to?"

"Neither."

"What do you mean?" I demanded. She was speaking in riddles.

"I don't think he wanted anyone to find out about you. He told no one."

How could she be so sure? Had he brought me here under the pre- tense of saving my family so he could turn me over to the king? Or to Durham? Is that why he hadn't told Durham the truth about us? I could feel tears of betrayal forming, but I blinked to stop them.

CHAPTER 17

[LANEY]

"Where are they, Curwen? They should be here by now," I demanded as soon as they came through the door. I was sitting on the stairs, thinking of all the possible scenarios of what could have happened to them.

"Laney, please calm down," Curwen begged. "You're not helping the situation." Was he not concerned, or did he just hide it well? Was it just a part of who he was—to remain calm under pressure?

It wasn't part of who I was.

"It has been five hours since we all left each other this morning. They should be back by now! Shouldn't they?" I appealed to Sheldon for support.

"Maybe we should go look for them," Sheldon suggested feebly.

It was obvious that Curwen was the boss of this operation.

"We're not going to the gardens," Curwen said firmly, decision made. "Just give me a minute to think."

We all remained silent, giving him what he'd asked for.

"Dan," he addressed my father, "we really should go ahead and take you home. It's not safe for any of us for you to stay. This may be our only chance. Corey and Annabelle are waiting."

My father gave a firm headshake. "They can wait a little longer."

"You're putting everyone in more danger, Dan," Sheldon tried to persuade him. "They'll come for you soon if we don't return you to the warehouses."

"*I'm not leaving without Lizzy*," he resolved. "Don't mention it again."

He spoke with such authority and determination, his command had to be obeyed.

"So, what do we do?" I asked. "What about Hollister?"

Why was Hollister everyone's last concern?

"Hollister?" my father asked. "Are we going to get him too?"

"Why wouldn't we?" I asked defensively.

"They took him somewhere last night," he explained, emotionless. "I'm not sure if they ever brought him back . . . "

Why hadn't he said this sooner?

My stomach dropped. My knees went weak. Sheldon grabbed my arm and led me to a chair. Then he turned to my father and asked, "How do you know? You're not in the same barracks."

"I saw through the tiny window near my bed. They took him somewhere. I fell asleep before I could see if they brought him back."

"Did you not keep watch over the monitors?" I demanded, my anger directed at Sheldon.

"The monitors?" Curwen asked, his eyes suspicious. "Sheldon, what did you do?"

Once the words left my mouth, I realized I had revealed our secret. But I couldn't care about that. And Sheldon appeared unfazed by it as well, unconcerned about Curwen possibly being upset or any of the potential consequences.

"I took her to see Hollister on the monitors," he confessed with boldness. "And we need to go back there now to see what else I can find out. Not just about Hollister, but about Leela, Mara, and Lizzy."

Curwen didn't speak for a long time, lost in thought. He wasn't bothered that I had seen the monitors, or that was the least of his concerns at the moment. "You're right," he finally agreed. "You need to see what else you can find in the system. But what do we do about Dan, since he won't let us take him home yet?"

He was annoyed with my father's decision because it wasn't a decision made in the best interest of everyone. It was a decision made from the love he had for my mother. Thinking of Hollister, I could understand it. I wouldn't leave that place without him either. Curwen didn't get it.

"We have a few hours before we need to figure that out. Let's just go," Sheldon said.

As we walked to Sheldon's house, I fell into step beside my father, hoping to start a conversation to find out more about his time in Antonia.

"Laney," he muttered, looking around him, "this place is rather beautiful, isn't it?"

"In appearances only," I replied coolly. "How are you, Dad?"

"Better than I was, but not the best I could be."

He put his arm around my shoulders, and I leaned my head on him.

For the first time in years, my father was clean-shaven; I missed his auburn beard, but I hadn't noticed its absence until that moment. Had they made him shave it, or did he choose to get rid of it because of the heat?

"Dad, tell me what happened."

"I don't really know," he replied. "One second, I was setting up tables for your engagement party, and the next second, I was here. One second, it was daylight, and the next second, it was nighttime and so hot. I didn't know that such heat existed. I'm used to it now though."

"So, you don't know how you got here?" I looked at his face.

He shook his head sadly. "I just keep telling myself it's a bad, never-ending dream . . . like maybe I had a stroke, and now I'm in a coma . . . having this nightmare. It could happen, right?"

"No, Dad." I shook my head. "You're not in a coma. This is really happening. This place is Antonia, and you get here by traveling through lightning . . . "

It sounded ridiculous coming out of my mouth. I had a difficult time believing my own words. Maybe my dad was right; he was in a coma, and I was just part of his nightmare.

"Travel by lightning? You mean I was struck by lightning?" he asked in disbelief. I nodded. "Well, maybe that's what put me in a coma," he suggested, sounding like a little kid.

Did he really think he was comatose? It seemed like he had spent a month making himself believe his theory, and I didn't know how to convince him otherwise. He would just have to see when we traveled home.

"So, what happened when you arrived here in the night?" I asked, hoping reliving the memories wouldn't make him have some sort of panic attack.

"They separated us into groups and assessed our skills and abilities. They assigned us a number and a service location. Then they made us change our clothes. Each group received a different color to wear." He glanced down at the clothes he wore now, seeming relieved that they were no longer bright orange.

"Had you seen Hollister before last night?" I tried to ask calmly, though I was anxious.

"Once or twice. But we were never able to talk. He wears yellow; that means he works in the fields. They have it the hardest, but they're all strong, capable young men."

"There are women in the fields too," I told him. "I've seen them . . . and I saw Hollister."

"Oh?" He was curious.

"Curwen and I went to the fields to look for him, and I saw him from a distance. They shocked him with his collar." It was almost too hard to say, the words choking me as I remembered. I felt him shudder, and his eyes grew wide with fear.

"Did they ever shock you?" I asked.

"Only once," he admitted, ashamed. "When I saw your mother, I couldn't stop myself. The men and women are kept separate. But once, they brought me into the female barracks after the women had left for the day so I could replace some old, rotted wood in the doorframes."

I nodded, encouraging him to continue. Curwen and Sheldon were listening too.

"The guard left me there to do my work while he went and talked with the other guards. He didn't realize the barrack wasn't completely empty. I saw your mother lying on a bed some distance away. I knew she wasn't doing well if she was excused from her labor. I went to her—I couldn't stop myself. I had barely touched her hand when the shock collar crippled me to the floor. The voltage is so high, especially for us big guys."

I didn't know when the tears had started running down my cheeks. Tears glistened in my father's eyes as well. He added, "Needless to say, they never let me near the women's barracks again."

I squeezed his arm, acknowledging his pain.

We were almost to Sheldon's house.

"How are Corey and Annabelle?" my father asked, changing the subject.

"They were fine when we left them, except that Annabelle hasn't spoken a word since that day. . . . She saw Hollister get struck by the lightning, and it traumatized her. But," I attempted to offer some hope, "she promised to talk again when we all return."

"Well, let's hope that we do," he said, doubtful.

"Curwen could take you home to them this afternoon, right now," I dared to broach the subject again. "Just think how happy they'll be to wake up and find you home!"

"We've already been over this, Laney. I'm not going without your mother."

"We're working on getting her," I said.

"Yes, but it seems like they're having some complications with that, and I'm just letting you know, I'm not leaving here without her. I don't want to hear about it anymore."

I let it go, knowing that when it came down to it, my father didn't really have a choice. If Curwen wanted to take him home, he could simply push the right combination of buttons, and the lightning would come for him. His coma would be over, and he'd wake up in the woods near our home. I imagined Corey waiting for him in one of the rocking chairs on our back porch.

When we entered the house, Sheldon went directly to his hidden closet in the pantry, not wasting any time. The monitor screens still showed barrack twenty-seven. I wished I could have sat there last night, watching. Then I would have known about Hollister long before my father happened to mentioned it.

"You're going to look for Hollister?" I prompted, anxious.

"Hollister can wait," Curwen said. "We need to find Leela and Mara."

Sheldon didn't acknowledge either of us, but made his own decision. "I already have access to the barrack's security footage," he explained.

"So, I'm going to scroll back through it quickly to see what happened last night. It will only take a couple minutes."

I hovered over Sheldon's shoulder. Curwen paced back and forth on the tile floors. My father sat at the kitchen table, still and quiet. He had always been like that—silent and patient in the midst of urgency, the calm in a storm.

He rewound the footage to the previous evening. Hollister was still lying down while other men, other slaves, began to return; the workday had ended. Hollister sat up, shook hands with some of the men. They ate some food, or rather some slop that masqueraded as food. He even smiled and laughed once or twice.

Sheldon fast-forwarded it. The men were all in their bunks now, and the sun had set. Because the lights were out, it was difficult to see what happened next. But there was movement in the darkness. Hollister rose and exited the door, where two guards were waiting for him.

Leela and I had been tucked under the covers in a comfortable bed, talking—and sometimes laughing—in this moment, when Hollister was being led somewhere unknown. This is when my father had seen him, through a tiny window in another barrack. It was hard not to feel like we could have been doing something to help, making better use of our time.

Sheldon fast-forwarded it again. The hours passed by until finally, at about 2:00 a.m., the barrack door opened again. Light shone in from outside. Two guards practically carried Hollister inside. His arms were around their shoulders, and they propped him up on both sides, dragging his feet across the ground. He couldn't walk on his own.

"What did they do to him?" I cried, attempting not to become hysterical. But every fiber of my being felt compelled to hit something.

My father didn't even need to see the screen to understand what had happened. He explained quietly from his corner in the kitchen, "There are rumors about some scientists. Sometimes they take some men at night to be tested, to see if they're suitable candidates."

"Candidates for *what*?" I asked, directing my question to every man in the room.

The scientists weren't just a rumor. Curwen heard the guard yesterday, threatening Hollister—*327 has it coming. If he so much as looks at me wrong one more time, I'm sending him to the scientists.* And Sheldon's body had become tense when I'd mentioned the scientists before.

I repeated my question. None of them would look at me. My father shrugged. Sheldon opted out of any response by focusing on the monitors. Eventually Curwen said, "We don't really know. I think most people assume it's to find a cure for the Queen's Disease."

Just then, Curwen's phone rang. We all held our breaths, hoping it was Mara on the other end. *Let it be Mara. Let it be Leela.* He glanced at his phone and then shook his head to indicate it wasn't.

"Hey, Durham," he answered it.

"Where are you?" Durham asked. The volume was turned up so we could hear.

"Why? What do you need?" Curwen asked, avoiding his question.

"I need you to not be home."

"Why?" Curwen's eyes became wide with concern.

"Because there are guards outside your door. They're about to search the place."

"We're not there," Curwen confirmed.

Sheldon hissed from his closet, "But the shock collar is!"

We had left it there so the tracking system would show that my father was still at Curwen's house, where he was supposed to be working.

"You've got two seconds to tell me if I need to intervene," Durham said. He was offering to help, even though he didn't know what was happening, what we had been up to. A dad trying to bail out his kids.

Curwen hesitated.

Sheldon ripped the phone from his hand. "Durham, get rid of the shock collar on the kitchen table."

"Got it. Meet me at Phaedra's," he replied. Then the call ended.

Curwen grabbed the phone roughly from Sheldon, angry at him for interfering.

"What's your problem?" Sheldon exclaimed. "I'm trying to buy us some time."

"We don't need Durham involved in this," Curwen said through clenched teeth.

"Too late for that," Sheldon replied as he returned to his chair in the surveillance closet, obviously not in a rush to get to Phaedra's, focused on his current mission—to figure out what had happened to Leela, Mara, and my mother.

This part seemed to make Curwen feel useless, pacing around as he waited for any information Sheldon could give him. Curwen was the planner, the strategizer, the leader when Durham wasn't around. Even though Sheldon wasn't in command, he was invaluable to the group.

"Hollister's been in his bunk all day," Sheldon announced. "Whatever they did to him made him unfit for work today. So, he's still in the barracks."

"Good. Now find Leela and Mara, please," Curwen ordered impatiently.

"Where do I even begin?" Sheldon mumbled under his breath.

Curwen wasn't amused. "Start with the police blotter. There must be some reason they're searching my house, and it can't be because of Dan—he's not due back for two more hours."

I took a seat at the table with my father, and I held his hand. Where was Leela? I wished we had some sort of twin psychic connection, but I didn't feel anything, good or bad. All I knew was that I couldn't, I *wouldn't*, leave that place without her either.

"Okay," Sheldon began, "I found something. There's a report of an incident in the gardens this morning. Two arrested. One taken to the infirmary. No other details. Neither the names nor the charges are listed."

"Can you look up the infirmary intake records?" Curwen asked.

"Already on it," Sheldon replied, one step ahead.

I hesitated, but finally asked, "If they've been arrested, can we bail them out of jail?"

My father answered first, with bitterness in his voice, "No, Laney. This isn't a place where you're innocent until proven guilty. There's no such thing as a fair trial here. Especially for those of us who are not from here." He cut his eyes at Curwen and then continued to look down at the floor, already defeated. I wished he would agree to go home to Corey and Annabelle *now*.

"Is that true?" I directed my question to Curwen.

He nodded. "Pretty much. Gigandet will decide the fate of any prisoner."

"Well, you know Gigandet!" I countered, a surge of hope rising in my chest. "Leela told me you talked to him yesterday in the gardens. You could plead on their behalf." I felt like I was begging when I shouldn't have had to—he should want to do everything in his power to help. But he didn't respond.

"Here she is—3126," Sheldon proclaimed, pointing at the screen. "She was admitted to the infirmary this morning."

My mother. My heart beat quicker. "Does it say why? What's wrong with her?"

"It lists heat exhaustion as the reason for admittance. But she wasn't brought in until eleven thirty this morning. She *was* brought from the gardens, though."

"So that means Leela and Mara should have seen her then, right?" I asked.

"Yes," Curwen stated, his voice strained, worried. "They had plenty of time to get there to see her before then. So, they must have been arrested in the process of trying to rescue her."

"Wait a second," Sheldon said, soft, but steady, his mouth agape as he stared at the screen. But then he didn't say anything else. He turned to look at me and my father, his eyes darting back and forth between us.

"What is it?" I whispered, afraid of the answer.

His eyes glossed over, and he blinked rapidly to hold back tears.

Why was he crying? I didn't want to know.

My father spoke, anger in his words: "Just say it, son."

Sheldon gave my father direct eye contact, giving him the respect he deserved. "The patient status for your wife has just been updated. I'm so sorry, but she's deceased."

"No, you're lying!" I shook my head at him, tears already streaming down my face. I jumped up from the chair and bounded over to the monitors, wanting to see proof with my own eyes.

Deceased in capital, bold, red letters.

I nearly fell over, but Sheldon caught my arm. Curwen grabbed my other one, and they both led me back to the chair beside my father. *My father. His wife. Our mother. Deceased.*

He pulled me close. We embraced. We sobbed. We wailed. We cried, the kind of gut-wrenching cry that can't be described, the kind of sounds that can only come from the depths of someone who has just lost a part of themselves.

I didn't know how long we stayed that way; minutes seemed like hours. I didn't know where Curwen and Sheldon had disappeared to, leaving us alone to grieve in private.

All I knew was that as soon as we pulled back from each other—our eyes bloodshot, our voices hoarse, our faces stained with tears—there was a pounding on the front door.

CHAPTER 18

(LEELA)

Mara was asleep in the corner. The sun had just set, so we were locked in complete darkness. There was no light from the moon or the stars to illuminate the prison cell. I only knew Mara was there because of her steady breathing and the fact that I could reach out and touch her.

After her revelation about me being the one to break the curse, she had retreated back into herself, distancing herself from me all over again. I had hoped that we were forming a friendship, or at least a mutual understanding, when she'd told me about her parents, but that had disappeared when she saw the mark on my neck.

Did I believe in this curse? Or was it just an old Antonian myth? I reasoned that it didn't matter if I believed it—the Antonian people did. Was I really the answer to the disease spreading among the people, the disease we had told Durham our parents had died from, the disease that our kind was immune to?

If Durham had known, what would he have done with me? How would he have used me as a pawn in his cause? I shuddered to think. I assumed the king would just want to marry me, to break the curse, as Mara had explained. That thought made me shudder as well.

Why had Curwen kept it a secret? He had purposely omitted it from the Antonian fairy tale he had told us in our living room. That night seemed like years ago rather than days. I missed the warmth of Annabelle's little body curled up next to mine.

If his intentions were to keep me from being discovered, why had he allowed me to come here? *I think you should stay here*, I remembered him saying. Y*ou're only going to make things more difficult.* Is this what he had meant? I laughed bitterly. Things were more than difficult.

Nobody had come for us yet. Surely they knew something had happened, something had gone terribly wrong, that we needed help. When we hadn't shown up at the meeting place, had they gone looking for us? Where were they now?

Mara could very easily have surrendered me to the king's authority. Another slave and a guard had come down to bring us dinner. She could have told them everything in exchange for her freedom, using me as leverage. But she hadn't, and I was grateful. Just like they had wanted me to be.

Question after question, scenario after scenario swam through my brain. Which was still aching. Periodically, a sharp pain would shoot across the front of my skull.

The more I thought about everything, the more confused I became.

I closed my eyes, ready to sleep the unceasing thoughts, worry, and confusion from my head. Not wanting to lie down in the dirt again, I sat with my back against the somewhat cool stone wall, my knees bent with my arms and head resting on them.

Engulfed in darkness, I began to pray for an answer to the current situation, a solution that would help everyone.

Suddenly, from behind my eyelids, my pupils detected light. My eyes flew open to see a figure coming down the tunnel holding a torch up high. His height and thin build let me know it was Whirl.

When he reached the cell, he sat in the same place as before. Although I was sure he knew I was awake and waiting, he didn't speak for several minutes.

"I know something you don't know," he taunted in a whisper.

Was he trying not to wake Mara? When I didn't respond, he sighed heavily.

"Don't you want to know?" he hissed.

"Sure," I replied with indifference. "Tell me what you know."

"Guess."

"No, thanks."

"But don't you want to know?"

"If you wish to tell me, I have no choice but to know it. But I won't play any guessing games, Rumpelstiltskin."

"Rumpel what?" he demanded.

"Nothing. Never mind." I rolled my eyes even though he couldn't see me.

"Fine, since you won't guess, I'll tell you." He paused, waiting to see if I would change my mind.

Mara slept soundly in the corner. For some reason, I felt better knowing that she was not a part of this conversation.

Whirl sighed again before he spoke. "We arrested four more individuals this evening." His teeth gleamed in the darkness. He was smiling with joy at his revelation.

I stopped breathing. Why was he telling me this? *For his own pleasure.*

"Two young men, an older man . . . and a young woman who looks just like," he pointed at me, "you." He laughed cruelly, but quietly. "What do you have to say about that?"

I couldn't breathe, much less speak. They had been caught. They had rescued my father, but then they had been arrested.

Or was Durham the older man? What had they been arrested for?

"Why were they arrested?" I whispered. There was no sense in lying—he knew Laney was my twin.

"For trying to help a slave escape. The older man was a slave. But, I'm sure you already knew that. Isn't that what you and Mara were trying to do today—help that slave escape?" he hypothesized.

"What happened to her?" I asked.

"You take an eager interest in the affairs of slaves, do you?" He scowled. "Why?"

"What happened to her?" I repeated, emphasizing each word.

He teased, "Do you really want to know?"

Did I? "Yes," I whispered, hesitant.

Bluntly, without emotion, he said, "She died in the infirmary."

"You're lying," I said. First stage, denial.

"No, I'm not. Three-one-two-six is *dead.*" He called her by her number deliberately, to provoke me. Was he lying or telling the truth? Was this part of his game, his interrogation, to see how I would react? *Was she really dead?*

No. No. No. I had just seen her; I had just touched her. Had it been for the last time?

All my composure dissipated. It felt like the blood was being drained from my body. I gasped for breath. Clutching my stomach, I heaved, quickly leaning over to throw up in the corner. Whirl looked away, repulsed, trying to keep from retching as well.

I wiped my mouth with the back of my hand as I turned to look at him.

The answer I'd been praying for found me, and I knew what needed to be done.

Glaring at him, I said, "I'd like to request an audience with King Gigandet."

He scoffed at my words. "Are you serious?"

"Very."

"Why?"

"Because I know something he doesn't know."

"You know we could force it out of you," he threatened.

"It'd be much more efficient just to let me talk to the king . . . "

"Why can't you talk to me?" He was offended that I was attempting to go over his head.

"Because my business is not with you, but with the king."

"The king is my business. Besides, aren't you like your friends? Why would you consort with the king?" His questions began to annoy me.

"Like I said, I know something he doesn't know. And I won't say another word until I'm in his presence."

He growled in frustration. "I'll see what I can do. But you better not be playing any games. This information that you have—it better be worth an audience with the king."

"Oh, it is," I assured him.

He rose quickly and walked away, leaving the torch behind in a holder on the wall. I was grateful for the light.

I won't cry. I won't cry. I won't cry. Not until I knew for certain that my mother was gone, I would not shed a tear. I blocked out any sentimental thought or concern. *Can't think about Corey and Annabelle without a mother. Can't think about my father without his wife.*

Can't do it. Won't do it.

How could Mara sleep through this? I moved closer to check. Her breathing was still deep and regular, sound asleep. No matter—I didn't need her to interfere anyway.

Despite the heat, my skin had goose bumps, and my body shivered in the dark. It felt like I had a fever. I fixed my hair around my shoulders and straightened my dirty clothes, desiring to look the best I could if I was presented to the king.

The wait was short. Soon, I saw Whirl's shadow around the corner at the end of the tunnel. Would the king be willing to speak with me? Or would he refuse, forcing me to speak with Whirl instead?

A guard followed close behind Whirl. That was a good sign. He wouldn't need the guard if I wasn't going to be transported somewhere.

Every footstep reverberated off the stone walls, sounding so loud, yet Mara did not wake up. Even when Whirl scanned his card through the door lock and it beeped open, she did not stir.

"Let's go," Whirl commanded. I stood up and walked two steps to the open door. "Turn around."

"Why?" I asked, now trembling.

"So we can cuff you." He grabbed my arm and turned me roughly. "And don't try anything stupid. It won't go well for you."

After the cuffs were tightly secured, they spun me around, and each of them grabbed one of my arms. They wore black leather gloves which pinched my skin. I hated them touching me, but I focused on the floor beneath my feet to resist fighting them.

Whirl shut the cell door quietly behind us—apparently, he didn't want to disturb Mara either—and it automatically beeped locked. He carried a torch in his free hand, casting shadows upon the walls as we walked to the end of the tunnel. It was longer than it had first appeared, but we finally reached the end, seconds ticking by like hours with the pounding beat of my heart.

There weren't any other jail cells along the tunnel, as if we had intentionally been isolated from the other prisoners, placed in the deepest, darkest corner beneath the palace. Why? Did they consider us such a great threat?

We turned left and ascended a small staircase to a thick, metal door. I was glad I hadn't wasted my breath trying to shout for help. Nobody would have heard me. We were truly alone down there and at the mercy of Whirl. Now Mara was all by herself.

The door had to be opened by a series of access codes so it was impossible for someone to steal a keycard and gain entrance. Only specific individuals knew and memorized the codes. Once opened, it led to a wide, short corridor. The walls and floor were made of white stone, and it was brightly lit with fluorescent bulbs. This was where the other cells were, lining each side. They were sealed with thick plexiglass rather than metal bars. It was completely different atmosphere from the dungeon we had just left.

There was another guard standing just beside the door. Whirl ordered him to blindfold me. Why was it necessary? Was Laney, or my father, in one of these cells we were about to walk past? Maybe my mother was there. My breath quickened. I wanted to *see* them, to know they were alive. But everything went black with the thick blindfold.

Finally, we took some steps forward. Whirl went slowly, prolonging the agony. We must have passed at least four cells, but I heard nothing. A few seconds and steps later, though, I heard my name, a muffled scream from behind the glass. Laney screaming my name.

"Is he with you?" I yelled into the air, not wanting to mention my father by name, not wanting Whirl to gain any information.

"Yes! But she's NOT," she cried back, obviously in tears. Did that mean our mother was not with them, or *no longer with us*? I couldn't. I couldn't fall apart, not when I was going to talk to the king. *Deep breaths, deep breaths. Maybe that's not what she meant.* I didn't respond to her.

A few steps later, someone else yelled my name. Curwen.

"Where are you taking her?" he demanded. "Where are you taking her?" A loud noise, the sound of him hitting the plexiglass, frustrated that he couldn't get to me.

Then another voice. Sheldon. "Leela, what have they done to you?" he cried. "Are you okay?" No. I wasn't sure I would ever be okay again.

They were all saying, yelling, different things. But where was my father's voice? I couldn't hear it among them. But Laney said he was there.

Whirl commanded, "Shock them into silence now."

"Nooooo!" I screamed, struggling against their strong grips. Their voices ceased. They were wearing shock collars now. Why hadn't they put collars on me or Mara?

Another door beeped open, a gush of cool air hitting me. Then we were somewhere else, and the blindfold was swiftly removed. We were in a lobby of sorts, more white stone walls and tile, a cold place, like a mausoleum.

On both ends were two grand staircases that led steeply upward. I had no doubt that they led to much grander places. Which one would we take? Oddly, they both seemed inviting.

Whirl and the guard attempted to pull me in different directions.

"This way, Allen," Whirl demanded, frustrated. The guard had not yet spoken a word, but now I knew his name. We headed for the staircase on the left.

The staircase curved and narrowed as we reached the top. We stood on the landing while Whirl knocked on the huge, wide wooden double doors. Without pause, two guards opened both doors simultaneously.

I knew they were guards even though they were not dressed like any guards I had previously seen. They were clothed from head to toe in the brightest, purest, almost glowing white.

I instinctively knew that was the color of the palace, of royalty, of anything connected to the king. But why did Whirl not wear white if he was the king's most trusted advisor? He wore the same black as every other guard.

Once we passed through the doors, I was shocked at the splendor in front of me. As impossible as it seemed, the walls, floor, and high ceilings appeared like gold. Encrusted in them were jewels of all sizes and colors. Some were so tiny that they resembled a fleck of glitter, while others were as large as my palm. Where had they found such large jewels? I tried to imagine how majestic it would look during the day, with the light shining in from the floor-to-ceiling window at the end of the grand hall.

Allen finally spoke. "Where are we taking her?"

"To the king's library," Whirl replied curtly. A library? The king had books. Were they books from our dimension, books that were forbidden to ordinary citizens, like the ones in Curwen's locked bookcase?

They guided me across the enormous hall and down a much narrower hallway that was dimly lit. At the end of it was another wooden door. Something in me knew this was the last door, the one that would lead to the king, and my feet became more hesitant with every small step. How must I have looked—my blond hair caked with blood, my face and clothes smeared with dirt?

This time, Whirl didn't use a card to grant him entry; he simply knocked. A guard opened the door from the inside. We entered slowly. Whirl and Allen gripped my arms more tightly, rubbing them raw, ensuring I wouldn't break free.

The room was large, resembling an old-fashioned library, with wall-to-wall and floor-to-ceiling dark, stained, wood bookcases, complete with ladders to reach the highest shelves. There was plush crimson carpet beneath my feet, and the ceiling was painted a glossy gold. There were no windows, which created a very cozy and private feel to the room, and it was lit by lamps and candles placed at strategic locations to cast a soft glow over the place.

And there was a fireplace burning brightly in the center of the wall to my left. From where I was standing, I could feel the heat exuding from the flames, but it didn't bother me. It was comforting.

Near the fire were two luxurious, high-backed chairs. Seated in one was the king. Like I had thought in the garden the previous day, he was an average-looking man, a blank slate, someone whose attractiveness had to be determined based on an assessment of his personality.

In the chair beside him was a beautiful woman. They were leaning in close to each other, speaking softly and laughing. When they noticed our presence, they sat back and stared at me with interest. The smile he had so lovingly bestowed on his lady friend disappeared when he looked at me. It wasn't a rude or unkind look he gave me—it was just that I was not the object of his affection.

The woman appeared simply angelic. Her frame was small and slight. Her fair skin contrasted beautifully with her cascading brown hair, and her cheeks held a pink glow the same bright color of her lips.

But her eyes drew me in—they were the most uniquely dark-gray eyes with a subtle tinge of blue. The firelight flickered in them. Her smile had faded as well, but she still had a kind yet curious expression.

"Whirl, Allen, you can release her," the man, the king, said. He had a gentle voice, softer than when he had spoken to Curwen yesterday. They let go of my arms. "And, you can all wait outside," he added.

Allen and the other guard left without a second thought, but Whirl hesitated, obviously upset that he would not be privy to this conversation.

"But, sir," Whirl feebly protested. The king needed only to give him a stern glare. Whirl exited without further comment. He wasn't the king's most trusted advisor.

Only three of us remained: the king, his lady, and me.

"Come closer . . . Leela, is it?" the king asked for confirmation.

I simply nodded because I couldn't find the words.

I walked closer, but I didn't want to sit in the free chair because it was so nice and my clothes were so dirty. I couldn't imagine how appalling I looked in comparison to the lady sitting beside him. Was she the king's beloved who would die if he were to marry her?

If the curse is true. Which it isn't.

It wasn't difficult to see that they belonged together. They didn't have to touch or speak or look at each other, but the connection was still obvious. These two truly loved each other, and I felt unworthy to be in the presence of such intense feelings. *Like Laney and Hollister.* Even though the king and his lady weren't speaking words, I felt like they were still acutely aware of what the other was feeling and thinking. It was intimidating.

"Well, Leela, I'm King Gigandet," he said, "but you can call me Gigandet."

"I don't believe I could be that informal, sir," I spoke softly.

"You can because I have given you permission to do so," he countered, "and this is Elodie." He looked at her with a loving smile when he said her name.

"Hi, Leela," she greeted me. Her voice was like music.

How could any man not fall in love with her?

"Well," he said when I stood silent. "You requested an audience with me, so please speak. You've broken many Antonian laws, yet I still agreed to see you, so please don't waste my time."

"And please sit down," Elodie added. "Chairs can be cleaned." She was perceptive about my apprehension.

I took a seat, perching on the edge of the chair. "I have a proposal to make," I started. There was no sense in prolonging things. I would be direct and honest, but choose my words with caution. "Your guards have arrested several people today. Do you know about them?"

"There is nothing my guards do that I don't know about," he stated with confidence. "All of them, and you, attempted to help two slaves escape. Four of you, including the two slaves, had false identification cards. And all of you attempted to resist arrest. . . . Well, except for that poor, weak female slave who died."

Mama. She died. "Did she really die, sir?" I blinked back tears.

He realized his blunder—talking so carelessly about her death.

I closed my eyes, focused on my breathing to maintain composure. There would be time for tears later.

When I opened them, Elodie was staring at me with her piercing gray eyes. "You're not Antonian, are you?" she asked gently. "Who was that slave to you? Your family? Your mother?"

I heard the king's sharp intake of breath—he didn't know everything. Elodie could read a situation better than he could.

I nodded—no sense in lying. "Yes," I said with boldness. "And I have a proposal to make."

CHAPTER 19

(LANEY)

As soon as the shock wore off enough that I could move, I crawled onto the hard cot. Lying there, the fluorescent lights burned my retinas, so I covered my face with my arms.

Where were they taking Leela? Was that the last time I would see her? We had already lost so much. Had we lost our lives as well? Would we be put to death? Was my sister—was Hollister—dying now, as we remained trapped in these cells?

They had busted open the door to Sheldon's home and had instantly handcuffed each of us without any chance for explanation. Sheldon had just enough time to close up his secret surveillance closet before the door opened. Even if they all went up in flames, they would protect the resistance.

This *resistance*—what did it stand for, what was its cause?

We'd never asked, too focused on our own personal mission.

Would Durham find out what happened and be able to help us? Or would he stay out of it, distance himself, for the sake of the *resistance*? Were the children he raised more important than his cause?

They had marched us in handcuffs through the living quarters and then through the meeting quarters. The Antonian people gaped at us and ushered their children inside, away from us criminals who would corrupt them.

When we passed the houses of the resistance, the ones with the flowerpots in the windows, the people recognized Curwen and Sheldon. There

193

was something different about the way they stared, the way they stood, a defiance in their stance, a look of encouragement in their eyes.

But what good was their encouragement? We weren't going down for the cause of the resistance. We were going down for the unity of my family. They couldn't, or wouldn't, help us in this fight.

Sheldon and my father were locked in the cells across from me. Curwen was in the one beside me. Why hadn't Leela been in these cells? Where were she and Mara being kept? We had only been there for about two hours, but shortly after arriving, all three of the men had gone silent—no more plots to discuss, no more plans to figure out, defeated.

And even though this was the end, even though we had failed, it somehow didn't register in my mind. I felt like we weren't finished yet, like some sort of miracle would occur. My mind imagined Hollister finding out that we had been arrested. Then he would come to the rescue, with an entire army of rebel slaves behind him. Impossible, I knew, yet such a beautiful image of hope.

Just then, I heard a sound, the door opening again. I tried to jump up quickly, to see who it was, but I fell back onto the cot, the blood rushing to my head. My father had not budged from his cot; he had been seated in the same position since we had arrived. He hadn't even gotten up or said anything when Leela came through—I had wanted her to hear his voice, to be reassured.

Sheldon was already standing, his forehead pressed against the plexiglass, straining to see who had entered the bright, white corridor. The tall, lanky man appeared—the one who had led Leela through here thirty minutes ago, the one who had ordered us to be "shocked into silence." He had four guards with him—I guessed one for each of us. Was it our turn to die now? *Was Leela dead?*

"All of you," the man shouted, "stand at the entrance to your cells, your backs to us!"

I stood up slowly, obeying the man's command. But my father didn't move. *Please don't make this harder*, I internally pleaded with him, as if he could hear me.

"Up now!" He beat on my father's cell. "Or we'll leave you here to rot!"

That's probably exactly what my father wanted.

"Dan, please listen to him," Sheldon begged my father, not desiring anyone else to be hurt. My back was to them, so I couldn't see them.

I heard, "Daddy, please get up."

It was my voice, but it wasn't me speaking. *Leela*. She wasn't dead. *Like Mama*.

"Silence!" the cruel man yelled at her. "You do not speak!"

My cell beeped open. One of the guards ordered me not to move while he cuffed my hands again. The other guards did the same for Curwen, Sheldon, and my father, who had finally complied.

I turned around to see Leela. She smiled at me, but Cruel Man swiftly slapped her across her cheek, knocking her off balance; her guard steadied her. Cruel Man demanded that she lose the smile and look only at the floor.

When it appeared that both Curwen and Sheldon wanted to come to her defense, Cruel Man said, "None of you speak a word unless you are told to. Keep your eyes downcast. You will walk in a straight line with the guard that has been assigned to you. If at any time you disobey these commands, each guard has permission to shock you and to increase the voltage with each subsequent offense. If my directions are clear, say yes."

We all said yes.

"Good." He smiled wickedly. "Line up in this order. Leela. Curwen. Laney. Two-nine-one-six."

He refused to call my father by his name, even though he knew it. We stepped out of our cells and stood in the order he had instructed.

But what about Sheldon? His name hadn't been called.

"Guard, take Sheldon to his new location, please," Cruel Man said with a smirk at the rest of us, at Curwen especially.

"No, no!" Curwen cried, wrestling against his guard's grasp. "Where are you taking him? Take me instead! *Take me instead!*" Curwen's guard shocked him—not too strongly, but enough to make his knees buckle. But his eyes pleaded with Cruel Man.

Did he know Cruel Man? He knew the king, so he must know the leader of the king's guard. There was something unspoken in the looks they gave each other. It appeared that Cruel Man despised Curwen long before any of this happened.

Sheldon's eyes were wide with fear and confusion, unsure of what was happening, where he was being taken next. I could tell Curwen felt responsible for Sheldon, like an older brother for his younger brother; he felt it was his fault for getting Sheldon involved in this mess, and he was willing to sacrifice himself. But what if Sheldon was going to a better place than us?

"It's fine," Leela said firmly. "Stop resisting."

"Shut up!" Cruel Man slapped her again. This is when I realized that she wasn't wearing a collar, like the rest of us. The back of his hand was the extent of her punishment. What did she mean—*stop resisting*? What did she know that we didn't?

Sheldon's guard was dragging him the opposite direction, toward the door that Leela had first appeared through. Where did it lead? Leela knew, but she couldn't say.

"Back to your feet!" Cruel Man shouted at Curwen.

His guard helped him to rise. He glared at Cruel Man with a look that said *I will kill you* as Sheldon disappeared behind the mysterious door. Would Sheldon be tortured or killed for assisting us? It was too much to imagine.

Cruel Man gave the order for us to move out. We exited through the same door we had entered, the same door Leela had gone through blindfolded when she'd come through earlier. There were stairs to the right and to the left. We took the ones to the right; they led outside.

It was night. The stars were out. What kind of stars were they? Did they have the Big Dipper? Were the constellations the same in other dimensions? I wanted to look up, to see for myself, but kept my eyes on the ground, like we'd been instructed.

Where were we going? For the first time since I had been in Antonia, I felt a chill and had a shiver go up my spine. There was a sporadic breeze. We were on a paved walkway, headed toward the rear of the castle. On one side was the wall of the castle; on the other side was the outermost wall of the gardens. Did Curwen know where we were going? Had he been here before? I didn't dare ask.

It seemed as though we walked forever; my feet were exhausted from all the walking in the past two days. At some point, the castle wall on my right ended, and there was an enormous courtyard. We continued on our path, though.

Mama should be on this path with us. Maybe it was better she wasn't. She had died in a hospital—there was no telling how we were about to die. Would Hollister die too, maybe in some kind of lab experiment with the scientists? I couldn't think about it.

And Corey and Annabelle—how would they ever know what had happened here? Would the Antonians go after them as well? We had been careful not to mention their names; perhaps no one here would ever know they existed. What kind of lives would they live without us?

Good ones, better ones than us, I hoped.

We eventually came to a thick stone wall, the outer most wall around the castle estate. Guards stood every ten feet around its perimeter, both inside and outside. Some of them glanced our way in curiosity for a split second before returning their eyes to the ground. It appeared that they had a fear of Cruel Man, of angering him in any way—something I could relate to after this evening's events.

There was a gate, which Cruel Man had to open with a series of codes. Always more codes. How could they remember them all? The Advanced Ones, the gifted children who lived at school, I bet that was a memory skill they had to possess. Were Curwen and Sheldon Advanced Ones? Had Durham sent them to that school?

So many random thoughts run through your mind when you're about to die, things that don't matter, things that you will never know about or need to know about. *Worries that hold no substance.* I could think of no other reason why they would lead us outside the city gates, in the dark, other than to execute us. Isn't that what Curwen had said—these acts were *punishable by death?*

Once the gate was finally open, we filed through.

I could see the end of the path now. It ended, and then the grass began. Once again, the most beautiful rolling green grass I had ever seen, a field that stretched out for a couple of miles until it reached the tree line of a dense forest. Beyond that, there were dark silhouettes of mountains contrasting against the midnight-blue velvet sky.

"Eyes down," my guard ordered, elbowing me roughly in the ribs. I didn't think he wanted to resort to shocking me because he spoke quietly enough that Cruel Man did not hear.

There were several figures standing in the middle of the vast field, but I couldn't make them out. Eventually, my eyes registered, as we approached, that all of them were wearing black (except for one), which indicated that they were more guards. Were they the firing squad prepared to shoot us all down, one by one? I felt sick. *Please let them blindfold us.*

The other figure was wearing white, very easily visible in the darkness. When we were close enough, I realized he was wearing a crown. This was the king. He was here to watch our deaths. Was this entertainment for him?

He was as Leela had described him, an average-looking man. He didn't appear to be an evil dictator or a benevolent ruler. There just wasn't much about his appearance that revealed what kind of man he might be. He had to open his mouth and speak for that to be determined.

After assessing us, his eyes unreadable in the dark, he finally spoke. Looking at Cruel Man and pointing at us, the king asked, "Whirl, what is this? This is an unnecessary display." Then, speaking to the rest of the guards, he ordered with a wave of his hand, "Remove their cuffs and collars."

Whirl—that was Cruel Man's name—appeared embarrassed, angry, confused.

"After you've been released," King Gigandet said, "sit in the grass while we wait for the others to arrive. Don't attempt to run. There's no point. You won't get far."

We sat. Our guards backed farther away, joining the other guards to create a large circle around us.

Others? What others? Did he mean Sheldon? Mara? Durham? Phaedra? Hollister? Or did he mean others completely unrelated to us, others who had been sentenced to death for their crimes?

"Whirl," Gigandet called, "you can be dismissed. You've been on duty for too many hours. Allen can take over."

Whirl looked alarmed. "Sir, I would prefer to see this through," he objected.

What did he want to see through? *Our deaths?* Certainly, for him, this *was* entertainment.

"You've logged too many hours," the king replied with more firmness. "Are you asking me to break my own laws?"

"No, sir. I would never, but—"

Gigandet cut him off, "Then *go.*"

This couldn't take much longer, could it? Did he really care so much about his labor laws, or was there another reason Gigandet wanted Whirl gone? I wasn't sorry to see him go. Neither was anybody else—I could tell from the collective sighs released by so many of them once Whirl was out of range. The guards' shoulders relaxed, and the tension left them.

Curwen ventured to open his mouth. "Gigandet, may I please speak with you?"

"No. You may not." Knowing Curwen's persistence, the king added, "And don't ask again." The king wouldn't even look at him, disgusted with his betrayal.

Now Leela dared to speak, "Sir, may I hug my father and my sister, please?"

So, he knew 2916 was our father. Did he also know that his people had killed our mother?

Gigandet paused for a moment, glancing from Leela to me to our father. Then he nodded. "Yes, go on." Was he a benevolent ruler after all? How could he be? He had only spoken to Leela with kindness. He didn't seem mean; he seemed desperately sad with the haunted eyes of a heartbroken man.

Leela lunged past me, throwing her arms around our father's neck. It took a minute before he reciprocated, wrapping her up in his big bear hug, the one that was so familiar to us. I assumed I had permission to join them, so I did. They made room for me, the three of us sitting together in a tight embrace, weeping softly and whispering apologies, apologies about our mother, apologies about our failure, apologies that everything had ended up this way.

How could the king not see the impact, the sad consequences of his actions? Could he not see that we were human beings with just as much value as himself? Did he not see that?

Surely, a benevolent ruler would.

When our current session (there would be many more—if we didn't die) of family grieving ended, my father asked Leela, "Did you see your mother?"

"Only for a few minutes." She explained, "She was in a very confused state of mind. Not really understanding what was going on or that we were trying to help her. I passed out before I could see them take her away. I'm sorry. I'm so sorry I couldn't do more."

"It's not your fault," I assured her, casting a glare in the direction of the king.

"Do you know how she died?" she asked us.

"The infirmary report listed that she was admitted for 'heat exhaustion.'" Anger welled up inside of me at the thought of it. "But I doubt that can be trusted."

"She wasn't doing well. It probably is true," my father muttered. We sat together, still and quiet for a minute, like a moment of silence for her.

Finally, I asked, "Leela, do you know who we are waiting on?"

She had a twinkle in her eye, and she smiled broadly—the first time I had seen such a smile on her face in weeks. "Ask me what you really meant to ask me," she insisted.

I hesitated, not willing to even hope it could be true. I whispered, "*Hollister?*"

She smiled softly, gently nodding her head, her eyes brimming with tears.

"So," I tried to understand, "we all get to . . . die together?"

"Laney, we're not dying. We're going home," she revealed.

I shook my head at her in disbelief; I'd been preparing to die. But she simply nodded more vigorously, willing my doubts away.

"How?" I whispered, aware that Curwen was listening as well. Was he coming with us?

"I've spoken with Gigandet," she said. "He's granted us permission to leave."

"What about Curwen, Sheldon, Mara?" I asked.

"I'm not sure. It appears that Curwen will come with us," she explained in a cool tone, as though she didn't want him to come with us. "But that Sheldon and Mara will stay here. I'm sure they'll be released from prison."

"How can you be sure? Will they be safe once we're gone? I can't imagine they won't be punished for their actions." Sheldon had become my favorite Antonian; I didn't want him to be harmed for helping us.

"They'll be safe. I'm sure of it." She sounded so confident, it was hard doubt her.

Just then, there was movement on the horizon—three figures headed in our direction.

Hollister.

I stood up in anticipation, despite the king's previous command for us to sit. Leela grabbed my arm, pulling me back to the earth. "Hey," she whispered, "I told the king that he's my brother, mainly because once you two are married, he will be . . . but don't do anything to make it appear otherwise. I want nothing to hinder our escape from this place."

"All right," I agreed. "I won't." I pulled my arm from her grasp, my eyes never leaving the three figures coming toward us.

My twin knew I wouldn't be able to control myself, so she asked, "Gigandet, when our brother arrives, do we have permission to hug him also, sir?" How could she maintain such a posture of respect to that man? *Nothing to hinder our escape.*

"Only once he has reached you," he said.

With every step they took, my heart pounded harder, faster. I could hear it in my ears.

I could make out the features of Hollister's face now, close enough, but not within the confines of our guarded circle. How could I not run to him? Leela and my father knew my thoughts, and they held my arms.

"Please let me go to Hollister," I begged the king. "I'm not trying to escape."

He looked at Leela. "Your brother, huh?"

"Well . . . he will be one day," she offered as an explanation.

He had an amused yet sad smirk on his lips. "Let her go. At least one lady can be with the man she loves."

Leela and my father released their grips. I shoved past the guards and ran like I had never run before. When I reached him, I threw my arms around him without a second's hesitation. He did not immediately respond to my embrace, his arms up at his sides, trying to find some balance from my impact.

But then he crushed me to him, not as strongly as I'd expected. He was still weak from whatever they had done to him last night. But it was tightly enough that we were squeezing the breath from each other's lungs. It was love.

His chin rested on the top of my head. I hadn't realized how much I missed the weight of his head until that moment. I had missed his scent, his hugs, his eyes, his face, but the little details—like the weight of his head—had escaped me.

We relaxed our embrace a little to allow our lungs to fill with the warm air, which suddenly smelled much sweeter to my senses. But we did not pull away or look at each other. We just stayed like that, *together*.

CHAPTER 20

[LEELA]

Watching Laney and Hollister, tears springing to my eyes, I ran through my conversation with the king, the one that had taken place less than an hour earlier.

"*I was brought here in an attempt to rescue three people I love very much—my parents and my . . . brother,*" I began.

"*So, the other slave we arrested is your father?*" the king asked. *Surprisingly, he was not yet angry, as I had feared. I nodded.* "*And where is your brother?*"

"*He was assigned to the fields. Number 327.*"

"*And you want me to let all of them go?*" *He was shocked by my audacity.*

"*Yes, sir. And the others who helped us.*" Curwen, Sheldon, Mara. "*It's not their fault they helped us. We made them.*" Even if Curwen was going to betray me.

"*You want me to not only release slaves, but traitors also? How will that help me enforce the law? I have never had such rebellion. I can't let it go unpunished.*" *He pounded his fist into his palm. While his words held passion, I did not think they held anger, so I decided to force my case. It might be my only chance.*

"*But, sir, their actions were not meant to be acts of treason. They simply wanted to help us because they have good hearts.*"

"*Good hearts are ones that can obey authority.*" *He saw everything in black and white.*

"*No one has to know that you released them,*" I pleaded. "*They can leave tonight, and you can tell the public whatever you like about their disappearance.*"

"*Why do you keep saying they and their?*" Elodie asked. *Again, she was perceptive.* "*Do you not intend to go with them?*"

"No. And I don't want them to know that I'm staying here."

"Why aren't you going with them?" the king asked, his curiosity piqued.

"That's the exchange."

"All of them for you? Six for one? Doesn't seem like a fair trade," he said. Always good to know what he thought of my worth.

I smirked. "I'm more valuable than you know. I know how to find what you're looking for. Who you're looking for."

He gave Elodie a quick glance, then returned his eyes to mine. "Who am I looking for?"

"The one whose neck has the mark in the shape of three—"

Holding his hand up, he said, "Stop."

He and Elodie were locked in an intense gaze, conversing with their eyes again. It was a private conversation I should not have witnessed, but it made things more clear, almost as though they were speaking out loud.

They were so in love. How could he marry someone else just to break a curse? What would happen with their relationship? Would they separate and never see each other again? Would it be too painful to be near each other?

He couldn't marry her because that would kill her. But if he didn't marry the person with the mark, hundreds or thousands of his own people would die. If the curse is real. Which it isn't.

Would this beautiful young woman spend the rest of her life mourning the loss of her love? Could she ever find someone else to love as much as she loved him? I had no doubt that another man could easily love her, but would she ever be able to love him back?

I could have almost shed tears for them, if I didn't have enough of my own sadness to cry about. Why couldn't she have the mark? I wished I could transfer that mark from my skin to hers. If it really matters. Which it doesn't.

But it belonged to me, and I had to use it as leverage for now.

Their silent conversation went on for what seemed like minutes, when it was only seconds. They turned to look at me. Elodie smiled, but there was deep sadness in her eyes. Gigandet was stoic, revealing no emotion on his face.

"You have a deal," Elodie stated, somehow knowing it would be too difficult for Gigandet to say those words.

"Guard," he called, "take her out of here." He gestured at me. "Tell Whirl I'll speak to him soon with instructions."

I rose to leave. I admired Elodie. But would she hate me later when she knew I was the one coming between them?

That's what I thought about when Gigandet let Laney run to Hollister. His words—*at least one lady can be with the man she loves*—made me think of Elodie. Where was she now? Laney and Hollister were together again—the way it was supposed to be. But it was probably the last time I would get to witness their togetherness.

They would go home, get married, and have a family. I would see none of it.

I etched their images into my memory.

As I watched from a distance as they lovingly embraced, I couldn't help but feel a tiny tinge of jealousy. I glanced over at the king to discern his reaction to their display of affection.

He was definitely affected. But not in the sense that he disapproved; he longed to express his love for Elodie in such a way. His eyes poured forth a mixture of sadness, longing, envy, and despair. *Where was Elodie now?* I pictured her dark-gray eyes like storm clouds, drenching the earth beneath her feet.

Curwen had inched his way closer to me. He dared to grab my arm. "Leela, are you okay?" he asked gently.

"Please don't touch me," I said without emotion, pulling my arm away.

Whatever his reasons or intentions, he had lied to me. Whether he truly would have sold me out to Durham or Gigandet, I would never know. Or whether he would have kept it a secret, like Mara had suggested—I wouldn't know that either. No matter how he tried to explain it, I could never trust that he was being honest.

"Leela," he attempted again, "are you okay? What did you talk about with Gigandet?"

That's all he really cared about. He wanted to know how much Gigandet knew about his treasonous acts. He didn't want to know if I was okay. I didn't answer him.

He had brought me to Antonia under the pretense of a lie, and his motives were still unclear. Had it been his plan to turn me over to the king? Had I found a way to outsmart him, a way to get freedom for everyone I loved by turning myself over to the king?

Did he realize I wasn't going back with them?

Did he realize *I had decided my own future*?

I would be the king's bride. *Well, until I find a way out of it, a way to unite him with Elodie instead.* Then maybe I could go home.

Home. Corey and Annabelle. I hadn't given myself the opportunity to think about them. If I couldn't find a way to make it home, I would never see them again either. I imagined all my siblings ten years in the future—Laney and Hollister with children of their own, Corey engaged to be married, Annabelle just beginning high school.

I didn't get to keep my promise to them. They wouldn't get their mother or one of their sisters back again. *But they will be okay. They would have good lives.*

And I would miss it all.

Then I remembered Annabelle's drawing—the one of me wearing a crown, the one she had given to Curwen. Had she known this was going to happen? Had she known I wouldn't be coming home? *Home.* The weight in my chest felt heavier.

Blinking back tears, I walked over to the king. "Gigandet," I whispered, "do you think we could hurry up and get this over with?"

He turned to me with sympathy in his eyes. "Sure," he replied softly. "Allen, you and the guys move out," he instructed the guards.

Gigandet pulled Curwen's phone from his pocket and handed it back to its owner. "Take them home," he ordered.

When Laney and Hollister returned to us, I embraced Hollister, grateful to have known him my entire life. "You'll have to help Annabelle speak again," I whispered in his ear.

His eyes looked confused, but he would soon understand.

I waited to see where Curwen would stand among our small group. He stood next to Laney.

Curwen. Laney. Hollister. Father.

It worked out perfectly. I went to the end to stand beside my father.

"Curwen," I requested, "please count to three before you do it. I'd like to prepare myself."

"I'll stand beside you . . . give you support, if you need it," he offered.

We were both remembering the intense pain I had experienced on the journey to Antonia. Avoiding the pain was the only thing I was looking forward to.

"No!" I protested. "That's not necessary. Just count to three please."

"Okay. Fine." He remained beside Laney, feeling rejected.

I held on loosely to my father's arm, ready to let go at the count of two, knowing he wouldn't grab onto me; he didn't know he was supposed to.

"Everyone ready?" Curwen asked after he finished pushing all of the codes into his phone. He was an expert lightning traveler; I only hoped he wouldn't try to come back for me.

We all said yes.

"Okay. One . . . two . . . " I released my hold. "Three."

The lightning shot down from the clear night sky with fierce determination. I was blinded by the light, inches away from me.

I ran as far as I could. But it was so fast.

One second later, they were gone.

The white lightning was sucked back into the sky.

I lay on the ground, where I had fallen, and stared up at the stars.

There was the Big Dipper, and the Little Dipper, and that ever-faithful North Star that my siblings and I had followed, navigating our way through fields and woods. Life would never be like that again—the laughter of Corey and Annabelle trailing behind me on a cold October night, being able to see our warm breath as it hit the air, leaves crunching beneath our feet.

I didn't have any coherent thoughts. Just images and memories flashing across my mind.

My head couldn't think. But my heart felt it all.

For the first time in my life, I understood what my sister had meant about feeling things without thinking about them first. In that moment, I was not the master of my emotions; they mastered me.

I heard the king's footsteps approaching, and I sat up quickly. *Show no weakness.*

He spoke softly, "Okay, Leela, you got what you wanted. Now, how do we find the one with the mark?"

He doesn't want to find her. But duty required him to.

I pulled my hair away from my neck. "Here I am."